# CRIMSON COBBLESTONES

Crimson Cobblestones



This book is for entertainment purposes only.

Printed in Oliver Springs, Tennessee, United States of America

Library of Congress Control Number: 2024931637

Description: Crimson Cult Media, 2024 | 321 pages printed text. | Series: Hellfire Club. | Audience. Adult. | Summary: A fictionalized Benjamin Franklin attempts initiation into the Hellfire Club.

ISBN:  979-8-9880338-9-9

Subjects: FICTION_HORROR, HISTORICAL, PSYCHOLOGICAL THRILLER, OCCULT HORROR

Proem


Young men did meet, across the sea
of art and wit—high society
Hellfire's club, so named were they
T'were drunken sadists of debauchery
One man was not completely born
Till he had passed through death
A chasm of humanity torn
With his victims' final breath
For two hundred years, their name did grow
Yet seventeen souls were buried below
Beneath the floor of Franklin's home
And thus inspired the following tome

# Of Dark Persuasion

## Philadelphia Colony, 1739

*"Am I a monster that stalks in the night, justice comes swiftly with terror and fright."*

*-Timothy Turnstone*

Silence is the most deafening of sounds.

The silence after an admission of love.

The silence of a stillborn babe.

More importantly, in this moment, the necessary silence of one with everything to lose.

The creeping fingers of night curled around the edges of the day, dragging the sun down in a bruised smear across the horizon.

Cobblestones stole the last warmth they could as Philadelphia yielded to slumber beneath the watchful eye of a swollen summer moon. Not all within those somber streets would find peace this evening, for one of dubious intent moved among them with purpose in the deepening dark.

The man in the crimson cloak slipped between shadows, carefully choosing his path. The well-worn cobblestones of Philadelphia's town square were littered with patches of stubborn grass—weeds far more resilient than the denizens that called this city home. It did a fine job dampening the clack of his wooden shoes.

Years of sneaking up on unsuspecting women had honed his skills of stealth, but now he needed more than a talent for an unexpected laugh. He crept softly down the street, attempting silent footsteps, as discovery could mean the difference between life and death for him.

Or another.

Darkness hid many unscrupulous deeds, and tonight he was especially thankful for it. The shadows of this night disguised his purpose— a necessary execution.

The stolen axe trembled in his iron grip as he tried to quell his fear. The smell of freshly baked pastries and breads threatened to overwhelm him,

sending a wave of nostalgia to the tip of his tongue. He'd tasted the buttery sweetness of those warm buns with cinnamon and sugar since he was a child.

But never again.

Tonight, he came for the baker who made them. The man in the crimson cloak paused.

A moment of doubt arrived.

If he chose to follow this path of violence, he would unleash primitive and forbidden yearnings with severe consequences. He must begin with this deed in order to stand among the people he admired. The pursuit of knowledge and control warranted a sacrifice. In order to live a life of grandeur, he would consequently surrender all prospects for a heavenly afterlife. If such a thing even existed.

Peering through the grimy window around the back of the baker's house, he watched the man at his table. Gayle Williams was well known, and generally well-liked, except by the girls whose bottoms he pinched. And them.

Those he served required this kill. He dared not question it.

Flickers from the oil lamp illuminated his pinched and haggard features. The baker was a portly fellow, unsurprising given his chosen line of work. He'd never taken a wife nor learned to clean himself from the look of things. His shirt was untucked, breeches unbuttoned, and both of his shoes were strewn about the floor, leaving the man with black-bottomed feet.

What atrocious, yet fitting attire to die in.

The stench of this filthy abode overpowered even the most delectable smells from the bakery at the front. Clearly, his fellow Philadelphians held no concern about buying bread from such an unclean man.

His unkempt home would serve as the place of ritual; the doorstep a sacrificial altar. The baker, Gayle Williams, was little more than a goat to slaughter in his eyes.

Tonight, the earth would drink his blood.

Fear of sin and "Hell" were too often used as a reason to abstain from darker desires. Yet, if such cravings existed within himself, surely they were present in others. The burden was heavy, but the outcome would be well worth the cost.

He watched as Williams hunched over, reading a passage from what looked to be an open bible on his desk– yet his eyes kept darting to the door.

This was the night of decisions. For this night, the cobblestones could run crimson.

The sudden yowl of a cat, hissing and spitting to the right, startled the man in the crimson cloak. So much for stealth. His skin seared with scratches from the holly bush next to the back door..

Knock. Knock. Knock.

He tapped on the door with the axe's blade, leaning over to the window to watch as the baker rose from his chair and hobbled over, visibly drunk.

The man in the crimson cloak chuckled.  No angel knocked on Gayle Williams's door this night.

With the Devil's own luck, he could finish this deed unseen. He turned as the back door crashed open, the silhouette of his prize blocking most of the light from inside with their bulging presence. "Come on out you cock robin!" the baker yelled.

A fleeting thought, as elusive as a phantom's whisper in an abandoned home, danced across the corners of his consciousness, leaving behind a shiver of apprehension. The chance to choose a different path still remained. He

could turn away, untouched by guilt or shame– or he could fulfill his given purpose. One insignificant life would pave the way to the remaining five required for sacrifice.

This was only the beginning. He rose from the bushes to exact Gayle Williams' sentence.

This is what they wanted. No, what he wanted. To stand among those wrapped in Hellfire with pride.

He had made his decision, and the choice was sin.

The baker stepped back, but the man in the crimson cloak grabbed him. Gayle William's spluttered prayers and pleas for mercy were a pitiful sound. Alas, his cries to god would go unheard.

One quick swing and life as it had been would cease to exist.

One quick swing and he would begin the transformation into one of them.

The shocked expression of his prey would not be so easily forgotten, nor would the swish of the axe through the crisp night air. His hand trembled, ever so slightly, to which he tightened his grip.

"To the bitter end..." he whispered.

On impact, the baker's skull cleaved in half, the blade slicing clear to his lip. The gollumpus man fell through the threshold, the sound of his blubber slapping the floor as repulsive as the death gurgle that escaped his split mouth.

Mouth agape and eyes wide until the last twitching ceased, the baker died. It could have been anyone at all, as this was merely the price of entry. The other five sacrifices would be chosen with additional care.

Tonight, it was the baker's blood that pooled and ran in rivulets, mixing with the grime of the floorboards and the dust of the earth.

His own blood thundered in his ears.

What calamity his hands had caused. He experienced a heightened

awareness of his surroundings, the crimson flood upon the floor inching ever closer to his custom birch clogs. Tonight, he had been reborn into something

far greater than himself. Soon, he would join them and achieve transcendence.

Silence rang in Philadelphia once more.

The silence of a stolen soul departing for the afterlife.

The silence of his conscience.

More importantly, in this moment, the silence of one with everything to gain. Stepping away from the grisly scene before him, his senses settled with the knowledge that soon he would feel nothing at all.

# A Meeting of Chance

Charlotte peered out of the lone window of the library, pressing her nose against the glass, leaving a small smudge on its cool surface. Like so many other days in Philadelphia, the sky hung low and heavy, weighted like a wool blanket draped over the city. It was heavy. Thick. Oppressive. She longed for days when she could feel her heart beating about something. Days when the wind was real and the people were loving and she felt alive again.

Perhaps today would be different. "I am more than my hysteria," she whispered into the glass.

The striking clock in the state house tower tolled, signaling the top of the hour– an opportunity for change. Below it, the long

shadow of a large sundial stretched across the cobblestone street. Charlotte

twisted the tarnished door knob of their tiny book haven and stepped aside as a stream of excited children, arms full of books, rushed into their mothers' welcoming arms. The patter of eager feet echoed through the hall as a chorus of childish giggles faded down the stairs. So sweet an embrace, that of a mother and child. One she hadn't known for too many years—not since Mother was stolen from them.

She caressed the spine of the leather-bound book they'd been reading,

11

feeling the worn ridges and inhaling its musty aroma. She carefully placed it on the shelf and allowed herself a moment of solace among the books she so loved—a respite from the small, yet ever present ache that tensed the edges of her heart.

Charlotte pulled in a steadying breath. It was time to venture out and meet with her best friend, Priya. She'd promised, after all.

Papa and Priya were always hatching schemes to get her out of the house. The purchase of a new dress was their latest plot, which seemed a foolish    solution to such an intractable issue. Evidently, her current attire was only "a step beyond rags" as Papa had pointed out, and he had cobbled together enough coin to change that. Certainly, her clothes bore the signs of wear, but while tattered clothing could be replaced, her inner turmoil was far more difficult to fix. The finest silks money could buy wouldn't mask the anxious thoughts and constant fears that kept her close to home. Plus, as much as she loved perusing the shops with Priya, trying on dresses next to her willowy, slender friend pinched her confidence just a bit.

No, she reminded herself. Not today. She would pull herself from the shadows and put on a cheerful front until it resonated with her genuinely. In addition to a new chisel and flowers for Mother's grave, she might even try on the leather shoes she'd seen last week, the ones with the golden braid and wooden soles. Perhaps she'd find marigolds, as those were Mother's favorite.

"We must pattern ourselves after the marigolds, Charlotte." She'd say to her. "When you plant marigolds in the garden, it helps the other plants to flourish and grow."

Grow. Serve. Avoid extremes in all experiences. Lesson after lesson Mother had given her about the deeper meanings in life, and how important an inquisitive mind was to raise consciousness. One must better themselves in order to assist "other flowers to bloom."

Charlotte had never forgotten.

As she passed the council's chamber, her steps faltered as a chill skittered down her spine. The tall and imposing man standing in the door was one who many admired.

But not her.

Time slowed, stretching and crawling and creeping as Charlotte focused on his figure. He had a square jaw, dark eyes that were sharply focused on a distant point with a disconcerting air of abusive authority. Seconds turned to minutes. She couldn't move. Couldn't breathe. Flashes of the misfortune that had befallen after Mother's death filled her thoughts.

It was the Mayor who led the false charges against her Papa.

Mayor Richard Payne, with his back turned, now blocked her way. He was an equally brilliant yet terrible man, one well-revered under false pretenses in their Philadelphia Colony. One many viewed as a visionary—yet the way he inserted himself into everyone's lives made her skin crawl. He was unsightly and stank of sweat and musk. A disheveled wig sat lopsided on his balding head.

Charlotte bristled, steeling herself.

It was supposed to be a good day. She had prayed it would be.

She concentrated on the floor before her and rushed past, hoping he wouldn't notice her as she slipped by. Please, no idle chatter. No comments about "growing beauty" nor comparisons to Mother.

Charlotte quickened her steps to get past him and avoid his queries as to why she had yet to bear children of her own, as he usually did. She chanced a sidelong glance. Sweat collected on the man's wrinkled brow as he turned toward her, the expression on his swollen features truly vexed. Whatever words of concern he and Minister Horvath whispered to each other were of a pressing matter and kept the two men distracted enough to leave her alone.

She swept through the canyon of the state house hallway, the large and less inviting building that housed their precious library, her fingers closing around the cool iron door latch.

The town square ushered her outside with its usual bustle of boisterous shouting and all varieties of smells, from the delectable to the revolting. The faint smell of horses and baked goods greeted her as a brisk wind nipped at her cheeks. Traders set out their wares, hawking mirrors, silver-plated utensils, curious clocks, and tea services. Their desperate cries mingled with the clatter of horse-drawn carriages, creating a cacophony of noise that assaulted her senses. One riskier fellow, Mister Robert Dawson, even sold illegal wigs in the street. Alas, most of the goods were imported from England, none of which would appeal to her hardened Papa. Worldly possessions meant little to him—other than Mother's.

For now, having bypassed the mayor's insidious gaze, she was ready to be swept along with the mid-morning crowd and their chaos.

A young family passing by—the strapping Papa arm in arm with his beautiful wife and two curly-haired daughters in tow—warmed her restless heart. What joy to have a confidant to stave off the darkness and children to brighten each day with laughter. How she craved a companion's love.

But true companionship was hard to come by.

Finding the elusive "one" seemed impossible among the ill-intentioned. She distanced herself from such people, avoiding the "walnut trees," as Mother had called them. Walnut trees were problematic for anything that tried to grow near them, their invasive roots spreading a toxic influence. Her grin faded.

What her life could have been if Mother had lived…had she been there to mold her, teach her, to help her understand why the emotions of others consumed her.

At last, the sun decided to grace them with its presence, peeking out from behind the clouds, flirting with the townsfolk, whispering of warmth, and yet remaining concealed.

Charlotte understood why the sun would want to hide from this town, but she could not hide from it herself. It was time to find Priya.

While a lively square was not altogether unusual on a Saturday morn, the crowd that swelled near the East End that faced the river was. People gathered around the bakeshop where the friendly Gayle Williams always saved her a sweet biscuit on library days. Cursed with the ability to tune into the emotions of others, for better and for worse, she could feel a rumble of displeasure. Her breath froze in her throat.

Walk away. There is trouble here. Head home and visit the square on Monday.

Yet, even with the warning that pulsed inside her head, curiosity pushed her forward. She saw the blacksmith's wife clutch her daughter's hand and half drag the child toward their shop, brow furrowed as she shuffled away.

"Lottie! There you are." Priya danced through the crowd toward her, her golden skin much like the buttery light that bathed a forest on a midsummer's day. "How were the children today? Are you ready to shop?"

Charlotte embraced her dearest friend, her heartbeat steadying and clenched jaw relaxing in her perfumed presence. Priya, her closest confidant since they first met in finishing school, always gave her solace. She smiled. "They were wonderful. We are reading one of my favorites." She held out the borrowed book from the library. "Beauty and the Beast."

Priya, her gleaming black hair arranged in elaborate braids, was as usual, dressed as if attending a ball. She tilted her head and raised a questioning eyebrow. "That sounds like a curious tale. Why should a beauty take interest in a beast? It certainly doesn't seem appropriate for children."

Charlotte rolled her eyes. She loved her friend but sometimes the lack of literary curiosity was irksome. But she did not judge her for it. Priya always managed to maintain an air of amusement, of merriment. Given her circumstances in early life as a foundling, it was nothing short of miraculous.

Charlotte grinned. "It's much more than that. It's a love story between a woman with complicated dreams and a cursed prince. By the end, it reveals that the huntsman, who some thought was the town hero, was actually the villain, and the cursed prince is good."

"I see your point. First impressions." Priya nodded. "But I much prefer the Three Princes of Serendip."

Charlotte shook her head and smiled. Priya never ceased to surprise her.

"Perhaps stories of the East Indies are beyond the understanding of Americans." She winked, eyes glowing with mischief.

Charlotte feigned indignance, then laughed.

Sharing wry grins, she linked arms with Priya and rounded the corner into Queen Village. They were an odd pair—the wheelwright's moody daughter and the Captain's adopted one—but the town had grown accustomed to them.

Together they headed toward the preferred shops for elegant assortments of the most fashionable millinery goods. On her Papa's Captain's salary, Priya could afford the finer things these shops had to offer.

Colorful window displays adorned the front of the buildings. They were large structures built specifically to house the shops. She spotted glassware, dry goods, and the cobbler's shop where she could find those new shoes. Priya turned from looking at the buttons and thread in the haberdasher's window and gestured across the street to three imposing figures walking among the crowd. "Oh look! It's Amie with John Priestly and his friend Ben Franklin walking by the docks. Don't they look dashing today?"

Priya lived for social encounters...especially when they were with dapper young men. It was amazing, given her vivacious nature, that they were friends at all.

"Amie! John! Come say hello to two damsels in distress."

So flirtatious, Priya was. Without a care in the world.

Priya's older brother, Amir Lanivet, or "Amie" as she liked to call him, had clearly heard her shout and wave. Priya and Amir were orphans when Captain Lanivet found them wandering the streets of Kolkata. Starving, hardly beyond the age of toddlers, he'd brought them back to the colonies where his wife took them in as her own.

Amir had grown into a handsome bachelor of some, but not prodigious, wealth while Priya stole more than her fair share of glances. Men went out of their way to speak to her, much to her brother's annoyance. While Charlotte viewed the towering masts of ships clogging the port as skeletal fingers reaching towards the sky, Priya saw them as opportunity markers.

Those ships held all varieties of her favorite pastime...men.

Charlotte groaned. "Must we, Priya?" Surely her friend could recognize the desperation in her eyes.

"Oh don't be so chuffy, Lottie. Allow the attention of handsome men to brighten your dreary day for once." The breeze carried the sharp scent of tobacco near as the laughter of the three men grew louder.

The dashing John Priestly turned their way. "Distress, you say! And just

how are you in need of assistance on this fine..." he glanced at the murky sky, "well... cloudy day?"

Charlotte had little time to compose herself for the impending conversation. The three men had ascended from the docks and now stood before them, the perfect picture of well-polished, finely suited gentlemen. Men that silk-clad ladies would throw themselves at.

They were handsome, and worse—they knew it.

Ben and John opted for traditional waistcoats and frocks, but Amir stood out among the crowd. People stared, as usual. Unlike Priya, who also chose to follow the latest trends out of London, Amir frequented the shipments of banyans procured by their father. He often sailed for the United Company of Merchants of England, formerly the East India Trading Company. Amir strutted towards them, proud as a peacock, his velvety green robes almost as dazzling as his smile.

Charlotte chuckled, sensing her nervousness dissipate, if only slightly. Miss Nelly, her housemaid who was more like a mother to her since losing her own, would refer to these chaps as "Macaroni," and she wouldn't be wrong. Feathers in their caps indeed.

"Dearest Priya, what brings you to town this morning? Come to gossip among your flock of hens?" John Priestly's eyes held a roguish glint, and Charlotte sensed they held secrets none would ever know.

"Oh John, such nonsense! Your twistical tongue has no doubt learned of every detail surrounding the town's latest scandals already." Priya's curtsy was slow enough to provide the other two men with a prolonged opportunity to glance at her bosom. For shame. Amir narrowed his eyes.

"Well. I have minimal gossip. But let's not spoil the rest of the morning with such talk," John said.

Oh, thank goodness..

"Do you know my friend, Mr. Ben Franklin?" John continued. "He's recently returned from abroad. Finally finished traipsing about the English countryside in search of something none of us will ever be fancy enough to know, I'm sure." The three friends snickered.

Mr. Franklin rolled his eyes. "You're merely envious because the English weren't as fond of your...studies."

John Priestly cut his eyes for a moment at Mr. Franklin, yet quickly replaced his frown with a grin. He nudged his friend with an elbow.

"Mr. Franklin, at your service, my ladies," the man said with a sweeping bow, "But please, do call me Ben."

Charlotte fidgeted as Ben Franklin's attention landed on her, not uncomfortably so, but more in the way of curiosity piqued. "My ill-witted friend belittles my quest for knowledge and truth into a nonsensical adventure, but we'll let him have this one." He flashed them a pearly white smile.

Priya stood tall, her gaze meeting the young men's eyes, though she still stood a head shorter than them. "Ahh yes, Ben. It's been some time, but we remember you. Don't we, Lottie?"

Charlotte's lips curled into a bittersweet smile, her head giving a subtle, nearly imperceptible nod. Ben seemed to think it funny, as she caught the whisper of a smile just above his chiseled chin. His handsomeness was undeniable.

"We are dress shopping, you see. Not letting the day get away from us. Soon we will head for refreshment," Priya said.

"What luck!" John clapped his hands with glee. "We just came from ninepins and are headed to Aunt Beth's house for brunch. She sets a delicious table for every meal. You must join us! And you as well, Miss Charlotte."

Brunch with Bethshua Franklin ranked last on the list of events she wished to attend. With her huge home and retinue of admirers, that society woman was the most intimidating person in Philadelphia.

"We wouldn't want to impose, Mr. Priestly," Charlotte mumbled. "We are not dressed for the occasion and your Aunt Bethshua would have no foreknowledge of our attendance."

Priya wilted. Perhaps they'll drop it.

John chuckled. "Nonsense! It's nothing to set two more places. There's plenty of room."

Of that there was no doubt. The sprawling Society Hill manors and

townhomes owned by the Franklins were a wonder to behold.

"Since brunch is a tad impulsion du moment, and you already have plans, then I beg you to join us for dinner. We're celebrating Ben's return. Aunt Beth will be delighted—as will I." John Priestly clearly intended to win this battle. How bold to invite ladies to another family's home for dinner, even if John and Ben were like brothers. Amir grinned.

Ahhh. And there it was. A quick wink from John towards Priya. The nail in the coffin. Her friend practically fell to her knees in the street.

Priya turned to Charlotte with pleading eyes, wordlessly begging to have her whole year made by attending a macaroni affair such as dinner with the Franklin family.

Dinner. At a Franklin abode.

Perhaps, Charlotte mused, she needed a bit of a reprieve from her mundane existence. Perhaps it could be—dare she consider it—fun?

She'd prayed for today to be different, after all.

"There's no arguing with a gut-founded man when it comes to dinner. Do join us." .

A soft sigh escaped her lips, surrendering to the irresistible charm of their infectious grins.

"Fine. So long as we do not tarry for long. Papa will wonder what misadventure Priya has gotten us into if we stay too late."

Ben's sharp, inquisitive eyes met hers once more. "Splendid! I shall send a carriage to collect you both at say, five o'clock?"

So generous, this Priestly man. He must have an interest in dear Priya. Amir stood still, watching his friend.

"Oh thank you, John!" Priya chirped. "Five o'clock sounds lovely. Now come, Charlotte, we must truly go find you a new dress. See you this evening, gentlemen."

"Enjoy yourselves." Amir chuckled. "Alas, I must excuse myself from any invitations this evening, as I have a date with an unparalleled beauty... and I promised to show her my hookah." He grinned. John Priestly raised his eyebrows, biting his lip to stifle a laugh.

And with that, they were off again. Priya dragged her in and out of every shop on the street, and Charlotte finally chose a dress of beautiful chambray rose, with intricate lace work detailing the neckline and sleeves. A sizable yet delicate bow adorned the bosom. She thought it too much, but Priya promised it looked divine. It hugged her curves nearly beyond comfort, but the color and lace were too irresistible to pass up.

What an interesting turn this day had taken. Brunches, dinners, one small conversation and now she would dine on Society Hill this very evening. Delectable smells drifted over from the market, causing her stomach to emit an audible groan. Instantly, a voracious hunger consumed her.

Charlotte turned to Priya. "How about a quick visit to see Mr. Williams at the bakeshop? His ratafia cakes are delicious."

They made their way there only to find a lengthy queue stretching down the street.

Odd. Mr. Williams typically opened earlier on weekend days to accommodate the crowds. Mrs. Duloe, dressed in the finest silks England could provide, stood at the end of the long queue. She was an old friend and regular client of Papa's who owned not one, but two luxurious carriages that required frequent wheelwright services. The sound of their wheels on the cobblestones was a familiar melody to Charlotte's ears.

Her lips curved into a forced smile, a reluctance to engage in small talk palpable. The bakeshop's windows were shrouded in darkness, as was Mr. Williams' neighboring residence, an unusual sight for a man who prided himself on his early morning baking routine.

Men knocked on the front door.

An idea sprang to mind.

"Has anyone gone around back to check on Mr. Williams at his home? Perhaps he is taken ill or suffers from a sharp head pain?" She wouldn't dare accuse him of a hangover publicly, but given his history—it wouldn't be the wildest of reasons he wasn't around.

Priya smirked and raised an eyebrow. "We know how he likes his rattle skulls."

Mrs. Duloe glanced behind them. "Not that I know of, darling. Everyone knows he doesn't like to be bothered. Perhaps we should send someone?"

Charlotte seized the opportunity. "No, no. I'll go. Best not to frighten the man." She turned to Priya. "If you'd be so kind as to hold my book and packages?"

Priya held out her hands. "Of course, Lottie."

Charlotte passed the queued crowd and slipped beyond the garden gate to the baker's home. Mr. Williams was a single man, and judging by the clutter of his yard, quite untidy. Her stomach clenched. Perhaps those weekly sweets weren't a good idea after all. A flash of silver amidst the litter clogging the path caught her eye. Interesting. It was a cufflink.

Charlotte knelt down to pick it up and gasped. She turned it carefully in the light, scrutinizing each angle and detail as she searched her memory for where she had seen its unique markings before. The shock of it paused her steps as she recognized the symbol from ten years ago—crude lines in the shape of a goat, with an inverted cross on its forehead.

Coincidences were never random, but rather, they were the threads that wove together the tapestry of fate, binding us to a destiny we cannot escape. For years she had searched for similar markings. She knew it didn't really burn, but with the silver in her hand she might as well have been holding fire. She wrapped her fingers tightly around the cufflink, pressing the metal into her skin. It was coming home with her. A connection, even if small, was one step closer to finding out the truth behind her mother's demise.

She rounded the corner and headed for the baker's back door, but stopped. She could almost feel the brush of her mother's hand against her cheek, like a whisper on the wind, reminding her to have courage.

Dear God.

Blood pooled upon the cobblestones.

# A Shocking Display

*T*his cannot be.

Charlotte's hands shook uncontrollably as she stared down at the visceral scene before her. Heart pounding, unable to breathe, but unable to stop, Charlotte stepped closer to the swollen legs lying in a puddle of blood at Gayle Williams' back door.

Get away from here.

Fear held her back, yet stronger curiosity pushed her forward. The buzz of flies met her ears and when she inhaled, the putrid stench of death choked her.

Good God, it was awful. With little warning, sickness claimed her. She heaved, clutching her stomach as she retched into the bushes.

How has no one seen this yet?

She ventured a glance beyond the splayed legs, where the head of Gayle Williams was split in two.

Visions of Mother flashed before her eyes.

Her hands. A pool of blood. Lifeless, glassy eyes staring at nothing.

The horror of what Mother had experienced in her final moments had lingered in the air that day. For whatever reason, Charlotte could feel it then, and now. The pain. The agony. The desperation of one who knew their final moments were upon them.

Dissolving into a scream that tore her from the inside, she heard the thud of footsteps. The fire from within crawled up her neck and to her ears.

"No. No. No! Take me away! Take me away from here!"

Warm arms surrounded her, squeezing tight.

As quickly as it had begun, the violent vision of Mother was over. The deep pressure of the hug gave her comfort.

Breathe, Charlotte. Breathe.

A solemn calm washed over her. Peace cometh, pain goeth–a simple phrase she often repeated to calm her mind.

"Lottie! Oh my sweet girl. Shhhh. Shhhh. It's all right. You're all right."

Her face buried deep in his chest, she smelled the familiar freshly cut wood mixed with musk and spices.

Papa? But why was he here?

People of the town rushed around the corner toward them now.

"Good God!"

"What happened here?"

"Murder! Murder in Philadelphia!"

Papa led her across the street to the little bench beside Mrs. Tavisham's garden. On any other day Charlotte enjoyed distantly watching the activity of the square from this spot, a safe way for her to participate among the outskirts...but not this day.

"Papa, what are you doing in town?"

"Summoned by a client, dear one." Their years of struggle had added lines to her Papa's face, but never dimmed the determined hope in his eyes. He wiped his sweaty brow. "I'd only just met with Priya when we heard your scream."

Mrs. Duloe swept across the street followed closely by a troubled-looking Priya.

"My God! Darling what did you see? Are you all right? Are you injured?"

"I've got her, Ophelia. Thank you." Papa waved the clucking woman back and again turned to Charlotte. "How did you come to venture back there, dear one?"

"I– I was merely going to check on Mr. Williams, to see if he was ill. I never thought—"

"Well of course we couldn't have known." Priya sat beside them, packages in her lap, wringing her hands.

She breathed. In. Out.

Gently wiping the tears from her cheeks, her Papa whispered soothing words, just as he had after childhood nightmares.

Peace cometh...pain goeth. Charlotte straightened, wiping the remaining tears from her eyes. "Papa, the sight of blood startled me, but I am recovering my wits."

With the evident concern in his eyes, he wasn't convinced. Papa turned to Mrs. Duloe. "Ophelia, I see Mayor Payne headed this way. Please tell him I would like a moment to ensure my daughter is well before he begins his questions."

Charlotte noticed her Papa's jaw clench at the mayor's approach. His hatred for the vile man still simmered below the surface.

"Of course, Thaddeus." Ophelia Duloe waddled away.

Priya sat to her left and grasped her hands. "Lottie, are you truly void of an anxious heart?" Lines of worry creased her brow.

She wasn't, but she wanted to be, or at least appear so.

Her racing heart had nearly settled.

"Yes, yes of course." She turned to look at him. "We will speak with the mayor and then Priya and I will prepare for dinner this evening."

"Dinner?" Papa's brows lifted in surprise.

"Yes...with the Franklin family. Priya and I have been invited to a social engagement. I wouldn't want to disappoint her by not attending."

Priya blushed. "Lottie-. "

"I'd like to go." Charlotte tucked stray curls behind her ear, hoping to mask her shaking hands.

Papa and Priya both studied her. She wasn't sure how she had managed to remain outwardly calm, but a sense of normalcy would help her reset the day and clear the visions from her mind.

Typically, her affirmations worked to calm her, but today nothing could wash away their stain.

Papa stood. "Priya. Stay with Lottie. I must speak with Payne. Lottie, I'll meet you back at home, if that's all right?"

Priya nodded. "Of course, Mr. Scott."

"I'll see you soon, Papa." She embraced him and watched as he walked away.

Priya handed over Charlotte's items. "I wonder who did it." Priya questioned, instantly returning to her usual charm. A wicked sense of amusement flashed in her best friend's eyes. "I wish I could have seen it."

Settling the parcels on her lap, Charlotte's cheeks heated. She wasn't all right, she'd only stated it to ease Papa's worry. But surely Priya knew that? "Doesn't the murder bother you at all?"

Priya's lips parted in surprise, then melted into a smug scowl. "What happened to being all right? Of course it bothers me! But you can't say you're entirely surprised, Lottie. The man had enemies. Gambling debts. Most likely he smacked one too many bottoms of the married ladies in town and some hot-headed husband came to teach him a lesson."

Charlotte bristled, thinking of the sweet cakes. "For shame! Gayle Williams was a delightful man. A little flirtatious, but never dangerous. Certainly not as malicious as this murderer now on the loose."

Priya's eyes had darkened, lost for a moment in what Charlotte knew were memories of what her best friend had witnessed while living on the streets of Kolkata. Priya cast her gaze to the ground and held her hands in her lap, suddenly becoming enthralled with her painted nails. "You're thinking of your mother, aren't you?"

Of course she was thinking of Mother. How could she not?

Priya sighed. "I'm sorry, Lottie. I didn't think of what this would bring up for you. They'll find out what happened. They'll find the killer."

Priya reached out and squeezed Charlotte's hands, as if she tried to absorb her pain.

"Well, Priya," Charlotte muttered. "I hope you're right. Perhaps this was a squabble gone awry and Philadelphia isn't going to have another rash of murders."

Like Mother's.

Priya flashed her a look of concern. "Shall I walk you home? We can speak of something else to take your mind off of this gruesome business."

No. She wanted time alone with her thoughts—to dissect them, work through them—to immerse herself into the darkest possibilities in order to steel herself for whatever terrors might come.

"No, but thank-you, dear one. Go home and prepare yourself for our pleasantries this evening," she said, managing a smile. "You'll want to look your best for Mr. Priestly."

It was late afternoon and the town square had finally quieted as she and Priya parted. Mothers clutched their precious babes, headed home to start supper. The Statehouse emptied as the council finished for the day. She noticed Madam Delphia, one of Society's elite, whispering with a beautiful woman in a crimson red dress that she didn't know. The clouds had again overtaken the sky, casting a grim curtain. A low canopy of fog drifted through the streets, the evening's cool descending upon Philadelphia proper.

Gravel crunched beneath her feet as Charlotte walked towards home, absorbed in her thoughts. The shock of a grisly, premature death, taken by the hands of a fellow townsman, was disquieting.

Gayle Williams had been butchered like a pig.

Charlotte quickened her pace as she glanced over her shoulder, unable to shake the chilling thought that the killer still roamed free. She must not question God's purposes but would never understand why he allowed death to take the innocent.

She shuddered, clutching her packages. A chilling thought indeed.

Murder was a tragedy she knew too well.

Some say time heals even the deepest of wounds, yet her memories remain indelible stains, never bringing peace. The death of the jolly baker served as a stark reminder of what she needed for closure. Ten years and the culprit unknown, she hadn't ceased searching, and she wouldn't– not until she knew the truth.

Charlotte shivered and quickened her steps.

Earlier, her thoughts had turned to love, safety, and a dinner party with the Franklins.

But now, it seemed, she would again have reason to fear the shadows.

The walk from the town center to Quarry Street and Third where she and Papa lived was a quick journey. Three streets to the left, then three streets to the right. She had assured Priya that she would be fine alone, yet, as the daylight faded and the air turned brisk, perspiration dotted her brow.

No need to be frightened. It was merely a walk home. The same walk she had taken hundreds of times at the edges of town, sided by thick woods.

But not with a murderer on the loose.

Three streets.

Her footsteps quickened with each heartbeat. Whether it was the cold, or something else, the hair on her arms and nape of her neck prickled.

Two streets now.

Then turn left.

To her left, she had to pass the poor Baker's shop again. No wonderful smells of bread and muffins wafted through the air this crisp evening. No sweet biscuits saved for her.

Lightless. Lifeless.

As she rounded the corner, a sudden bark startled her. A wagging tail disappeared around the corner. She must have frightened him, too.

She should have taken a different path, to avoid it. Why hadn't she?

Oh God. There they were, bloodstained cobblestones by the door.

A few steps forward. Get past his house.

A few steps forward. Not far from home. Though she breathed a sigh of relief, something made her pause and glance at the town shut-in's manor. It was a quiet place. A place of loneliness. The formerly fine manor had fallen into disrepair, with crumbling walls and a sagging roof. Charlotte had never laid eyes on the wealthy woman who lived there—no one in town ever had.

Yet, whispers of witchcraft and devilish rituals surrounded the enigmatic woman. She sent out for her necessities and never set foot outside. No one knew where she came from or who her family was.

At one time, the front yard had burst with rare imported flowers of every hue. The air was once thick with the sweet scent of yellow jasmine, which had climbed the trellises that lined the garden. Forsythias and irises used to spill out of overflowing planter boxes, their vibrant colors a riot against the often gray sky. Charlotte thought she could still smell the sweet perfume of the peonies by the gate. She was struck with a faint memory of walking around in that garden. But no, that couldn't be possible. Perhaps it had been a dream.

A man-sized cross, wooden and worn, drowned in the wild thorns of a dead rosebush, the flowerbed a soggy matting of wilted stems. She recalled Mother pointing out the rose cross, rumored to mark the Rosicrucian Order - witches, the minister called them. The once-lush blooms were now withered and dry, their petals curling in on themselves and colors faded to a dull brown. She fought the temptation to pluck a rose and crumble it to dust. How satisfying it would be to let the ashes fall through her fingertips.

A looming figure stole her breath. It emerged from the shadows, indistinct in the mist. Charlotte strained to make out its features as her heart raced.

But it wasn't a figure...it was a statue, just off the cobblestone path. She'd never seen it there before.

She squinted through the fog for a better look.

Dear God. It wasn't a statue. It was a woman—dressed in black.

She was shrouded in mist, her black veil trailing along the ground like a darkened river.

A skeletal arm stretched out from beneath the veil. Long, dark fingernails sprouted from a bony white hand. From fear or from witchcraft, Charlotte was unable to move.

The faintest sound drifted through the air. A cough, or more like a rasp.

She strained to hear it.

"Charlotte."

# Far From Shadows

**B**reathe in. Breathe out. In. Out.

Nothing was coming. No one was chasing her. Just breathe.

Perhaps the visions were beginning again. Her throat burned. Her ears rushed.

Thank God. The front door of her cherished family home was within view. The meetinghouse blue beckoned her, similar to the inviting hue of a cloudless summer sky. It promised familiar warmth and safety behind the peeling paint. She arrived at the parsnip door and reached for the leather latch string, ready to lift the bar and enter. Papa and Miss Nelly would soothe her. They could prune the unseen vines that tightened around her throat with each breath.

Why must she endure this affliction of the nerves, this weakness that left her vulnerable to the terrors of the world? If only she didn't crumble as easily as the dried rose from the garden with any small pressure. Papa once told her that Mother had suffered from the same malady. The fiery surge up her throat and the sudden rush in her ears were the harbingers of her anxiety, ruling her life with an iron grip. Of all the traits Mother could have given her, this was one she would gladly return.

With one more step over the threshold, she entered her sanctuary, her haven of peace and safety at last.

Miss Nelly's embrace upon her return was as comforting as the warm rolls she had baked for dinner.

"Sweet lass, are ye al rite? Ye look to have crossed wi' a spirit!"

She must have looked something dreadful for Nelly to greet her so.

"On the way home, I—I saw…"

No. She was home now. She would not allow worry to vex her. No need to bring up the grotesque woman in black. Perhaps she had imagined her. She focused on the dinner invitation, grasping for it like a life preserver in her swirling thoughts.

"Nothing. I saw nothing."

Papa and Nelly shared a worried glance. Both had known her mother and were no doubt concerned that she was falling into the same mental bog that had plagued her near the end.

"Yer no' all rite, child."

Surely Papa had told her of the baker. Nelly was the closest thing to a mother Charlotte had now. Her homely smile melted away all fear of witches or spirits. The wick to their candle, Nelly had kept her family's spirits alight for as long as she could remember—since Mother and Papa had employed her. She'd come from Boston nearly 20 years ago, among the first of the Ulster Scots to arrive in Philadelphia. Since then, she'd been a blessing beyond description.

"A paircel!" Nelly stepped back and clasped her hands. "Cud that be a new dress fir our beautiful Lottie?"

It was an attempt by dear Nelly to take Charlotte's mind from whatever bothered her, and it worked.

Charlotte smiled, calmness settling in her chest, her heart no longer racing in an attempt to escape its cage. "Yes, I purchased a dress, and, truth be told…" she flushed, "I have somewhere to wear it this very evening!"

She met Papa's gaze. So gentle and kind, her beloved Papa was worn thin by time and sorrow. He didn't speak of the past very often, but that was certainly the cause of his frequent spells of silence, entrapped in his own memories. Some evenings, once the work was done and their own chores tended, he would sit by the fire with a cup of hot tea that would usually grow cold long before it touched his lips.

"My Lottie." Papa's outstretched arms promised another warm embrace, his calloused hands closing around hers. "Feeling better?"

"I am well."

Papa narrowed his eyes, so stern and serious. "Earlier you mentioned dinner tonight but did not say how those arrangements came about? I would like to hear more, if you would have my blessing."

She managed a smile. "Priya and I ran into John Priestly and Ben Franklin today. They were with her brother, Amir." Butterflies fluttered in her stomach. Come to think of it—more like moths.

Now she must convince Papa that this was a good idea, an ironic twist of events considering she still needed to convince herself she was excited to attend.

Soft flickers of flame illuminated Papa's furrowed brow. Was it anger that she saw? No, the lines of his forehead were shadows of concern.

He closed his eyes and drew a long breath. "A courtship? Surely not, sweet Lottie. I am hardly acquainted with either man."

Charlotte bristled. "Papa, there is no need to treat me like a glass egg. I am a woman grown!"

Nelly swooped in. "Now Thaddeus! If tha child wishes to kipple wi' a young lad, she could have chosen a much poorer match, in more ways than one. She needs a bit o' joy to brighten her days, don't ye ma dear?"

Charlotte's stomach tightened. Farewell, butterfly moths. "Oh no! No...no...nothing like that." She studied their faces as they examined hers. "Mr. Priestly invited us to share dinner with them at one of the Franklin homes. It's Ben's Aunt Beth, I believe. Ben Franklin has returned and they intend to celebrate his accomplishments abroad. If the rumors are true, he's quite the diplomat."

"And you intend to celebrate him, too?" Papa raised an eyebrow. The shadow of a smirk crept across his scruffy, weathered face, as if he knew something she did not. Always the skeptic, especially when it came to the town elite.

"Why...yes." She crossed her arms. "Yes, I do."

Papa's voice was laced with suspicion as he asked, "Will the governor attend this soiree de celebration? The mayor? You know the kind of company that Franklin family keeps." With narrowed eyes and pursed lips, Papa turned his attention to the fireplace, one hand upon the mantle to support his weight, or perhaps—his worry. His other jammed at the coals with an iron poker.

Charlotte crossed the room and rested her own hand on her Papa's shoulder. "He didn't mention who else would be there. Mr. Priestly is taken with Priya, and if she were to have to go alone, she'd never forgive me. She surely needs an escort, a trusted friend, to accompany her. Someone to keep her from making too much of an impression. You know as well as any how she can ramble herself into a corner."

"Thaddeus, plaise." Nelly clutched at her apron.

He turned a sharp eye and settled it upon Charlotte. "If this is what you wish, then I willingly oblige—but be careful among society's finest, my dear one. They are not all they seem."

Papa's misgivings surrounding Philadelphia's elite were certainly concerning, yet it was the gentry that typically received his scorn. He had always been wary of those who held themselves above others, those who revealed in their own wealth and power. This dinner was with the Franklin family, and they were an upstanding lineage of high moral character. She had nothing to fear.

Still, with his approval, even begrudging, her heart soared with joy. She planted a kiss on his scruffy cheek and with a quickening pulse, hurried off to prepare herself for the evening's festivities.

Once in her room, she realized the burst of emotion and paused to understand it. Merely hours ago, the thought of dining with the Franklins had filled Charlotte with unease. Now, however, an allure had taken hold of her. Something of substance could come of this night for Priya. Perhaps this was one of those moments only found in stories in which a life was changed forever. Though the thought of socializing knotted her stomach after such an ordeal, the prospect of disappointing Priya was even more distasteful. Charlotte resolved to push through her discomfort for her friend's sake.

Nelly knocked to ask if she needed help with her dress.

Forcing a grin from ear to ear, she let the kindly woman in. A

long-standing confidant in her life with whom she planned to share every detail of her evening.

The murder slipped from her mind entirely.

AUNT BETH
SAMUEL
MR. FRANKLIN
SARAH
MRS. FRANKLIN
ELIZABETH
THOMAS
CHARLOTTE
BEN FRANKLIN
PRIYA
JOHN PRIESTLY
MADAM DELPHIA

# *Whispers of Wealth*

Dinner with the Franklins was a far cry from the simple meals Charlotte was accustomed to.

'Twas an excessive affair.

Where Charlotte found comfort in the humble furnishings of her own home, judiciously selected by Mother and Papa when they first wed, this grandiose manor on Society Hill featured the finest walnut furnishings of Queen Anne's style. Beadwork cushions in tones of clotted cream sat on every chair. Light flooded the room through the floor-to-ceiling windows that were taller than many trees she had seen, but just as breezy. The red ochre walls were covered with gold-framed portraits of surly, but handsome men, graceful beauties, and children in frilly lace dresses. No doubt they were members of the Franklin family, long passed.

Aunt Beth, her dewy skin as supple as a woman half her age, held court at the head of the longest table Charlotte had ever seen. The centerpiece was a colossal lobster no less than four feet in length from claw to tail. She'd had lobster before, remembering its firm yet smooth texture, tender and sweet, dipped in melted butter and served on a platter. The ones she'd had were much smaller, of course. Perhaps that's why the Franklins had one on their table now. A crustacean of this size must have cost a great deal more than the smaller ones found at the market.

Aunt Beth glanced from face to face. Her brother Josiah, Ben's father, sat beside Aunt Beth. He smoothed the napkin tucked into his linen shirt and waistcoat. "My dearest sister, thank you for the glorious spread you have provided to welcome back our Ben. You have outdone yourself!" She would wait for them to reach out and start their meal. The sheer number of cutleries before her was a daunting sight. Surely someone would begin soon.

Mr. Franklin nodded at their hostess, a smile dancing under his mustache. "Pray tell this lobster did not come from that ferret by the docks?" He chuckled at the offense registered on Aunt Beth's painted face.

"Of course not! I'll not be serving those cockroaches of the sea in my home. This is a mere decoration, brother." She narrowed her eyes, her thin lips curling into a sly grin.

Charlotte set her fork back on the table. Hopefully no one saw her mistake. She sheepishly glanced around to see if anyone had noticed. Aunt Beth's amused stare struck her like lightning.

Damn.

Of course. Lobster was a lowly food, eaten by those less fortunate than the Franklins, and would likely be devoured by the servants who prepared their grand spread of delicacies, perhaps shared with the children, widows, and widowers of town.

That was why she had tasted it before. When Papa's business hit hard times.

"Oh Josiah! Come now, stop your pestering. Simply enjoy and celebrate the return of our son." Mrs. Franklin brandished her fork like a dagger.

"Weapons at the dinner table! Please excuse my wife for her lapse in etiquette and threats of violence!" Mr. Franklin chuckled once more, passing a wink to his beloved.

So, they were playful, Ben's parents. That was a good sign. It was reminiscent of the banter shared by her own.

Charlotte returned her attention to the mysterious Aunt Beth. Though visibly pleased to be surrounded by family, and graciously accepting of her two unexpected guests, she sat mostly silent. Floral arrangements of pink angel's trumpets were delicately placed behind her on the buffet.

There was a fierceness in her probing eyes. Charlotte recognized the same look in Ben's.

Once the gargantuan lobster was removed, the sumptuous meal started with spoonbread and sweet potato muffins, setting the tone for the dinner to come. Next came creamy peanut soup, topped with roasted peanuts that provided the perfect crunch. But which spoon? Charlotte glanced around the table again.

Directly across from her, Ben spun his third spoon idly. A whisper of a smile played about his lips.

The third spoon it was. Best to take smaller bites so as not to appear gluttonous—an impossible task when each spoonful brought with it a wash of exquisite joy. No' another bite into yer mouth until the former is swallowed, Miss Nelly would say.

The Franklin family laughed, told jokes, and rejoiced at Ben's return. How wrong Papa was. The Franklins were exactly as they appeared to be. Playful. Kind-hearted. Generous. She was among good company.

Charlotte whispered in Priya's ear, "If only Papa could see this side of Society Hill."

Priya raised her eyebrows and nodded in agreement, her mouth too full to respond.

The Franklin family had taken their places in a well-rehearsed routine. Ben's older brother, Thomas Franklin, and his wife, Elizabeth, were seated close together in the middle. They graciously tried to include her in conversation. Thankfully, they already knew Priya. Thomas owned the Apothecary where her brother Amir had chosen, to the great shock of all, to apprentice.

From the head of the table, their hostess spoke, her gaze fixed on Ben. "What troubles you, nephew? Is Yankee pot roast not to your liking?"

Ben surveyed his portions. "I do not enjoy the taste of flesh, Aunt B... remember?"

Aunt Beth gasped, a hand flying to her chest. "Oh dear, it slipped my mind! Do tell me the rest of your meal is to your liking?"

Ben nodded. "No trouble at all. My plate overflows with delicacies and my cup runneth over with wine." He winked. "I'll be sloshed before the night ends. So kind of you to look after my needs."

Bethshua Franklin grinned. How pearly white her teeth were.

Charlotte glanced at her plate. It brimmed with samplings of succotash, squash medley, and green beans tinged with a tartness that tasted of apple cider vinegar. A variety of cutlery remained before her, and with ten courses she would surely use them all. It would be a social faux pas to use one out of order.

Priya was, as expected, a delight to the entire room. Spoon in hand, she carried conversation with Madame Delphia and John Priestly with ease. John could hardly peel his attention from her. Charlotte studied the tablecloth in front of her and tried to choose a matching spoon. Heavens above, the steamed pumpkin pudding was delicious.

"Such a delight to join you all this evening!" Priya took another sip from her cherry wine. "Charlotte and I are unaccustomed to such lavish dining, and we are much obliged for the invitation."

Ben's sullen sister, Sarah, sat next to Madam Delphia at the other end of the table. She lowered her glass slowly, her eyes fixed on Charlotte like a predator stalking its prey. "I must admit, it is unusual to invite a lady into someone else's home, but we cherish our John, and I can't say this is a first."

Priya's smile faltered for the first time that evening.

"Now, Sarah—" Samuel, Ben's other brother, interceded. "Let's not patronize our guests." He ate with speed, shoveling food into his mouth. This family had so many members, Charlotte had a hard time keeping it all straight.

"Were you near the baker's shop today as they discovered the body?" Samuel asked, turning toward Charlotte with a mouthful of game pie, a mischievous grin playing about his lips.

Where before the room had chilled her, it was now exceedingly hot. "We were, though we were blessed not to suffer the sight of such atrocities for long." She shared a withering glance with Priya.

Mr. Franklin signaled to the servant boy. "More cherry!"

Yes, please, more wine.

Aunt Beth cackled into her glass. "The sight of such atrocities? My dear girl, you're correct in fearing such sights."

Mrs. Franklin's eyes grew wide. Aunt Beth continued. "Pray tell, girls, have you ever heard of the Salem debauchery?"

Priya nodded. Speechless for once.

As was Charlotte, trying hard to force down the bit of pork she had just swallowed. The taste turned bitter in her mouth, tainted by the unspeakable horror the accused suffered.

Aunt Beth raised her voice. "I was there. I witnessed the heresy myself." Her nostrils flared. "Twisted bodies, dead livestock. I myself suffered from hysterical blindness and convulsions!"

The clinking of silverware upon fine china ceased.

After basking in the silence for far too long, Aunt Beth continued, lowering her voice. "Do you know the Devil, girls? Have you seen what his presence can bring?"

The drums in her chest began their tapping. The color had drained from Priya's face.

Mrs. Franklin rested a hand on Aunt Beth's arm. "Bethshua, I think that's enough. Let's not frighten our guests."

Aunt Beth continued. "My testimony sent Martha Corey to the gallows."

"More wine!" Mr. Franklin bellowed. His eyes flitted about the table. "Dear sister, let's not dwell on events thirty years past. We live in the present, and that's where our minds should be! To Ben!"

"To Ben," the table echoed, followed by the clink and clatter of silverware.

Sarah raised her glass for more wine, but Elizabeth stopped her, placing a hand on Sarah's wrist to lower it. Samuel noticed, as did Thomas and Mrs. Franklin, judging by their expressions.

While the meal had resumed, the tone had darkened. There were unspoken secrets at this table. Charlotte could feel them.

Mrs. Franklin turned to her, smiling. "John tells us you were busy at the market today?"

"Yes!" Priya clasped her hands together. "We purchased the very dresses we are wearing."

Oh, Priya. Widen the unspoken canyon that separates us from them.

Ben lifted his eyes to meet Charlotte's. A softness lingered behind them. Somehow, they made her feel safe.

"You chose well," Ben muttered.

His smile reappeared, seemingly meant for her alone.

But surely not.

"Oh yes, absolutely beautiful you both are!" Madame Delphia's chair strained as she scooted to the table. If chairs could speak, hers screamed.

Excessiveness leads to excessiveness, it seemed.

"Perhaps you can wear them to the Franklin Ball when the time comes? The Gentleman of College acapella group from William and Mary will be in attendance. It shall be divine," Elizabeth Franklin whispered.

"How does your Father fare, Miss Charlotte?" Oh dear, Delphia again.

"I'd heard there were many wheelwrights in town now. And after—" Delphia paused, "does that diminish his patronage, pray tell?"

The heat rose to Charlotte's cheeks. She surely matched the shade of her dress by now. How dare Delphia allude to Mother.

"We do fine, Madame. Papa has many long-standing customers that require his services."

Delphia sighed. "That's lovely dear. I send many carriages around this town on business."

Oh, it was known. Madame Delphia scandalously ran a "companion" service for Philadelphia's elite.

"The next time the blasted cobblestones wreak havoc upon one of our wheels, we will send word to him," Delphia said.

Whether it was a smile or sneer plastered upon Delphia's face, she couldn't tell. It was a backhanded offering. The way it was spoken could

have been considered charity for the poor or genuine interest. Either way, the chasm of wealth between their families was emphasized all the same.

Charlotte forced a smile. "That would be lovely, Madame Delphia. Thank you."

Please don't let this wicked woman call upon Papa with her tainted, sinful funds.

Priya leaned in, bosom in full view yet again. "That's highly generous of you, Mrs. Delphia."

Charlotte lightly kicked her under the table. Priya scowled.

Delphia surveyed Priya with newfound interest, as if truly seeing her for the first time.

"Josiah, I've a joke for you!" John Priestly spoke, right on cue. "Why do they call an engagement a match?"

Priya rested her chin in one hand, staring at John with longing in her eyes. The elder Franklin swallowed another bite of his prime rib. "It's hard to say, my boy. Why?"

"Because it is so easily broken!" The table dissolved in forced laughter. Priya's smile melted into a frown. Charlotte squeezed her hand, sensing her disappointment.

Thomas signaled to the servant boy to bring the fish muddle. "Now Ben, do tell us of your travels in London."

She glanced at Ben. His eyes met hers, if only for a moment, before turning back to Thomas.

"Well, brother, I am pleased to announce that our American Philosophical Society was successful in discussions with the Parliament of Great Britain. I expected a fight over certain legislations, but our fellows were largely at peace. I learned a great deal while there, and hope to return one day in good company."

So, they were loyal to the crown. Of course they were. Perhaps Papa was correct in their seditious nature of high society, after all.

She found herself unexpectedly satiated, only to be confronted by the arrival of the syllabub, which would be a shame to leave unsampled.

# Seduction of Society

As the lamplight dimmed, Charlotte and Priya prepared to depart. They were alone in the foyer.

"Priya, heed my warning, steer clear of Delphia. She's a wicked woman and not one to involve yourself with."

Priya opened her mouth, but as she started to speak, Aunt Beth approached them.

Charlotte knew she needed to thank her for the evening, but what could she say?

Her best friend spoke. "Thank-you again, Mrs. Franklin, for allowing us to intrude upon your family affair. The food was delicious and the company was lovely." Confident Priya, as always.

"I appreciate your manners, dear one. John seems quite taken with you." Priya's cheeks warmed with a crimson glow.

Aunt Beth spoke again. "Perhaps we will meet again soon. I would be delighted." The smile she offered seemed genuine, in stark contrast to her demeanor at the dinner table. Without another word, their hostess swept away. Curious.

John Priestly and Ben entered the foyer, debonair as always. Headed to brandy and cigars, no doubt.

John bowed low. "Your carriage awaits! Let me escort you to the door, my fair lady."

Priya giggled as she wrapped her arm in John's.

As they departed, Charlotte found herself alone with Ben.

"Shall we, my fair lady," he said, extending his arm. The cheeky grin made its appearance once more.

She chuckled. "Are you contesting my fairness, kind sir?" A joke. Two could play this game.

"I wouldn't dare insult you, Miss Charlotte." He stared into her soul. "Come. Take my arm. Let me escort you to the carriage, if you please."

She took it. Strong as stone. Safe.

"Thank your Aunt Beth again for us, 'twas a lovely evening."

Ben nodded. "Perhaps I will see you at the library soon? You read to the children there, if I'm not mistaken?"

How did he know that? But of course—everyone in this town knows everything.

"Perhaps." She smiled. One step up. Lift the dress in. There we go. Priya leaned out the window, sending inappropriate whisperings to Mr. Priestly on the street below. How forward they were.

"Come along, John. Leave the ladies to their evening."

Ben to the rescue yet again.

As the coachman signaled the horses, Madame Delphia burst forth from Beth Franklin's home. Blustering and bulbous, she lifted her skirts almost as high as her nose in the air.

"Hold please! I must speak with the girls."

What the devil could she want with us. Surely nothing good.

"Miss Priya, Miss Charlotte. I'm sorry to delay your departure."

Was she, though?

"I couldn't help but notice the connection between yourself," staring with interest at Priya, "and our John."

Priya flushed as red as the rose bushes beside the front gates.

"You do know I play somewhat of a matchmaker in the, shall I say, better half of town?"

The way she influenced better was a bitter stab to the heart. Once upon a time, Charlotte's family had been close to the elusive better club, but after Mother, and the town suspecting Papa, their fortunes took a turn.

Priya, who knew better and evidently did not care, leaned closer to Madame Delphia. "Yes, I have some knowledge of your matchmaking." Her eyes sparkled with mischief. "But how does that concern us?" Her voice was but a whisper.

"The quickest way to a man's heart is through his breeches, my dear."

How forward!

"These other hens will beat around the bush and waste away their youth chasing after dreams, destined to wind up chained to the home by a husband and babies." Delphia gave them a knowing look. "Don't waste your years. I can teach you how to capture John Priestly, or any other well-bred fellow and make him yours. That's what you want, isn't it?"

Priya nodded. She was the only one to do so.

"Think about it. You've got a pretty face and I'm sure an even prettier pair of legs."

The audacity of this woman astounded her. She longed to silence Delphia's poisonous ideas, but held her tongue, determined not to let the woman provoke her.

Delphia continued. "Your flowers are worth a lot, my dears. You could do well for yourselves under my direction."

Charlotte bristled. Absolutely not.

Delphia turned to her. "How doth a man experience your pleasures, Miss Charlotte?"

Her cheeks burned and she did little to hide her scowl. "Through the church." Selling her virtue was unthinkable, no matter the temptation of status or wealth.

Delphia narrowed her eyes.

"Send a messenger if you ever take an interest—don't worry, I'll cover the cost."

And off she went, like a squat, painted toad, headed back into the Franklin abode.

# The Price

*"Five bodies and blood were the asking price, unto his Lord, he
would sacrifice"*
-Henry Meanwell

In damp catacombs lit only by an oil's fire, lost to common knowledge and relegated to whispered rumors, he stood with the congregation. They had met for generations and no longer would he merely observe. Though it had been a decade since the last offering, none present had forgotten the rites.

For the first time in recent memory, the man in the crimson cloak recognized the faintest hint of nervousness scratching and clawing inside him. He swallowed.

To stand among those who'd achieved what he had only dreamed was something of a revelation. These men and women would soon be peers if he could accomplish what must be done. However, should he fail—his own head would roll. Great was the cost. But greater still was the reward.

Their velvet robes were black as pitch at midnight, hoods draping over their eyes. In time, he would earn his own and join them as a senior member of the order.

Enlightenment always exacted a price and the wisdom of their lord demanded sacrifice. In the same way god had required his children to burn offerings of animals, so too did Lucifer, their Lord, dictate oblation. However, while god requested cattle and sheep to fulfill his covenant, Satan needed a more fitting donation; the souls of many.

Either way, it was blood magic differing only in the source of succor.

Did not their savior invite his fellowship to dine of his flesh and drink of his blood?

People differed from cattle in the way they perceived the world and acted upon it, and nothing else. The first death was exhilarating. He'd no remorse for the sin. In fact, it had been shockingly easy and dangerously addictive.

Already, he yearned to take another.

It was the beginning of something more, a test of mettle before the true trial could begin. Tonight, he would embark upon a series of tasks much larger than himself; greater even than humanity as a whole.

Their high priest spoke to everyone present. "Brothers and Sisters in blood, we gather this night to elevate our fellow, our missionary, into a higher order. He has taken the first step upon the path we have all traveled, the path of execution. This crimson cloak has done what was asked without question and without penitence." The others released a low hiss. "I submit he be given the opportunity to prove his worth. To begin the rite of damnation, with our approval. With my blood, I offer my approval."

A dagger flashed, illuminated by the flickering flames. The priest revealed his freely bleeding palm for all to see.

One by one, thirteen elders raised their own blades and hands, ready to agree or disapprove.

The man in the crimson cloak held his breath. This was the moment he'd yearned for, yet a tendril of fear gripped his heart. Should he be rejected, the sole path forward was death.

Seconds passed, each slower than before, but by the end all but two sheathed their ceremonial knives. The rest dripped crimson as the first.

Success.

Their priest spoke again, the tremble of excitement and bloodlust shaking

his voice. "By Lucifer's umbral light, this one is accepted into the fold. Name the five and let this crimson cloak begin his hunt!"

Half of those surrounding him cried out in a beautiful chorus of chaos. "The Harlot!"

"The Fool!" A woman cawed.

A gruff voice growled. "The Enemy!"

"The Servant!" A trio called at once.

The familiar, buttery smooth voice of a woman he knew intimately spoke the last. "The Lover."

Braziers blazed as their passionate priest raised his hands for emphasis. "Five souls delivered to the Master in exchange for his blessings. Five mortals slain for our cause. Return with the last for consecration through blood and earn the black cloak of enlightenment!"

The man in the crimson cloak dropped his hood and knelt before the thirteen, dozens more in the darkness beyond.

He rose in triumph. "I will do so with a heart of joy. The Master will know this servant as his own." His fate was sealed.

# The Constable Calls

The carriage lantern bobbed in the night as a second moon. It was impossible not to wonder at the stars, the pinprick wonders on the endless blanket of the night sky. What caused their changes so routinely? She imagined a celestial hand painting the cosmos, racing across the canvas of the night with strokes of pink, purple and blue. But Papa and Nelly discouraged such thoughts. For God, the author of our being, created the skies, they would say. Yet, even with her faith, something inside Charlotte spoke of more.

Priya's head thumped the window with each jolt over cobblestone. Her hands clasped together in a knuckle-white grasp.

"Priya? What troubles you, dear one?"

Priya sighed. "My heart yearns for John, but I've nothing to offer. Even with my Papa's sizable dowry, I've nothing much of value when it comes to high-brow conversations. Politics. Worldly matters." She lowered her eyes to study the floor.

"But you are the value, my sweet friend." Charlotte rubbed her arm. She hoped her words could soothe her friend's aching heart. She understood how it was to feel insufficient and lacking. In finances, and in mental fortitude, among many other things. Charlotte knew the feeling well. She had little to offer a man herself, a man like Ben.

Wait...say no. How soon the tall, serious, macaroni man had infiltrated her fleeting thoughts.

Charlotte sighed. "Didn't you see the way he cast his gaze upon you? He could hardly stay on his side of the table all evening! I half expected to find the two of you sneaking away, and I'd wager if you could have managed it, you would have."

Priya lifted her tearful eyes. Her lips narrowed into a playful, feigned scowl.

Charlotte pressed. "I saw him linger any time you were near. He brightened at your very presence!"

"But what of you and Mr. Ben Franklin?" Priya asked.

Oh dear.

"What of it?" She scoffed. "There's nothing to ponder. He simply assisted an overstuffed maiden into a departing carriage."

Priya grinned. "And paid a compliment to your new dress."

Charlotte laughed. "Oh look! Quarry Street and 3rd. Such relief to escape frivolity."

"You've had more excitement today than you've seen in a fortnight!" Priya hugged her and leaned in close, her breath tickling the outer edges of Charlotte's ear.

"And what of Madame Delphia's offer?" Her friend sat back with questioning eyes.

Charlotte froze, scandalized that Priya would give that vile woman's words a second thought. "Speak not, and shall I say, think not of that preposterous, wicked invitation again. You have no need of Delphia to capture Mr. Priestly's heart. You've already won it."

If ever a time she wished Priya would heed her warning, let it be this night.

The well-worn path that led to her home whispered signs of early autumn. Even in the dark she could see the forgotten leaves scattered about the walkway, blown in from the breeze, dashed across the ground like the hopes of many common girls that sought after wealthier men.

But she and Priya weren't common girls, and they certainly weren't in need of Delphia's Faustian bargain. Charlotte bristled remembering her audacity. Priya wouldn't actually consider it, would she?

"Good-bye dear one. I will see you in the morning at Christ Church."

"Goodnight, Charlotte."

Light flooded the pathway, revealing the gnarled branches from the wilting tree in the front yard. Her childhood swing swayed in the breeze, long since forgotten. Papa's shadow cast long across the ground, his thin set lips and sullen expression in clear view. In the distance, she heard the slightest rumble of thunder. God must be playing ninepins again. Papa waited in the door. His embrace warmed her as the cool night breeze nipped at her back.

He tilted her chin, surveying her. He could always tell if she was happy, or more often than not, fighting back the darkness within.

"Beautiful blue eyes. Like your mother's." He held the door and ushered her inside.

Nelly sat waiting, no doubt having flown through the evening housework so that she could hear every detail of the "festive boord," as she had called it earlier today. Her maternal aura yielded to a childlike glee when it came to telling stories of adventure and romance. Every bedtime memory contained Nelly recounting tales of love and fairies and wild forest creatures who did the most wonderful things. Her thirst for life was rarely dampened by the routine of daily housework.

Nelly loved to sit by the warm, crackling fire in her room. She would prop her feet to toast her toes, and read the books Charlotte brought home from the library—or tell tales from her own homeland. Papa had taught her to read in secret, much the same as the way Mother taught. Papa was kind to Nelly.

"Al rite, Lottie. Spar not a detail. Speak of yer macaroni dinner with the festive Franklins. Did thay feed you enough?" Nelly laughed, the sound of it a windchime in the breeze.

"Nelly...you wouldn't believe the enormous lobster they had. It wasn't even part of the meal! It was but a mere decoration upon the table." She hadn't the time to process everything that had happened at the dinner. Aunt Beth. Ben. Delphia. Her unease lingered, but there was no need to trouble them with those thoughts.

Papa chuckled. "You're impressed by a lobster?" As he settled in his favorite chair, a sudden disturbance erupted at the door.

Knock. Knock. Knock.

"Oh, come on then! No' in tha middle o' Lottie's story—but who's come a callin' at this late hour? Are ye lookin fir anybody, Thaddeus?" Nelly flew from annoyed to concerned with alarming speed.

Her thoughts turned again to the grisly discovery that morning. Murder. Gayle Williams. The image of the mangled body behind the bakery flooded Charlotte's mind. She shivered, the metallic scent of blood still fresh. What vicious fiend could commit such vile acts? She said a silent prayer for the poor man's soul.

The fire returned to her throat, this time immediately reaching her ears.

A crumbled rose, indeed.

She took a few short breaths, steeling herself for the unknown.

Papa crossed the room, checking to make sure his gun was in the corner by the door. As always, it was.

Knock. Knock. Knock.

The sharp rap at the door was insistent this time. Urgent.

Lightning flashed and illuminated the room. The deep roll of thunder would have shaken her if she were not already suffering a tremble. The storm had arrived.

In more ways than one.

Papa delayed, his hand clutching the latch string. His knuckles were white, his face more so.

He opened the door as another crack of lightning pierced the sky, illuminating their sudden visitor—but who?

Their unexpected guest stepped over the threshold and into the light, revealing a friend, not a foe.

"Robert Cobb!" Papa's shoulders sank back to their normal height and

thankfully his gun lay untouched in the corner. "What serves you to call this night?"

Constable Cobb.

He wasn't holding any axes, so that was a comforting sign. Her heart still raced, but thankfully upon his entrance, it started to slow. Robert Cobb was a longtime friend of Papa's. 'Twas unusual of him to call at such a late hour, but with murder afoot, she was glad to see him.

The Constable placed his hat on the table and set to the daunting task of undoing each button on his coat. His eyes, the color of clay, searched the room.

Papa continued, "Seeking shelter from the storm, old friend?"

"Nay—well yes—but I was also hoping we could converse about the latest tragedy to befall Philadelphia. I've arrived from Boston and just come from a grisly scene. Are you aware of the murder of Mr. Gayle Williams?"

"That I am, Robert." Papa settled at the head of their table. He leaned back in his chair and gestured for his friend to join him. This was no formal affair. This was an old friend.

Constable Cobb spoke again. "He was discovered on the back doorstep of his home, covered in piss and head split in two."

Papa exhaled. "We know. It was Charlotte that found him."

Nelly's eyes widened and she valiantly tried to stifle a sharp intake of breath. So Papa hadn't told her, then.

"Thaddeus, tell me, did Mr. Williams have any enemies you might know of?" A perplexed shadow covered his slightly sunken face.

Papa sighed. "To be honest with you, he was generally well-liked around the town, but had a nasty habit of trailing his hand across one too many matron's bottoms, you see."

Interesting. Papa and Priya were of the same mind. The murder of Gayle Williams was likely a husband's anger come to call. Perhaps it was.

"Anyone in particular in mind? I'm completely in the dark here, Thaddeus. There weren't any witnesses—well, legitimate ones anyway. Your townsfolk

informed me of a woman dwelling in that house with the rosy cross." His gaze expanded and Nelly leaned in with renewed interest. "But it doesn't seem as if she's welcoming to visitors."

Papa pondered. "Have you spoken with Samuel Franklin? I believe he owns the soap shop on that street?"

Sudden recognition flashed into Papa's eyes.

"Charlotte! You came from the Franklin home! What did they have to say of Gayle's untimely demise? Had they any news or suspicions among themselves?"

She thought back to the dinner. Lobster, Cherry Wine, Samuel, Sarah.

And then, of course, Ben.

"It was briefly mentioned, Papa, but nothing of importance was discussed. No witnesses or suspicions, that I recall. Merely gossip."

This town was surely good at that. If gossip could power a carriage, none of the delicate feet of Society Hill would ever tread cobblestone again.

Robert Cobb lowered his voice, practically whispering to Papa. "Could it be the devil's own, Thaddeus? The same that claimed your Catherine?"

Charlotte rose. She couldn't listen to their theories of ritual deaths again. "If you'll excuse me, Papa, Constable Cobb...the events of today have thoroughly exhausted my energy. I shall excuse myself to bed in preparation for the Sabbath."

She would pray for less excitement tomorrow.

As she left the room, Charlotte intended to retire, truly, but hearing "cloven hoof" halted her footsteps.

"A cufflink, you say?" Papa's voice faintly carried into the hall.

"Yes, it could be the symbol of a deer, or even cattle, but you know the depictions of Lucifer. as well as I."

"But what about the symbols? Were there any markings similar to those we found on Catherine's skin?" said Cobb.

Dear God. Mother.

"Nay," Constable Cobb said, "Gayle Williams had none."

Tomorrow. Tomorrow she would tell them about the cufflink she had found by Gayle Williams. She wouldn't forsake the thin thread of her peace that barely held. She would tell them, just not tonight. If this murderer was the same that claimed Mother, she would make certain they would not overtake this town again.

# *She Heard My Frist Breath, I Heard Her Last*

*"Lottie...oh Lottie..."*

The soft whisper of a familiar voice floated around her. It permeated to the depths of her soul.

"You seek and I shall hide. Count to ten and then come find me."

Mother. Her hair. The sweet perfume of rose oil and lemon that she always dabbed on her neck after a wash. Papa loved the way she smelled.

Mother rushed away, clutching her petticoats. She had the most beautiful smile, with bright, blue gemstone eyes to match.

Charlotte followed the cheerful echo of laughter, through the large rooms with white-washed walls, down the endless hallway. Where could Mother be?

She entered a hallway lined with windows, stretching unnaturally long. Crimson draperies, the color of dried blood, hung from the ceiling to the floor.

"I'm coming for you, Mother!" She peeked around each doorway, expecting Mother to jump out and cause a fright.

But room after room was empty.

A sudden sense of loneliness enveloped Charlotte as the narrow walls of the hallway seemed to suffocate her slowly. Perhaps they were closing in. Her heartbeat quickened with her pace, footsteps pounding the floor as she

started to run.

She glanced out of the broken windows. Rose bushes stared back from the other side. Had Mother gone out to the garden?

Her own breath in her ears was deafening. She must have stopped running. With the end of her footsteps came a dark, crushing, silence.

Birds outside the window opened their beaks, but sang no song.

The hollyhocks swayed, but no breeze touched her cheeks.

She reached out and ran a finger across the broken window pane.

Pain.

Her fingertip pooled with blood. She touched it to her tongue, but tasted no iron.

And then—she heard her.

"Charlotte…"

A sharp jolt wracked her middle.

"Mother! Where are you, Mother?" Fire roared up to her ears, the rush of blood coursing through her veins.

It was only a game. We were playing a game. Mother was here. She was. She had to be.

Throat on fire. Ears pounding. Pain.

"Charlotte…come find me, little love."

The hallway stretched beyond her reach, the lights dimmed and the air turned cold. The hairs on her arms prickled, but from fear or from cold, she didn't know.

Without warning, the door at the end of the blackened hallway swung open.

Slam.

Charlotte stilled. Hairs pricked at the nape of her neck. This wasn't right.

A figure stood in the doorway, its hooded robe as black as the wing of a crow. Was that a mask? She couldn't tell. The dark void beneath the hood

revealed no discernible face, only a deep blackness where features should be. One thing she knew for sure—this wasn't Mother. The looming figure lunged, crossing the hallway in one step to land in front of her.

Her hair whipped away from her face. A putrid odor of decay wafted from the robes as it drew closer, threatening to choke her. Its fetid breath washed over her face as the hooded figure loomed, coating her tongue with the taste of grave dirt.

Outstretched arms and pale hands emerged from under the robe. Soft, long, slender fingers tenderly curled around her arms.

A visceral scream escaped her lips.

"Mother!"

The crash of her head against the wall as she lunged awake was surely enough to wake the household. Her heart still pounded, clamoring to break free from the prison of her chest. The surroundings were familiar. Her chair. Her desk. Her bed.

Charlotte was home. Relief flooded through her, but her heart needed time to catch up. 'Twas a dream. Nothing more.

Mother had not come to her in a dream for a long time. She couldn't shake the feeling that maybe Mother was trying to send her a message from beyond.

But if this was merely a dream, why did her finger bleed?

The Tenth
Chapter

# For Judgement



To startle the peaceful sleep of one held dear is an experience met with hesitation. Often, intentionally slowed and softened movements, or the slight pause of a hand intent upon awakening a beast, occur when there are consequences to the cause. How would the awoken react? Suppose that age is taken into account, considering the waking of a child differs significantly to that of rousing an elder.

Something intriguing stirred in waking the soft, serene slumber of the sacrificial lamb headed to slaughter. Blonde curls spilled across the pillow—an insolent, weak husband by her side. A terrible protector, it seemed. Not that it came as a surprise. He'd made it all the way into their bedroom without displacing a speck of dust, and was almost disappointed there would be no struggle. These circumstances were too easy.

Yet, the one he came for had cast her stones, and with her judgment had sealed a gruesome fate. She should have known better.

For tonight, Elizabeth Franklin, it is your turn to die. And this will not be a quick death, like that of the vile Gayle Williams. A quick kiss between axe and skull and that troublemaker succumbed.

No, this...this will be as slow as a raindrop melting down the steeple of the church you hold so dear. Judgment was a sin. And you, Elizabeth, cast the first stone. To startle the peaceful sleep of one held dear is an experience met with hesitation. Often, intentionally slowed and softened movements, or the slight pause of a hand intent upon awakening a beast, occurred when there were consequences to the cause. How would the awoken react? Suppose that age is taken into account, considering the waking of a child differs significantly to that of rousing an elder.

Something intriguing stirred in waking the soft, serene slumber of the sacrificial lamb headed to slaughter. Blonde curls spilled across the pillow—an insolent, weak husband by her side. A terrible protector, it seemed. Not that it came as a surprise. He'd made it all the way into their bedroom without displacing a speck of dust, and was almost disappointed there would be no struggle. These circumstances were too easy.

Thomas, her husband, snored ever so slightly, prompting a quickened resolve.

He knew there wouldn't be much time after waking her, thus a moment of hesitation took hold. A delay for the sacrificial lamb. One more moment for the bitch who elevated herself above the rest.

He took care not to drop the cloth meticulously covered in the silencing aide--a tincture of seaweed and eucalyptus. Two ingredients not easily procured, but effective in rendering the unsuspecting immobile. Easy now. He leaned in and brushed the cloth to her lips. Her eyes fluttered, but did not open.

Good. Let's close those eyes forever.

The weight of his hands pushed her back into the pillow, one pressing the cloth over her mouth and nose, the other covering her eyes. She needn't know who was taking her, just yet. He raised a leg and placed it on the bed to balance weight and lay his body over hers. She pressed into the bed.

We need not disturb the husband. He only had to hold her down until the silencer took hold. An encouragement for her to yield to the horrors yet to come for her. By his hand.

Her skin was soft, like the velvet of a lamb's ear, and she was delicately

petite. So thin. If not for the softness of their over plump bed, his weight would have crushed the air from her lungs by now. Even so, her frail frame hardly struggled as he waited.

Too many fall into the trap of naivete, raised to think the silencer will provide an instant escape from pain, or the means to control—for nefarious purposes, of course. But he knew better. The silencer needed time to take hold.

Her body was warm underneath him. There were possibilities here.

Unnatural...unnerving...unwilling...grotesque possibilities of pleasure.

No.

Not this night. Time was a swift thief, and had already stolen a portion of the evening away. Those he worked for would anger if he further disturbed her. His task was clear. He must use what little time remained to accomplish another costly deed. What once would have been concern for his eternal soul, was now in question. Gayle Williams assisted in lifting that holy weight. The weight of humanity. The weight of choice. The weight of who society deemed it appropriate for him to be.

But not anymore.

Elizabeth Franklin stilled. The silencer had done its job. Now it was time to move her frail frame downstairs. He was well-acquainted with the basements beneath Society Hill homes and their suffocating confines which provided a conduit between the wealthiest of Philadelphia. Most used their damp, dark alcoves for storage quarters or concealment at the first sign of trouble. Occasionally they served as a hiding place for forbidden romps with a forbidden partner. It wouldn't be prudent to be seen. Some in the town whispered rumors of catacombs, long hallways with walls filled with sacrificial bones and native skulls.

He knew the answer.

A chair sat in the center of the room. How convenient. Elizabeth was light enough that it hardly moved when he set her upon it. She was a doll delicately placed upon a shelf. He must work with haste now, as the silencer only worked for a short amount of time.

Around the arms. Tie the ankles. Tie the wrists. The rope was rough against her porcelain skin, scratching and maiming her with its braided claws. The gag across her mouth needed to be tighter. Her head lolled from side to side as she tried to rejoin the world of the living. The silencer was already wearing off, and soon she would awaken.

But she wouldn't be awake for very long.

He left her eyes uncovered because he took great joy in the thought of her watching. He wanted her to know it was him. To understand the consequences of her judgmental actions and corrupted "grace." To spurn one is to spurn all.

Elizabeth regained consciousness. Her eyes went round, full with an undiluted understanding and fear of her predicament. They were also filled with questions and tears.

She struggled against the ropes around her arms and the filthy rag in her mouth. Coming from the floor, there was no doubt it tasted of muck and mire. A rat scurried by. The putrid smell of the basement staggered him. Elizabeth's arms showed a hint of trailing blood as she attempted to wrench free. Such a fitting end for one of high society. She tugged at her restraints, but luckily the rope ties held. 'Twas a useful skill indeed. Her pleading eyes brimmed with tears, no doubt wondering why this was happening.

Fortuitous that her daft husband was the most highly equipped apothecary in town. Bark of the willow tree, that he had slipped into her tea earlier today, had surely thinned her blood by now.

There. A slice to each wrist and one small slice to the neck, but not too much, she needed to bleed out with time. The blade parted her skin as easily as it parted butter at the dinner table. He must be cautious, so as not to unleash a crimson tide. He wasn't cutting that deep. No instant release for fair Elizabeth. Droplets would flow tonight.

First, she would experience the sensation of dizziness. He placed a hand upon her heart. She had ceased her thrashing by now. The incessant thump, thump, thump in her bosom quickened, compensating for the volume of blood loss, trying to save her.

He smirked. It wouldn't work.

She stared at him with glossy, dazed eyes. Her limbs would soon start to tingle, and then go numb. Her body would reroute the blood into her trunk

and head, an attempt to save her organs. Then, she would fall into the deepest sleep she'd ever known. When her soft, luscious curls had touched the pillow tonight, seeking sleep and escape from daily light, She could never have guessed that it was for the last time.

He sat, and he watched.

Something inside the darkness recently unveiled, encouraged him to trail his hand across his member. It was pulsating with need. As he watched her release, he craved his own.

Her eyes rolled back in her head once more. No more parties. No more dancing. No more frivolity and fine dining. No more philanthropic pursuits that were self-serving in nature more so than actual righteousness.

He stroked over the cloth. Faster. Faster. Taking himself out of his breeches to feel skin on skin. Gripping his entire length in one hand felt better than two fingers. Concentrate on the head. Yes. Her blood dripped into a crimson puddle. As he throbbed, she drained. Maybe he would release onto her body. It was getting close.

But no. Then they would know it was a man.

Suspicions be damned. He stepped towards her, she was unconscious now, and he spilled his milky seed upon her. Fuck yes.

That was...surprisingly satisfying.

A darkness settled deep within. He was letting go. Letting it in. No need to resist any longer. This is who he was.

He was a monster.

# Death is a Certainty

The embrace of a warm bed worked wonders in thawing her frightened heart, reminding Charlotte of the precious solace and security that home offered. She never took these comforts for granted.

In her heart, Charlotte cherished the fleeting moments when she saw Mother, even if it was only in a dream. Yet, the terror that accompanied these visions was a constant reminder of the darkness that lurked within her subconscious. Why couldn't her dreams be filled with the same joy and light that her mother had brought to her life? They started out so peaceful, so light, as a bud bursting to bloom. Yet then they turned dark...poisoned. Her dreams were laced with memory but distorted with pain. Not only the pain of losing her, but also the pain her mother surely felt in her final moments.

She glanced out the window to clouded skies yet again. 'Twas a distant wish to think a sunray's kiss could wake her from the dark.

Nelly blustered in, her cheerful demeanor instantly brightening the room. It was time to prepare for the Sabbath. Maybe she would discuss her troubled dreams with Minister Horvath. Even though he kept company with dreadful Mayor Payne, he was a Godly man. A righteous man. He lived to serve his Lord and town. Maybe the minister could offer words of comfort and assist her in seeking solace in the word.

****

She and Papa walked the cobblestone streets to Christ Church. She needed to tell Papa about the cufflink, but not yet.

"You look dashing today," she beamed, hugging his arm. It was strong and comforting.

"And you, my dearest Lottie, are the picture of elegant grace." His warm gaze met hers. "That gown truly has you dressed to the nines. I'm thankful you were able to get it."

Ben liked her dress.

Charlotte searched the pews, wondering if Ben would be joining his family today. She regretted not taking more time on her hair this morning.

She paused at her reflection in a shop window.

"You're my beautiful rose, Lottie." Papa said.

She smiled. "You're too kind, Papa." But today was for God, not for batting eyelashes and catching the eye of Ben Franklin.

The sunlight teased across the church entrance, but illuminated a troubling scene.

Another gathered crowd. At God's house this time.

She sensed the frantic nature of the crowd, dressed in their Sunday best but their faces shadowed with dread.

The crowd gathered outside was small, and more somber than before. Papa's face was stern, all warmth turned cold with caution. "We should go inside."

"Papa, this makes me nervous. Is everything all right?"

"I fear for what it could be, but I've seen this panic before..."

Charlotte wanted to run. To return home, petticoats flying. But instead, a sliver of curiosity piqued her interest and drove her footsteps forward.

Charlotte's pulse quickened as she walked down the aisle. She clasped her hands to still them.

Please don't let there be a body.

They entered and Charlotte gasped. Gathered in the front row, far from their usual Sunday seats, was the Franklin family. A draft swept through the candlelit church, making the flames shudder and dance wildly. Instead of solemn worship for the one on high, all were tearful and ashen-faced.

But who was missing?

Please don't be Ben. She couldn't bear it.

"The Franklins." Her Papa flattened his lips.

"I must go to them to...offer comfort."

"If you feel that is appropriate, I shall join you."

As they began the slow walk up the aisle, she noticed who they were walking toward. Mr. and Mrs. Franklin stood over Ben's sister Sarah. She was seated on a bench, wrapped in the comforting arms of her brother Samuel. Ben, so tall he was easily spotted, rocked a sobbing child. Both looked as if their souls had crumbled that day, but she couldn't help but think of Ben as a Papa himself as he consoled the child.

"Thaddeus! I'm surprised to see you." Constable Cobb stood halfway up the aisle. Distracted, she hadn't noticed his presence.

Papa shot him a look. "When my dearest daughter requests that I attend church with her, I oblige, good sir." He settled his gaze on the somber gathering at the front of the church. "What say you about this morning? What has happened with the Franklins? I'm assuming they seek the Minister's counsel."

Constable Cobb lowered his voice. "From what I've been told, they had just arrived at services when word was sent from the Thomas Franklin household—they found his Elizabeth."

"What did you hear?" Charlotte pressed, concerned.

The Constable lowered his voice, "Things no young lady should witness."

Papa spoke low. "Natural or unnatural causes, Robert?"

"A servant of the kitchens went down for stored food, in preparation for their breakfast. She found Mrs. Elizabeth tied to a chair and completely drained of blood."

Dear God.

Papa sighed. "Another murder then."

Breathe deeply. Peace cometh. Pain goeth. The infernal blaze crawled up her throat once again, creeping, climbing, like a flame enveloping a tree. Now was the time. Her chance to tell him what she knew. "Constable. I found something near Gayle Williams' home the day of his murder."

The constable narrowed his eyes. "Go on."

She started again. "A silver cufflink, with the devil's horns and an inverted cross engraved on it."

The constable and Papa shared a worried glance.

Papa spoke. "A cloven hoof and the markings on Catherine—that isn't a coincidence."

Constable Cobb frowned. "I'm headed over to the latest scene. I'll be alert for any symbolism. Just waiting on the coroner to meet me here."

Charlotte stifled a groan. The coroner, Edward Robinson was known as a decent man and clearly fancied her. As if summoned by the mere mention of his name, he swept in through the church doors, his labored breathing and hunched back rising and falling with each inhalation. It was not his appearance that unsettled her, nor the greasy hair and crooked teeth, but the way he leered at her from afar. She had once caught the man watching her read to the children in the library, stalking outside the window. She shuddered and could not muster a smile.

"Hello Miss Charlotte," he wheezed. "I'm pleased you are here today." Edward Robinson reached to kiss her hand, but she pressed it close to her side.

"Mr. Robinson, there is no joy to be had today in the midst of sorrow. You'd do well to remember the feelings of others and cast aside your own." Charlotte scowled.

Papa shot her a scowl of his own. No doubt he was aghast at such unladylike behavior. Maybe it was her heightened state, but she was not in the mood for Mr. Robinson today. She wanted to get to Ben.

She glanced back to the front pews. She sensed his piercing gaze upon her. He must have noticed her entrance.

"Excuse me, gentlemen. I am going to speak with a friend."

Ben walked towards them now. Charlotte's pulse throbbed as she tried to steady her shaking hands. She was glad for the bustling crowd that might disguise the furious beating of her heart. His somber expression settled her.

She wasn't sure what made her do it, perhaps it was the adrenaline, but she reached out her arms to gather Ben Franklin in an embrace.

With the commotion at the front of the sanctuary, no one else had noticed, but Papa had.

Perhaps fate had crossed their paths on purpose. They'd hardly known each other before he left for England, but now, after a mere few words, she felt an attachment to him. She desired those few words to turn into more. To speak with him of his travels, her wishes, what life could be.

Life.

Murder.

Ashamed at her thoughts, she snapped her arms back to her sides. She must stay composed. Ben looked down at her and drew in a long, slow breath. "Good morning, Miss Charlotte. I'm assuming you've heard our terrible news?"

"Yes, Mr. Franklin, I'm so sorry to hear."

"Call me Ben."

She peered upward through her lashes, pressing her lips together.

"Ben."

"Is this in some way connected to the Baker's demise?" With horror, she realized the inappropriateness of her question. He was grief stricken and she was inserting herself into their family matters. "I'm sorry, please do not think of me unkindly."

He frowned. "Think not of it. This town is full of devils, it seems."

"I'm so very sorry, Ben. I offer my condolences to you and your family."

"I still don't understand why someone would do this," Sarah dabbed her eyes.

Ben sighed, "We all cared for her deeply, left-handed marriage or not. It seems there is a rogue devil on the loose, intent on killing." His eyes flashed with a hint of anger. It was quick, but noticeable.

A left-handed marriage. So Elizabeth was of lower social class than they. As most in this town were.

As she was.

She looked to the floor. He placed a finger under her chin, lifting her eyes to meet his.

Papa's burning gaze upon her back like rays of sun on a midsummer's day.

"Miss Charlotte, cast not sadness into your beautiful eyes." She stilled. Did he enjoy poetry, as she did? "Cry not that rose bushes are riddled with thorns, but cherish that thorn bushes have roses. Elizabeth was a rose. You are a rose. We will celebrate her life, though tragedy cut it short."

She could see the specks of black in those piercing grey eyes. Drawing a simple breath was a hardship. The spice-scented water wafting from his tanned skin intoxicated her. What was she thinking? He must speak with such endearing terms to all, but she was unconvinced that was the case.

She fumbled for the right words, her tongue suddenly feeling thick in her mouth. "What beautiful words."

Ben met her eyes with a sad smile. Though grief shadowed his face, his presence eased her anxiety. She smoothed her skirts, suddenly self-conscious under his gaze.

"Charlotte." The gruff voice of Papa shattered the moment. His footsteps were soft on the wooden church floor. She could hear the disapproval in his tone. Not anger—but a clear, unmistakable and venomous warning. His misgivings about the town elite were valid, it just...could he not see that there might be something here? Something unknown and exciting and stirring within her—so much better than her usual despair? Ben was not cut of the same cloth as the company he kept. She knew it.

Speaking of the company he kept, where was John Priestly? She followed Papa's gaze to the shadowy corner of the church. John and Mayor Richard

Payne huddled close, speaking in hushed tones with Aunt Beth. Amir stood with them, clothed in violet and peach tones today. The mayor's eyes darted about before leaning in to whisper in John Priestly's ear.

She faced Papa. Cheeks flushing red, a tightness climbing the sides of her throat.

Papa met her eyes. "I believe we need to go, dear one."

"Yes, Papa, of course."

Ben stepped toward him. "Mr. Scott, allow me to introduce myself properly. I am—"

"I know who you are."

"It was a delight to have your daughter join our family for dinner."

Papa sighed. Clearly choosing his words with care, so as not to overstep. He clasped his hands behind his back and the tension in his shoulders released, if only slightly.

"Let us not intrude upon your family's grieving. We shan't be rude. This is not the time to engage in frivolity."

That last word startled her. Frivolity. Seeing the Franklins' ashen faces, Charlotte's fervor evaporated. She shrank back, the image of their grief etching itself in her mind. Her childish excitement now seemed shameful. How quickly she had forgotten their grief. His grief.

Charlotte followed Ben's gaze to where her father stood rigid. Something unspoken passed between the two men.

Ben's jaw tightened as he looked away, but then quickly looked back at her and smiled. "I will see you soon, Miss Charlotte."

The Twelfth<br>Chapter

# God is our Refuge

The funeral gloves arrived at noon the day before—soft and silken against her skin. Charlotte twisted them at the wrists, the tight leather conjuring memories of another funeral, another pair of gloves.

Mother's funeral. They would visit together today.

Gloves such as these were traditionally sent to all funeral and graveside attendees, meant to be worn during both services. They were soft. Silken. She kept the gloves she had worn at Mother's funeral in a small wooden box in her room. Mother had given the box to her as a child, and it had a rose with a cross carved on the inside lid. Pastors collected thousands of gloves in their lifetimes, often selling them off after use. How many pairs of gloves did Minister Horvath own?

She held an inkling of suspicion that it was Ben who had sent them, but couldn't be sure. She stole a swift glance at him, standing beside the hole that would soon hold Elizabeth. A dirt bed, hard and cold, unlike anything Elizabeth had ever slept in before, topped with a six-foot blanket of earth and a duvet of grass. A far cry from the featherbeds of Society Hill.

She twisted them at the wrists yet again. The gloves were uncomfortable, a reminder of a time veiled in darkness not only for her, but for the entire town.

If she walked far enough down among the orderly headstones, through the daisies and across the moss, she would come to Mother's grave. A familiar, albeit painful, spot they frequented—Papa more than she.

Perhaps she would go and visit her today, and she hoped Dirch Johnson, the wheelwright's apprentice Papa had insisted escort her to the service, wouldn't follow her there.

"For I am convinced that neither death nor life, neither angels nor demons, neither the present nor the future, nor any powers, nor height nor depth, nor anything else in all creation, will be able to separate us from the love of God that is Christ Jesus our Lord."

Minister Horvath read the same lines of scripture for so many of the funerals, that even though she trusted in his Godly wisdom, the words rang with insincerity. "Do not let your hearts be troubled."

"Blessed are those who mourn." When she heard first the scripture quoted for Mother she was comforted. But in the years that followed, with dysentery and food shortages ravaging the poor, taking life after life, the words lost their power over her. She had attended far too many services.

Beside her, Dirch shifted his weight, his head down, bowed with reverence or boredom she didn't know. Surely half the town had joined them, as this service was attended by the presumed "notable" members of society– the neighbors from Society Hill. Standing with the council members and their wives was Governor Hellsmith, his dewy-eyed young wife clinging to his arm as she dabbed at her perfectly painted face. Her handkerchief probably cost more than many of the dresses worn here today.

Charlotte caught her breath. Behind Mr. and Mrs. Franklin, Mayor Payne and the offensive Madame Delphia were engaged in a whispered conversation. The way they surveyed the young ladies in attendance sent a chill up her spine. Against her better judgment, she moved a few inches closer to Dirch.

"God is our refuge and strength, a very present help in trouble. Therefore, we will not fear though the earth gives way, though the mountains be moved to the heart of the sea."

She bowed her head as he spoke the familiar verses. Though the words rang hollow to her now, she prayed others found solace in them... prayed this service would offer some semblance of peace amidst the shadow of another

murder.

Priya softly mourned with John Priestly, near the family but not among them. How quickly they had become attached, and publicly so. She wondered what had happened between them in the days since the dinner, for not even a week had passed and Priya hadn't come to call. The Madame fixed her snake-like gaze on Priya. She was a dangerous woman, no doubt about that.

Samuel stood beside Sarah, her expression absent of tears or emotion. Were they twins? They were always so close. She noticed as Sarah moved closer to Priya, whispering in her ear. Curious.

The sheer expense of mourning dresses that surrounded her was astounding, not to mention the rings supplied by the Franklin family. They were a token of remembrance, for Mrs. Elizabeth, having "knowledge lies betwixt death's veil and life's light" engraved upon each. A lavish gesture, but one to be expected from the Franklin family. She and Papa couldn't afford rings for all attendees of Mother's funeral, so Papa had commissioned only two rings to be made. One for each of them. She wore hers now.

"Faithful servant to the Lord and all of his children, Mrs. Elizabeth leaves behind a legacy of…"

There he was, his speckled eyes staring down at the ornately carved mahogany box where Mrs. Elizabeth lay. Eyes that perfectly matched the storm clouds gathering above. Ben had an arm wrapped around Thomas, offering brotherly comfort. She had tried not to notice him, but it was inescapable. Ben stared down at the box, his eyes cloudy with turmoil. Charlotte longed to embrace him as she had in the church, to comfort him. But propriety kept her feet rooted to the ground. By God, she would not disrespect Mrs. Elizabeth with more fanciful thoughts as they lowered her into the ground.

"Why do we mourn departing friends?

Or shake at Death's alarms?

'Tis but the voice that Jesus sends

To call them to his arms.

Are we not tending upwards too,

As fast as time can move?

Nor would we wish for hours more slow

To keep us from our love.

Why should we tremble to convey

The bodies to the tomb,

There the dear flesh of Jesus lay

And left a long perfume."

The perfume of any person that had passed on was not a scent she wanted to think about. Many were uncomfortable standing among the stones, among those that had gone on to whatever waits behind the final shut of their eyes, but not she. Perhaps it was because Mother was here, or perhaps because death appeared rather peaceful, but of all the things in the world that heightened her state, the burial grounds weren't among them.

The crowd dispersed and the Franklin family eventually left as well.

Charlotte turned to her escort, relieved that they could now depart also.

"I'd like to visit Mother, if you please." She wasn't sure why she said "if you please" considering she would visit Mother with or without his consent. Oh, the pressures of kindness for Papa's sake.

"Your Papa awaits, Miss Charlotte."

"Yet my mother has waited longer," Charlotte replied curtly. Gathering her skirts, she strode off without another word.

"I'll wait for you by the gate, Miss Charlotte." So cold. So stern.

As she passed each row, careful not to step across the graves, she read the names of those departed. Loving mother. Cherished husband. So many stories lay under the ground, immortalized by mere markings upon stone. Their lifetimes condensed into a few words. Toward the back of the grounds the poorer resting places solely contained a name. No script, no verse, no memories. What would her own stone say one day?

The familiar rose bush, planted as a marker, caught her eye. There she was. Mother. So often she had come here, wishing they could speak together on

life's troubles and concerns. If only Mother could bring peace to her fears. But, of course, these conversations were one-sided.

The Bible said that one day they would be reunited, but she was sure Mother had never truly left her. She felt her when the sun kissed her cheeks and when their garden bloomed. Mother loved tending that garden. So many memories of plunging their hands into the soft earth to settle seeds and encourage new life. Yet now Mother lay beneath the soil herself. Too many questions had gone unanswered, their family, life as they knew it—cut short.

Murder.

Enthralled by her thoughts, Charlotte flinched at a hand upon her shoulder. She turned.

"Dear God!" Grey eyes.

"Not God, Miss Charlotte, only a friend." He offered a soft smile. "Forgive me, I did not mean to startle you."

"Ben." Charlotte tried to ignore the rapid flutter in her chest. "No need for an apology, I was just..." She faltered, unsure how to explain. "My sincerest condolences to you and your family, again."

"Thank you for coming, Miss Charlotte. Are the gloves not to your liking? I couldn't help but notice your discomfort in wearing them."

So he had been watching her. She hadn't imagined it.

"Oh no! They're perfectly divine. The finest silk I've ever worn, and under such sorrowful circumstances. It's only that gloves remind me of my mother."

He stared intently upon Mother's grave. The flowers Papa had placed a few days ago had already started to wilt. "I look upon death to be as necessary to our constitution as sleep. We shall rise refreshed in the morning."

Interesting.

"Sometimes I believe that I can feel her with me," Charlotte said. So intimate. How was it that someone she hardly knew encouraged her to spill forth thoughts with no regard? She stared at the grave. "Do you believe in the afterlife, Ben?"

"We are spirits. That bodies should be lent us, while they can afford us pleasure, assist us in acquiring knowledge, or in doing good to our fellow creatures, is a kind and benevolent act of God." He turned to face her. "Our spirits will one day meet again, but just in case, I choose to live each second of this life as if it were my only."

Perhaps he had doubts, too? Sometimes it was hard to believe in God's love when he had allowed her mother to be taken away. She pushed those thoughts aside.

"If only those spirits could enlighten us as to the cause of their demise."

"What happened to your mother, Miss Charlotte? Did sickness befall her? If I am too bold with such a question, please forgive me."

Something within her wanted to tell him. She wished for him to understand, to share in her pain.

"She was murdered. Taken too soon, just as your brother's wife was cut from this world."

Horror flashed across his face. In the tender silence that followed, Charlotte felt the spark of a connection, as if their hearts grieved as one. "I did not know. I am so sorry, Miss Charlotte. How terrible for you and your father."

"Similar circumstances surrounded her death. No suspects, no cause that anyone could find. The town proceeded to cast blame upon Papa, suspecting he took her from us." Her thoughts turned again as to what exactly was the reason Mother was targeted with the rest of the victims ten years ago.

His face drained of what little color it had.

"That is the cause of our falling upon harder times. Once Papa had been a master wheelwright attracting the majority of orders in town. But the presumption that he had murdered Mother kept many townspeople at bay." Her cheeks were damp with hot, salty tears now, but it felt comfortable to share with him. What would Mother think of this man?

"Oh, Charlotte."

She wiped the tears from beneath her eyes and inhaled a sharp breath to compose herself. "Never mind my sorrow, kind Ben. Again, it is your family

who suffers the trauma of one taken too soon this day. Time heals the shock, that is sure, but it seems that sorrow tarries longer."

"I notice that your friend also tarries," he motioned in the direction of the gates where a sullen Dirch stood watching. "Your 'betrothed'?"

Was that a smirk?

"Nay. He is Papa's apprentice. At one time, we expected it to be so, but Dirch can be...a bit controlling in his desires."

Ben raised his eyebrows. There were questions behind his eyes, questions she'd rather not answer. Silence fell between them. They stood observing the grave. It was not awkward, but peaceful. They were but two mourners sharing the peace that comes with stillness together.

"I find it interesting that you don't feel the need to fill the voids in conversation," Charlotte said.

"At certain times, silence can be terrible, but at others it brings me a sense of calm. Peace to be alone in my thoughts, to ponder life. It allows me to contemplate what I imagine could be."

She couldn't ignore the intensity she felt towards him. She met his intense gaze of uncompromised intelligence head on for the first time since he'd joined her here. Unspoken desire. Or maybe it was just her. No, he noticed it, too. How quickly her emotions shifted around this man. He parted his lips, hesitating.

She leaned in, waiting for his next words.

"Miss Charlotte." The stern voice of Dirch Johnson slashed like a knife. "We must be going; the air will soon turn to a chill."

"Of course, of course," Ben said. If he were offended, he hid it well. "I appreciate your escort of Miss Charlotte to the service, Mr. Johnson. We appreciate her attendance."

"A pleasure, sir."

Charlotte cast a final glance at those storm cloud eyes, matching the distant rumble she heard from the sky. "I hope I will see you again soon, Mr. Franklin."

A thin smile crossed his pale pink lips. "Likewise, Miss Scott."

# Memories in Mahogoney

The scent of lilacs enveloped Charlotte as she hastened down the lane, gasping for breath. She'd be holding more than her sharp words and emotion during the ride, evidently. The floral perfume mingled with the acrid smoke of chimneys, accosting her senses. She paused to lean against a fencepost, its black iron hot from hours in the afternoon sun. The echo of horses' hooves on packed dirt drifted to her ears. Charlotte steadied her breaths, willing her heart to slow its frantic pace before continuing on.

The root cause of it was Dirch's presence, of course. How uncomfortable he made her anymore. They'd shared not a word for the journey in the same way she harbored no excitement for him in weeks. The last few yards without him provided a chance to remember.

Dirch's bland, dreary company or the cryptic thoughts of Mother's death– she couldn't decide which was worse. This day, she'd had the misfortune to endure both.

Memories of Mother flooded her mind, both lovely and horrible. Baking bread. Playing scotch-hopper. Her delicate hand resting in a pool of blood. Her stomach lurched at the last one.

Shadows stretched long across the dirt lane as Charlotte approached the familiar oak door. She paused, tracing the whorls and knots in the weathered wood before pushing it open. The comforting scent of beeswax candles and

hearth smoke greeted her. Nelly must have been baking bread earlier, the lingering aroma of rising dough still present amidst the musty books and her father's leatherworking tools. Charlotte slipped off her shoes, savoring the coolness of the wood floor through her stockings after hours in funeral finery.

To her surprise, neither Papa nor Nelly appeared to be in the house. Perhaps they were outside or away in town with the sun's smiling rays to burn away the gloom. Regardless, this was a rare opportunity to begin seeking answers to questions she hardly dared ask.

While she hadn't mentioned it to Dirch, her thoughts had swirled on the way home.

She knew so little of Mother's interests and involvements prior to the untimely death. Perhaps, with luck and God's grace, she could part that mysterious veil.

As she stood in the great room, pondering where to begin with what little time she had, a soft knock rattled the front door. She stifled a shout of surprise.

Lucidity replaced lunacy. Charlotte straightened her back, dropping her shoulders to raise her head high. Not every small noise was a harbinger of danger.

It wouldn't be Papa or Nelly, as they wouldn't knock before entering their own home. Charlotte chanced a glance out the window to see a young boy holding a quintal horn in the shape of a fan. Flowers spilled from each of its five vases. She exhaled deeply, all tension releasing from her spine.

No fiend, only the florist's assistant.

Charlotte gathered herself before opening the door.

"Hello mum. I've a delivery for a Miss Charlotte Scott, here." He held out the vase. "Would that be you, by chance?"

Her mouth parted, only slightly, before she remembered to speak. "Oh my!" She reached for the vase. "To whom do I owe my thanks, kind sir?" The orchids and lilacs intoxicated her, entreating endearment Dirch never had.

"A Mr. Franklin, mum. He stopped by and ordered them just now, paid extra to have them delivered straight away."

Impossible.

With a smile that would have been forced moments earlier, she thanked the young man and retreated inside to inspect the gift.

Flowers from Ben Franklin. How bold. How flattering. Could it be true?

Placing the ornate array on the table, Charlotte almost danced to the bookshelf where Mother kept a book on the language of gifted flowers. Such gifts held coded messages from the sender.

After a moment of tapping spines, she found her quarry and tugged it free of the rest. Metal rattled against wood as a key bounced between her feet. She recognized it immediately and thought of the chest.

Mother's trunk locked away memories Charlotte desperately wished to rummage. There would surely be answers waiting inside. But time was of the essence, now.

After a moment of indecision, she chose the surer bet. The box might hide what she needed, but the flowers held their own riddle and one that could be determined with certainty. What message did Ben send? Concentration on anything else would elude her until she knew.

White clover. "Thinking of you."

Charlotte smiled.

Green ferns of sincerity. White clematis, the mark of a mental beauty. She blushed. Pink orchid, beauty. Finally, her shaking hands clutched the book as she struggled to settle her breathing...multi-colored lilacs to elucidate the budding emotions of affection.

Affection!

She snapped the book closed and returned it. This couldn't be happening. Feelings of affection, so fast. And for her?

Time dwindled now as she knew that Papa and Nelly were sure to return at any moment. She must concentrate on the other task at hand.

Shortly after the private funeral, Papa had gathered many of Mother's most cherished items and locked them in the mahogany trunk. She had seen

that trunk at the foot of Papa's bed every day since and only dreamt of its contents. The pain of his memories had kept it shut, and Charlotte hadn't dared ask to see what was inside. Without his blessing, she hadn't dared to test it herself—until today.

With one small click and a creak which seemed a cacophony, Charlotte stilled her beating heart and lifted the lid, revealing her Mother's memories.

At first, she felt like a grave robber, stealing access to the thoughts of a dead woman. But as she shifted through Mother's treasures, her heart lightened.

A sharp pang wracked her chest as she noted white gloves of the softest silk she could remember, a duplicate of those she'd worn at the funeral. A small glass sphere with a delicate golden stopper held the remnants of Mother's signature scent, the citrus and rose, long ago dried up. A single tear rolled down Charlotte's cheek.

Shifting aside simple sketches and the beginnings of small water paintings, she noticed a stack of books stacked along the side. They were old, bound in leather, with titles she didn't recognize, even from long hours combing the library: Fama Fraternitatis, Confessio Fraternitatis, and Chymical Wedding of Christian Rosenkrautz, dated 1459. Charlotte opened the first, untying its leather cord. Inside, scrawled in crimson red ink, it read: "To my dearest daughters, Catherin and Abitha, this is The Fame of the Brotherhood of RC, an account of the German doctor and mystic philosopher Christian Rosenkrautz, the founder of our Rosicrucian Order. May it guide your hearts and mind to the truths of a joyous life."

Her mind whirled with questions. Rosicrucian Order? Minister Horvath made clear that those who followed in such teaching practiced in the occult. In mysticism. Their thoughts were not of the righteous world, and did not follow a Godly path.

Surely, this was a mistake. Mother had been a Godly woman, a wholesome woman.

Charlotte glanced in the chest once more. There remained more to uncover in the chest. Her heart sprinted as her mind whirled in a frenzy. There was a small golden cross, similar to the one that hung on her bedroom wall,

only this one held a small rose in the center rather than curling about the edges with thorns.

Rosicrucian. The symbol of a rose.

She shifted through the scattered papers depicting men, strange triangular buildings, and connections to the four natural elements. She found bottles of earth, flasks filled with water, wood chips surely used to make fire. Implements of... she couldn't bare to allow the term to cross her mind.

She wondered if Papa knew. Clearly he must have had an inkling of suspicious, considering he, himself, boxed these items up. The question was, had he hidden these objects out of horrified shame or secrecy?

Finally, she lifted her own greatest fear from the bottom, its smooth texture in stark contrast to the rough papers. A cloak, black as night, emitting a shimmery glint as she held it up into the sunlight not unlike the stars in a clear night sky.

This could not be.

She jumped at the sound of the back door clanging open. She must put these distractions away. Quickly! She must banish the thoughts from her mind. The clack of wooden shoes stepped upon floorboards grew louder. Papa was home.

In that moment, Charlotte once again felt like a criminal. But what she'd stolen could never be returned– forbidden knowledge.

Placing a satchel of herbs in her pocket, she hurriedly stuffed the rest of Mother's items back into the trunk and locked it. Perhaps she should hide. No, that would be too obvious.

"Lottie? Is that you? I could have sworn I saw Dirch upon the lane not too long ago."

Charlotte raced across the room, focusing her eyes and hands upon the curtains as if to straighten them. Papa materialized in the doorway.

"Oh yes! Hello Papa! I was only fixing the drapes, as the sunlight was overtaking the room."

Papa reached for her with a welcoming hug. Unsuspecting.

"Join us outside, dear one. We shan't waste this beautiful day indoors."

And with that, she followed her Papa outside. As the warmth of the sun helped shield the redness of her cheeks, she stifled the verse that battered her mind.

Thou shalt not suffer a witch to live. Perhaps there was a reason someone came for Mother.

# Fear the Fox

With the last of summer's warmth still lingering in the breeze, Papa was right that today was a day best spent together outside, removing the decaying summer plants. Pumpkins ripened while apples awaited picking before the coming frost. If the tomatoes and peppers and corn were left to rot, they would find slugs, bugs, and other maladies taking up unwanted residence in their soil over the colder months.

Papa and Nelly settled themselves beneath the apple tree, sharing a treat in the comfort of their secluded backyard. No whispers or sidelong glances could reach them here. Charlotte glanced at her hands, covered in soil, just as she remembered it with Mother. The rich, warm feeling of earth would always be a welcome to her heart, even if the dirt under her fingernails would send Nelly into a tizzy this evening. She chuckled. She would have to scrub extra hard when washing for dinner.

Charlotte wiped dirt-crusted hands on her apron and skipped over to the apple tree. "What are my favorite storytellers up to?" She settled in beside them, thoughts of the mysterious trunk momentarily faded. "Papa, it's such a beautiful day. Do tell us a story."

Nelly nodded. "Aye, Thaddeus! Plaise do. One of our favourites."

"How about a new story, my dear ones?" Papa asked, a playful glint in his wrinkled eyes. A soft smile greeted his whiskered, yet worn, face. The rare, full sunshine of today did him well.

"Now this tale does not have a happy ending, but, as many things in life don't, take this as an opportunity for a lesson in caution." He peered at Charlotte, intent behind his eyes. Did he know? Surely not.

Had Dirch gone to Papa and made something of nothing? There hadn't been time.

Nelly scoffed, waving her hands in the air. "Thaddeus, quit patronizin' an' get on wi' tha story, won't ye?"

"Let me tell you the tale of the Beautiful Bunny Rabbit." He had spoken with such a grandiose tone that Charlotte expected an epic adventure, yet "Bunny Rabbit" fell flat on her ears. Charlotte stifled a laugh at the inflated introduction.

"Deep within the forest, through the thickets and far off the beaten path, a community of animals thrived in peace for the most part. The deer frolicked with the rabbits and skunks and they ate breakfast with the raccoons. Chipmunks and rabbits and woodchucks and squirrels, all lived together in typical harmony. Off near the trees, away from the meadow, a family of rabbits lived in a burrow." He leaned back on the apple tree and crossed his legs. So casual and carefree, unlike Papa's usual stiff posture.

"Papa Rabbit was proud of his beautiful wife, Mother Rabbit, and their ten rambunctious bunnies. The eldest bunny, soon to be a doe herself, was the fairest bunny to live in the forest. Her whiskers were long and her tail was fluffy, and she practically befriended every animal in the forest."

Charlotte nodded along to Papa's story, but her mind kept returning to the strange artifacts buried in her mother's trunk.

Papa continued. "But, unlike her mother, she yearned for adventure, to see what was beyond the great forest where they lived."

Nelly leaned over and whispered in her ear, "Most likely fir the best!" Nelly wrinkled her nose as she giggled.

Charlotte tensed, shifting on the ground. Did Papa intend for this tale to serve as a warning? She was content to continue living her life as it was—and to be honest, it was terrifying enough already. There was no adventure needed, thank you.

"The rabbits played freely at dusk and dawn, when shadows kept them hidden...but danger always lurked for those who strayed too far when the sun was high. By noon they snuggled in the burrow in a large, warm ball of fur, safe from any larger predators that might come near. While they were surrounded by friends, there were still dangers that lurked in the forest, such as hawks, owls, falcons, and the ever-elusive..."

Papa narrowed his eyes, "...and sly, fox."

Ahhh, there it was. Dirch had spoken to him. If only Papa realized what a sly fox Dirch was outside of the wheelwright shop. "Dirch put you up to this, didn't he?" Charlotte narrowed her eyes. "I wish you knew him as I do, Papa."

He ignored her query and continued on.

"But one day curiosity overtook caution. Near noon, while her family slept, the beautiful bunny snuck away from the burrow's safety. She hopped through the familiar meadow, feeling the heat of the high sun upon her furry back. She hurried, as she needed to return before dinnertime at dusk. She was headed to the trees when all of the sudden, she spotted him, and he was more handsome than she could have imagined."

"Mmhmm." Nelly pursed her lips with suspicion.

"It was the fox. The fox ran to the beautiful bunny with such haste she had no time to hide. What brings you out in the sun, little rabbit?

I'm seeking adventure! I want to know what lies beyond.

Perhaps I can show you the way? The fox's teeth were dazzling, yet terrifying. The beautiful bunny knew she should turn away, but the draw of adventure's call was too great to resist. Take me away and show me what's beyond!

With a lick of his lips, the fox beckoned with his claws. This way, little rabbit.

They crossed through the trees, past the horrified faces of the deer and the badger, all the way to what looked like a fox's den. Surely this is not the way to adventure. The beautiful bunny had barely spoken above a whisper.

No, little rabbit, but it is the way to what lies beyond."

As the fox's teeth gleamed, Charlotte's stomach dropped, knowing the bunny's fate was sealed. Still, tears stung her eyes.

"And alas, the beautiful bunny made it home for dinner, though not the one she'd planned for." Papa crossed his arms, his message delivered in full.

Nelly's face had soured—still playful—but sour. "Well tha' was no fairytale at all, Thaddeus Scott!"

"Just a friendly reminder to watch out for charming snakes in the grass," Papa said with a shrug. He wasn't firm, nor stern, but still rather relaxed sitting under the apple tree. He might have been discussing the autumn breeze.

"You know, Papa." Here was her chance, but of course, here came the tightness in her throat. "Dirch may be more similar to the fox than you are aware."

"He's an exceptional man, Lottie," Papa frowned. "A hardworking man. He could provide for you, a future family, and keep you safe from the evils of this town."

She did well to hide her disgust. He would do better to suggest Edward the unsettling Coroner for a suitor. Say no, she shuddered at even the thought.

He sat upright and absently rolled his sleeves. "It's not your friend Ben that I worry about, my dear one, merely the company he keeps. That John Priestly fellow and certain Franklin family members have a history you know not of."

She thought of the trunk yet again—evidently they did too.

John's hushed exchange with the mayor resurfaced in Charlotte's mind. She pictured the Madame's piercing eyes and suppressed a shiver. Perhaps the elite's club had darker secrets than she realized. All of Society Hill were born and bred to keep company among themselves.

"One soiled egg does not a batch ruin, Papa." She scooted close and wrapped her arms around him. "There's nothing to fear. No interest has yet been spoken, and I promise I will bring him here first if he were to miraculously come to call. Fret not.."

He cupped her hands and smiled. "I merely want to protect you, dear one. You're all I've got left."

"Hmph!" Nelly crossed her arms in a huff.

"Oh come now, you blasted woman! And you, Nelly, but that goes without saying."

They fell to fits of laughter and basked in the fading sunshine that had turned to molten brass. The horizon drained of color and soon night would fall, and with the return of the shadows. Charlotte knew the crushing weight of her fears would return as well.

# Heart of Darkness

Charlotte jolted awake to stygian darkness. The candle on her bedside table had burned out hours ago. Moonlight streaming through the windows bathed the room in an ethereal silvery glow. She strained her ears in the midnight silence, searching for what had stirred her from sleep. The hair on her arms prickled. She had felt on edge since her disturbing discoveries. But tonight, a deeper sense of foreboding gripped her.

Charlotte glanced around her room. The wind whistled outside, branches tapping a haunting beat on the window. Her heart pounded as she pulled the covers tighter.

Sudden creaks and groans of the old house settling made her flinch. She tried to steady her ragged breaths, clutching her pillow like a talisman. Sleep would not return easily tonight.

Charlotte exhaled slowly, trying to quiet her racing mind. The wind picked up outside, moaning as it swirled around the eaves. She squeezed her eyes shut. Just tree branches brushing the outside walls.

As she finally relaxed a bit deeper into her pillow, a scrape sounded beneath her window. Charlotte's eyes shot open. She held her breath, listening intently.

Silence.

Her imagination was getting carried away tonight.

Charlotte was just about to drift off when a muffled thump hit the

front door. She stiffened, her earlier sense of dread returning. She waited, heartbeat thrumming in her ears.

There - barely audible - the crunch of footsteps on gravel outside. She clutched the covers to her chin. Should she wake Papa?

BANG. BANG. BANG.

Good God, what was that? She couldn't breathe. The embers in her throat burned, but not hot enough to absorb the rush of the ocean in her ears. Make it stop. Make it stop.

BANG. BANG. BANG.

Was someone trying to beat down their front door?

She'd locked it. Twice. Three times. She always, always, checked the door.

Dear God. Dear merciful God in heaven they have come. The murderers of Gayle Williams and Elizabeth Franklin, they have come!

"PAPA!" She pulled the covers up to her chin, gasping to allow the words an escape. "Papa, please!"

BANG. BANG. BANG. From the window this time.

Papa ran into her room, rifle in hand, pipe between his lips, ready to defend their home. A wafting scent of cherry tobacco entered the room with him.

"Lottie, stay in this room. Do you hear me? Do not leave this room no matter what you hear."

Charlotte's mouth was dry as dust, her tongue sticking to the roof as panic gripped her. A coppery taste arose as she chewed her bottom lip raw. She shrieked as a figure appeared, running through her bedroom door.

"Wha' tha devil is goin' on in this house!" It was Nelly, her nightcap fallen to the side.

BANG. BANG. BANG. The back door this time.

"They're trying to find a way in. You girls stay here, I'm going to end this killer once and for all!" Papa stomped from the room, rageful and ready.

Without warning, the banging stopped. Silence crept into the room

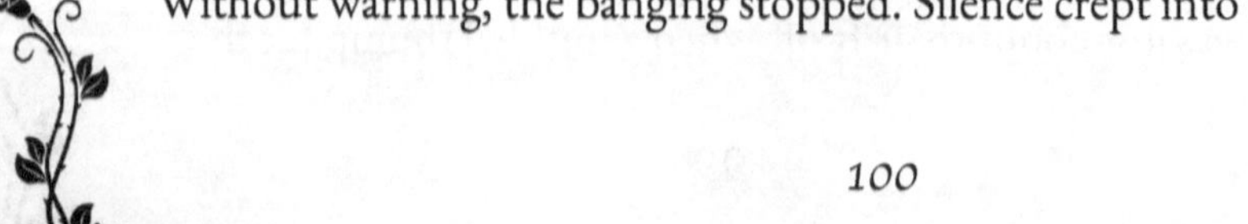

and surrounded them. No banging, no footsteps, no sounds of Papa or a gunshot. For the love of God don't let them have taken him too. She loosened the grip she had on Nelly as they clung to each other on her bed, her tears dampening Nelly's nightclothes.

"Maybe...we...should check...on...Papa." She wheezed with the effort of her words. Her head flushed with exhaustion.

Nelly whispered, eyes darting back and forth. "Child, we sit in this room 'til he comes fir us. We do no' move. I can protect ye here, but I can' do it out there in the dark. We wait. We wait together."

She heard the unmistakable sound of their front door creaking. Footsteps clomped down the hall as her heart hammered within.

Moonlight illuminated Papa's scruffy, concerned face in the doorway.

"Whoever they were, they are gone."

The tension released from her shoulders. The air gradually escaped her lungs with a whoosh.

"Rest not too easy, though." Papa's strong facade crumbled, revealing a man shaken to his core by the events of the night. "There's a message on our wall."

Nelly squeezed tighter, it was comforting and warm.

"I will take what is mine, it said." Papa scratched his stubble. Perplexed and perturbed.

"What is mine?" She couldn't imagine. "Perhaps an unpaid debt, Papa?"

"I owe no man anything." He lit the oil lamp on her bedside table. "Keep this one lit tonight. I will alert Constable Cobb and the council of this attack in the morning, but for the meantime, try to get some sleep while I stand watch." He slumped into the corner chair with the rifle still firmly in hand.

Nelly rose from the bed and turned to straighten the bedcovers. "Well tha'...was no' heartsome. Try to get some sleep, child." She kissed her cheek. "Thaddeus will give shelter to us."

She lay in her damp sheet, soaked with cold sweat by now. Just because

the excitement was over did not mean that her heart knew it.

Sleep eluded her as darkness descended, bringing with it a torrent of haunting thoughts. Across the room, still upright in his chair, Papa had drifted into his dreams, soft snores permeating the silence. She watched the flicker of shadows from the flame dance upon her ceiling, dancing with fire as the pagans did in the stories she'd heard as a child. Mother had told her that people were inherently good, to look beyond assumptions and search for their soul, but Lottie had a hard time believing that all people were good these days. Who would attack them? And why?

She glanced at the window, wondering if the sun were to rise soon or not.

Dear merciful God.

A face stared back at her from beyond the glass.

Her greatest fear had come to light. The one who cometh stood outside and watched her. Every time she glanced at the window at night, she prepared for the worst, imagined there would be a face, each time relieved to find it black with the night.

But this time there was.

The face moved out of the shadows and closer to her window. She couldn't move—couldn't breathe. There was a clear glimmer of teeth, split into a devilish, distorted grin.

Please, no.

It was the distorted face...of Dirch Johnson.

Charlotte's blood turned to ice as the face came into view. She blinked rapidly, hoping her eyes were playing tricks. But there was no mistaking that crooked nose and pointed chin- it was Dirch leering back at her.

Her mind reeled. She recalled his sly wink just yesterday and shivered. But why would he terrorize them like this?

Confusion and disbelief warred within her. But the malevolent hunger in his eyes appeared all too real in the moonlight.

Her breath caught in her throat as she met Dirch's crazed gaze. She

searched his twisted features for some sign of the man she knew, but found only the cold stare of a menacing stranger. Denial and doubt spun within her even as the evidence leered before her eyes.

Charlotte pinched herself hard, praying to wake from this nightmare. But the shadowy face remained, grinning malevolently. She squeezed her eyes shut, willing sleep to claim her from this torment.

A vision...that's all it was. A hallucination...she hoped.

# Claims of the Dark

White. It was as if she had sunk into a deep tub of whitewash or floated inside a fog. Perhaps if a raindrop had a soul, and knew what it was to be held within a cloud, this was how it felt.

But wait—objects began to sharpen. Charlotte found herself trapped within four walls. It was a large, square, eerily familiar room that stretched two tree lengths all around. The white room went on endlessly, the boundaries between wall and floor blurred until Charlotte could no longer discern up from down. Shadows danced and played tricks on her eyes, forming twisted shapes that lurked just at the edge of sight.

In the doorway, dressed also in a shimmering gown of a moonlight's glow, stood Mother.

She was thinner than before, a gaunt shadow resting upon her face, but still she held the smile, her flame-kissed hair, and blue eyes so dearly remembered. Mother crossed the room and met her with a bony hug.

Odd. There was no warmth in this embrace. No squeeze. Charlotte couldn't feel her.

Windows had formed on the walls, yet what lay beyond remained obscured in a blur. Mother wordlessly entwined their fingers, or at least, her eyes told her that, even if her hands couldn't feel it.

Mother led her across the room, a few footsteps ahead, and gently ushered

her out the door. What had once been a haze of white was now an explosion of luscious greenery. Moss, sage leaves, and dew-dropped grass grew thick between the trees. The trees themselves seemed alive, branches reaching, clawing, as if to trap Charlotte in their twisted embrace. The breeze was summer cool, still touched by a morning chill, causing her to shiver. Was it the cold, or was it her fear?

Foxgloves glittered in the soft sunlight and sparkling dew. Blue jays twittered love songs, creating an ambience of peace among the green, but Charlotte sensed a darkness within that peace. She followed Mother down the path and through the sprigs of purple lavender, arm outstretched as she grasped for her hand, farther away from the large brick manor that loomed behind them.

She'd seen that manor before.

"Come, Charlotte."

Her lips moved, but hardly the echo of a whisper met her ears.

Mother broke free from her grasp, fingers parting. She could feel again how she slipped away, much the same as the final time they touched in life. Mother's white chiffon dress was a contrast to her fiery wild hair and succulent greenery.

"Mother, please!" Charlotte cried out, though the sound barely left her lips. She reached for the floating specter drifting farther away, a profound sense of grief and longing welling up within her. But the woman gliding deeper into the hedge maze no longer seemed to hear her desperate pleas.

Charlotte's heart ached, yearning for the comfort and wisdom of her real mother. Tears blurred her vision as she chased the phantom, knowing that even if she caught up, the reunion she dreamed of could never be. She chased the billowing figure to a wall of the tallest hedges she'd ever seen—the entrance to what she recognized as a hedge maze, like the grandiose ones in Europe Papa had read to her about.

"Come, little Charlotte."

Little?

How could this be? Her legs were shorter. She was not her fully grown self, but a child again, not half as tall as the hedge. How peculiar this was. Small fingers. Long hair. She chased after Mother, running with the quick step of childhood. Whether spurned from youthful energy or fear, she did not know. Dark shadows from the towering hedges cascaded across the path. Turn left. Turn right. The floral scent grew cloying and sickly sweet, almost choking in its intensity as she moved through the hedge maze.

"Charlotte."

She could hardly see now. The further she ran, the larger the hedges grew, arching high above her creating a tunnel made purely of green.

"There you are darling."

It was Mother, cherry red hair floating in the air around her, as if she were swimming underwater and not standing in the tunnel of the hedge. Mother beckoned with a bony finger and darted out of the hedge tunnel.

"Mother, wait! Why do you flee? Come talk with me!"

She rounded the corner, escaping the dark tunnel and returning to the light. Mother floated down the maze, running her hands across the walls... walls made of roses. Walls that were covered in thorns.

"Mother! Your hands!"

She trailed behind as the ghostly shadow of the woman who gave her life ran her hands among the thorns. Her skin tore. Charlotte gasped at the shock of pain that greeted her own hands and looked down to find them covered in blood, yet she had not touched a single thorn.

Mother glided to the center of the path and, raising her arms to the sky, started twirling in a nightmarish dance while blood floated in droplets around her. She spun into the air, a twister of torn flesh and chiffon, growling and cursing in an unfamiliar tongue.

Mother violently slammed into the wall of thorns, her body rolling, faster and faster, as if down a steep hill, all the while cutting and scraping and ripping the skin from her frail frame.

She leapt from the wall and danced across the path, her white chiffon dress

soaked in crimson. A maniacal laugh echoed through the hedges.

Dark. Provoking. Female.

It wasn't Mother's laugh, of that she was sure. Surely, she too, was a ghost in this hedge hell, for she had stopped breathing long ago but remained upright.

Mother, or whatever demonic force masqueraded as her, parted her mouth and bared sharpened teeth. She raised her skeletal fingers, reaching out to grab, yet no longer did skin cover the bones.

Flesh dangled from her.

Even in this nightmare world, the blaze crawled up her throat. Charlotte covered her pounding ears, feeling the wet, slick blood coating her hair.

Mother snapped her neck to the side and grinned. She raised a broken cross to her heart, stabbing it again and again. From the wound, bloomed the brightest of red roses, dripping in blood. A low, slow hiss escaped through her bloody lips and Mother dropped the broken cross.

Then...she lunged.

Unable to move, unable to scream, unable to breathe. Her demon mother came for her.

# Silence in Society

Charlotte jolted awake, drenched in frozen sweat, coughing and sputtering, fighting for air. Slamming back to reality was a particularly jarring relief. She had kicked her coverings to the floor and rolled to the side clinging to the pillow.

That twisted creature wasn't Mother.

That maze was as familiar as the manor. Was it on the grounds of the Governor's mansion? She couldn't remember where she'd seen it before. The horrible vision clung to her thoughts.

Red hair. Further deepened in color by the splatterings of blood.

And roses.

Her view settled upon Christ's cross, hung on her wall from childhood. A symbol of hope and God's protection, carved with climbing vines and roses. A gift from Mother's sister. But neither the Lord, nor God had any part in the wickedness that filled her dreams of Mother.

Nay—nightmares.

Surely there was a reason why among the dark and twisted thorns, there bloomed the most beautiful of flowers. Or perhaps she should see it as a tempting rose protected by the deceitful pricks to punish those who wished to caress its beauty. Perhaps the Rosicrucians had betrayed her. Either way, the nightmare was a betrayal by the deepest of corners in her unconscious



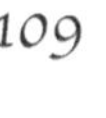

mind. She'd yearned to see Mother.

But never like that.

The scrape of chairs across wood sounded from down the hall and she heard men's voices, and by the sound of it, not a few. She remembered the moonlit face.

Dirch Johnson.

Was that a part of her dream, too?

Papa had insisted that he would call upon the council, but she couldn't have imagined they would convene here. It was surprising that he had actually called upon them, though, considering his general mistrust and distaste in their involvement.

She listened as they spoke. "And what would you have us do? Round up every man, woman, and child in Philadelphia, as sheep, and question them as to their whereabouts last night?"

Another voice. "What about the night watch?"

And another. "There is already an ongoing investigation."

"How do we know your visitor was even connected to the murders? And are the murders even connected at all?"

She heard them as she stepped closer. Every eye within the room, questionable as well as familiar, turned to her as she stepped into the light. Every chair they owned was taken so she would stand.

Papa rose to greet her, followed by the hurried shuffle of slight bows and nods from the others assembled. "Ah! Charlotte. I've called the council to assist us."

Minister Horvath, portly and tidy; the kind smile he offered under his door-knocker beard brought comfort. "What say you of the intrusion upon this household last night?"

The smallest disappointment still lingered concerning his words from Elizabeth's funeral, but she trusted that this man of God was here to help them.

Mayor Richard Payne sat by the fire, swirling what was no doubt a strong drink in his glass. Why risk the clouding of one's judgment at such an early hour? Of course, with the conversation being what it was, his consumption came as no surprise, and it was whispered that he enjoyed many from day to day.

Constable Cobb, stoic and well-dressed as usual but clearly uncomfortable with the gathered crowd inserting themselves into his lawful investigation. A grim elder Mr. Franklin was joined by his recently bereft son, Thomas, and the mysterious brother Samuel. Three from one family served on the council? That couldn't be right. Considering they served at leisure, it wasn't uncommon for the council to often encounter a change of membership.

Thomas looked awful, but of course he would with what he'd been through. Two other solemn men whom she did not know sat with them at the table. Probably merchants. New members, yet probably just as untrustworthy.

Rufus Spencer, Delphia's husband, sat quietly among them, thankfully not meeting her eye. Money clearly bought anyone a seat on the council these days. Some said his perversions swung towards the youngest of shavers his wife could procure.

Disgusting.

He was a small, otter-like man, and reminded her of a horrible fish recently discovered by scientists abroad. An angler fish, they called it. Male anglers attached themselves to a much larger, suitable female mate, sucking nutrients from her in order to survive. Eventually, with no need to see for themselves or swim, their organs withered away and they became a chunk of attached flesh—there to service their mate with sperm if the need arose. Of course, Rufus hadn't a need to provide sperm, as Madam Delphia was barren. Thank God.

And there he sat, a chunk of flesh among the council in their home.

Finally, her eyes came to rest on the attending member she had prayed wouldn't be there. His presence was clear the moment she had stepped in the room, but she had looked everywhere but upon him. The familiar prick of pins and needles crawled up her skin.

Governor Hellsmith. Evil harbored within this man. She knew not the reason, nor had ever been on the receiving end of anything suspicious, but deep within her heart she knew that it was true.

Papa knew it too, and perhaps that was the spring from which her misgivings came, but even today he had placed himself on the opposing side of the room from the Governor.

However, the Governor had heeded the call after their midnight attacker. Perhaps her misgivings in him were unfounded. Still, best not to play with fire lest they all get burned.

"Miss Charlotte, please share with us your take on last night." Minister Horvath beckoned to her and offered his chair. "I imagine you are still shaken." No doubt they had noticed how long she took to answer.

She settled her breath.

"I am unsure if the intrusion was an attempt upon our lives." She sat with as much poise as she could muster, given her nervous state, "but I fear we must exercise great caution moving forward, for someone clearly intended us harm."

"For what reason?" Mr. Franklin spoke calmly, without harshness, presenting as genuinely concerned.

"What reason did the killer have to come for Gayle Williams or Mrs...", she glanced over at Thomas and he looked to the floor, "Elizabeth."

Constable Cobb paused the scrawling in his notebook. "It seems we have upon our hands a killer of dubious, unrestrained intent of a serial nature. We may not yet have identified the connection, but rest assured that I will find it."

A man she did not know spoke next. "You'd better find it fast. The townspeople are at risk, even in their own homes."

"Elizabeth was taken from our bed," Thomas said, his voice trembling. "I slept beside her, neither alarmed nor awakened by the intrusion. How could they have slipped in so unannounced?"

Poor Thomas. How he sat among them and spoke at all escaped her reason, for after Mother, she could hardly rise from bed for weeks, and she was but a child at the time.

"Will the town's protection increase? An expansion of the night watch, perhaps?" Papa spoke with firmness. "So far, the murders have taken place at night, thus it appears the killer stalks among the shadows."

"We'll not want to cause a panic among the town, sir." The Governor's tone exuded authority.

Charlotte started at a sharp knock on the door. More council members? The familiar creak of their entrance made it clear that Miss Nelly was there, out of sight, but available to answer. Footsteps clamored down the hall and their newest guest revealed himself.

Good God. It was Ben.

"Ben! What a delightful surprise. I hadn't wished to wake you in leaving." The sight of his third son uplifted Mr. Franklin. Charlotte felt a similar flutter of uplift within her heart, but it didn't make it to her face.

"Pardon the intrusion, gentlemen." Grey eyes met hers. "Miss Charlotte." "Mother told me what had happened, so I came to offer my assistance. Was anyone harmed?" He looked to her. "Are you all right?"

"They're fine, Ben. None were taken last night, Thaddeus scared off the intruder."

Ben lowered his voice, but she stood near enough to overhear as he leaned into Mr. Franklin's ear.

"You should have told me, Papa."

The elder Franklin clapped Ben's shoulder. "I didn't want to startle you. The council has it under control. Besides, you're here now. Come sit."

Papa greeted Ben with a white-knuckled handshake.

The Governor wiped his sweaty brow. "Back to the matter at hand. We can't expand all of our resources until we are sure of what exactly we are dealing with. This is a large town. Would you have me post a man on every street?"

Charlotte's eyes went wide, her breath catching in her throat as the councilmen murmured in dissent. She hadn't expected such a wave of skepticism and accusation.

"Justice will not be served until those who are unaffected are as outraged as those who are."

My, how comfortable Ben was speaking to the Governor in such a way. Especially since he wasn't a member of the council. His political dealings abroad must have been impressive with such confidence. Intriguing.

"I shall see what we can do. For the immediate future, at the very least, we can post a watchman upon this street, and perhaps on either side of Society Hill. Would that suffice?"

Of course, protect those with the greatest ability to financially contribute to the town, and his next campaign. She stifled an eye roll.

"For a start, that will do."

"We appreciate the protection you've offered, Governor Hellsmith."

But wait.

"Papa—" She hesitated. She was certain that what she had seen last night was not a dream, yet a thread of doubt wove its way into her thoughts. If it wasn't Dirch, this would be a bold accusation to make.

All eyes were upon her, boring holes into her soul.

"I'm certain to have seen a face in the window, standing outside."

Dare she say it?

"A face!"

"Good God."

"Do you mean a shadow?"

The Governor raised his hand for silence in the room. "Whose face did you see, dear Charlotte?"

The way he called her "dear" made her skin crawl.

Charlotte settled her racing heart. "The face—was that of Dirch Johnson."

Stunned silence clouded the room. She could see it plastered on their smug faces and feel the doubt perspire from them.

"Dirch is a fine young man."

Papa sank to his chair and looked at her with saddened eyes. "You're confident in what you saw, Lottie? Without a shadow of doubt?"

"Papa…"

"Perhaps it was one of your dreams." He must believe her.

"I know what I saw, Papa. Dirch stood outside of my window last night."

"Isn't he an apprentice of yours, Thaddeus?" Constable Cobb raised a questioning brow. Thankfully, he remained unaffected by the politics of the town. Everyone knowing everyone and all of their business created long lines of loyalty in the proverbial sand.

"We must question the boy at the very least."

"You suggest that Dirch Johnson carried out the attack on your home last night? That he is the one responsible for the murders?" Mayor Payne spluttered in disbelief. "Clearly she's addled by the events of the evening."

"Mayor Payne, I beg your pardon! The council has asked what Miss Charlotte saw, and she spoke her truth. That is ripe enough for questioning."

Ben. Of course it was Ben. Charlotte's heart quickened at his defense, the sincerity in his eyes kindling a spark of hope within her heavy spirit. Perhaps she had found an ally among these quarrelsome men.

"Dirch Johnson is not the killer."

With such vigor they defended him.

"It is not my intent to besmirch any man's good name…"

"Lottie." Papa cast a warning glance in her direction.

Sophistication be damned. She would speak her truth. "…but I must say that in my own experiences—he may not be the man you think you know."

"Did he shoulder your advances then? Is this a lover's quarrel gone awry?" The chunk of flesh had spoken, and she wished he hadn't.

"Say, no."

"What's this? It may not even be connected to the murders at all!"

"Was it necessary to involve the council in such matters?"

The men were rising in tension now. "We know nothing of the sort. You cannot disagree that these instances are connected."

Charlotte clenched her fists, biting her tongue to restrain the torrent of outrage welling up inside at their dismissive words. How dare they imply she was addled or scorned! Heat flooded her cheeks at the councilman's crude insinuation. She averted her eyes, shame mixing with fury at the callous assumption he voiced before all.

"That's ENOUGH." Papa rose in frustration. "Please do not presume to speak to my daughter in such a way, standing in my home, Sir."

"Gentlemen." Samuel Franklin rose with the cool calm of a storm's center. It was the first time today she had heard him speak.

"We shall question Mr. Johnson of his whereabouts last night and proceed from there. The night watch will expand by ten men and we shall reconvene to discuss the interrogation in three days' time." He peered around the suffocating room, so thick with tension she could slice it with a butter knife.

"All agreed?"

The councilmen murmured in their typical, disgruntled fashion.

And these were the men they had chosen to follow.

"Agreed. Then we are adjourned."

As the councilmen shuffled to exit, Mr. Franklin and Ben sought her and Papa.

"Thank you for calling upon us, Thaddeus. I, again, am disheartened to hear of your troubles last night and hope you will not suffer such an experience again."

He thrust out his hand and Papa shook it. Mr. Franklin turned for the door.

Ben parted his lips, but paused. What would he say? He wasn't even supposed to be there. He had come to check on them.

On her.

She turned her attention fully to Ben.

"Mr. Scott—"

"Please, call me Thaddeus." Papa was full of surprises today. However, while the words were warm in intent, that same warmth didn't reach his eyes.

"Um...Mr. Thaddeus..Sir."

Her heart fluttered. Surely the confident Ben who had spoken so directly to the council and to the Governor wasn't nervous? For her sake?

"I apologize for the behavior displayed today by some of the council members. Please know their forward language is purely their own and not reflective of my family." His eyes shone with apology.

His heart radiated kindness.

"They sometimes get caught up among themselves. A flock of hens, as my friend John would say." He chuckled. "We were delighted to have Miss Charlotte for dinner not so long ago, and I thank you for allowing her to join us, Mr. Thaddeus."

"You're most welcome." Papa squeezed her hand. "She had a wonderful time." How long would they discuss her as if she wasn't there?

She cleared her throat, reminding them of her presence.

"Miss Charlotte, after the events of last night and an already taxing day today, I would like to extend my hand..."

His what.

"...in friendship and ask for you to join me in something more lighthearted in nature." He glanced at Papa. "With your father's blessing, of course."

Papa's face mirrored a shocked expression, as if he had delivered a stinging slap. He may have offered his first name, but agreeing to whatever this lighthearted affair might be would be a stretch. Ben was of the Franklin lineage, after all.

Of High Society.

One to be cautious of.

"The rainy weather of today will not do, so if it pleases you, I would like to come to call tomorrow. Would you care to join me, Miss Charlotte?"

She looked to Papa with pleading eyes. Please let him say yes. Oh please.

"Papa?"

He sighed. The hint of a smile played about his lips.

"Take care of her, Ben Franklin. Keep her safe and uplift her spirits."

The tension ebbed from Charlotte's body as Papa granted permission, a flood of relief washing over her. The promise of lighter days ahead with Ben lifted her battered spirit.

Ben chanced a wink her way. My God, how bold.

"I solemnly swear to it."

# Written as Silence

The glittering rays of sunlight shone through the lone window in a room that brought her endless joy. Ben had been correct in thinking the weather of today would provide a blissful setting for their lighthearted affair. The smell of old pages, well-worn and loved by the many hands that had held them before, enriched her senses and fulfilled her soul. Vanilla. Almonds. The books held the slightest hint of the woodsy pulp they were made from. An order had arrived from London two days prior, and as they sat reading in this small room in the west wing of the statehouse, the crisp texture of fresh paper, of the possibilities held within their covers, intoxicated her. Ben had brought her to the library.

Priya would scoff at the idea of courting among dust-peppered tomes, but Charlotte's heart soared knowing that Ben also enjoyed the enticement of tales unknown.

"What thou wouldst highly,

That wouldst thou holily; wouldst not play false,

And yet wouldst wrongly win."

The words of William Shakespeare, aged one hundred years by now, were like honey dripping off the comb as he spoke them. Ben was an intelligent man, transcendent beyond the constraints of his softer upbringing, and none too full of himself to admit enjoying the pleasures of the written word. It was undeniably intoxicating.

"Macbeth has always been one of my favorites. Anything written by

Shakespeare, really."

He peered at her over the pages. "I find that by studying the works of the many greats, I am able to improve upon my own writings."

"Oh, really?" She laughed. "A brother of the quill, have we? And what such tales are you inspired to pen?" She felt comfortable around him today, more comfortable than ever. "A knight in shining armor? The damsel in distress?"

He chuckled in response. "I cut my teeth on the works of Joseph Addison and Sir Richard Steele. They published periodicals in The Spectator, which my Papa had carried over from England to read."

"That's interesting—go on."

"And as I grew older, I dabbled in more poetic writings and stylized prose. I've found that printers are more interested in that form of writing as it draws the people in."

She was acutely aware of how deeply his gaze enveloped her.

"Would you like to know a secret about my writings, Miss Charlotte?"

"Well, of course, kind Sir." She flashed him a grin. "Do tell."

"I sometimes submit to printers using a name that is not my own. My brother owns a press, you know, and he would be scandalized to find that one of his most popular columns, penned by 'Silence,' was written by none other than his scallywag of a brother, Mr. Ben Franklin."

"You dog!" She laughed. "Such a devious nature to have in the pursuit of fine publishings."

He raised his hands in surrender. "Turn me in. Take me to the jailhouse and I shall henceforth be known as the Poetic Imposter! A criminal through and through."

"Shakespeare indeed." She reached for Macbeth, as it was her turn to choose a passage to read out loud, and noticed the hot flush of her cheeks as his hand smoothly slid across hers. Her skin tingled where they touched. Time froze, and in an instant, she became timid and exposed. She recognized her desire. Could he feel it too? Sharing secrets and flirtatious words in a room filled with tales of love was surely the happiest she had felt in a very long time.

She thumbed through the pages of Macbeth. Choosing a tragedy to read through might not have been the most romantic idea. She rose and made her way to the shelf full of books they had to choose from. She had seen one there, one she'd like to take home, but Ben needn't know of it.

She twirled to face him, sliding the book underneath Macbeth. "Ahh. Here we are. One of the best passages, and if I recall, it reminds me of you."

"I'll listen with interest then, m'lady."

M'lady, he'd added. She flushed.

"Your face, my thane, is as a book where men

May read strange matters. To beguile the time,

Look like the time; bear welcome in your eye,

Your hand, your tongue: look like the innocent flower,

But be the serpent under't"

Well that didn't end as she remembered it at all. Wide-eyed and embarrassed, she peered over the pages at Ben. He studied her with raised brows, a playful look of shock on his face.

"A serpent! You think of me as a serpent?"

"Of course not."

How humiliating. "I remembered this passage incorrectly, it would seem."

"It is a tragedy, after all."

"I am truly mortified."

He chuckled and leaned forward, resting his strong arms upon the table. "Shall we take a walk, Miss Charlotte? Look outside. The sun calls to us, don't you think?"

Thank God he wasn't offended. "A walk would be lovely."

What a handsome man he was, his mind and quick wit being of more intrigue than anything, but, of course, his chiseled jaw and soft pink lips did nothing to damage the vision.

As Ben gathered his belongings, she slid A Treatise of Witchcraft into her own.

Knock. Knock. Knock.

"Charlotte! Open the door! Charlotte! Please!"

Dear God—she knew that voice, and it sounded distressed.

"Please for the love of God open the door. I need help. Right NOW!"

Ben crossed the cramped room in a flash, footsteps pounding across the floor. In a flash, he opened the door, exposing a disheveled and panic-stricken Priya.

Charlotte rose. "Priya! What happened to you? My God, are you all right?"

Priya wore the tattered remains of the dress she had just purchased at the market only weeks ago. Her flesh flamed red, the dark shadow of bruises beginning to form. Tears stained her cheeks, her painted face smeared, and splotched.

Charlotte cupped her dearest friend's hot cheek. One eye swollen almost shut, accompanied by a cut above her lip.

Ben rose with a clenched fist and spit out the words in a sudden rage.

"Where is John? Did he do this to you? I will kill him." Priya sank into Charlotte's arms as she tried to help her friend to a chair. "No, God no," Priya sobbed. "It wasn't John."

Priya wiped at her tears with a corner of her ruined dress. "I cannot tell you how this came to be, but only that I need a place to hide. They'll come looking for me. I can't bear to see him again."

Charlotte struggled to hold back her own tears. "Please let us help you. Who did this to you?"

"Lottie, if I tell you..." Priya's concentration shifted away as she fumbled with the pieces of her dress. "Please, dear God above—I cannot."

"Breathe slowly."

Charlotte turned to Ben. "Please fetch me a cool, wet cloth and tell none what it is for. Come back without delay."

She settled her beating heart and waited for him to leave. Now, hopefully,

Priya would feel comfortable talking to her. And if she chose otherwise, that was perfectly acceptable, too. Right now, she needed to comfort her friend.

"Lottie, you'll judge me. I have sinned. I have done that which you will find abhorrent in nature."

"Priya. Let me help you. Whatever it is, you don't deserve such treatment. Was it your father? A stranger? The murderer?"

Priya released a long breath and settled into a stupor, as if she were in a trance. "Do you remember the night we went to the Franklin dinner? And Delphia?"

Oh no. Stay calm. Don't worsen this.

"Yes, I remember."

"I thought she could help me secure an offer of marriage from John."

"Oh, Priya."

"I sent her a message. Only interested in how she could help me. I thought maybe since she was close to all of the families on Society Hill, that she knew the way to make me suitable. A woman deserving of John's love."

Her heart shattered for her friend. "He was already taken with you, Priya."

"The first few meetings were wonderful. We spoke of elegance and grace and she taught me the proper etiquette of elevated life. How to sound like a lady. How to walk like a lady. How to...pleasure a man."

"Oh, Priya—why didn't you tell me? So that is why I haven't seen you of late?"

"I knew what you would think...what you would say." Priya gasped the words between her sobs.

"I think none of those things." Yet she couldn't help it now.

"Lottie. I saw them. Amir and John. I went to meet John at his home for breakfast and when I walked inside—"

Charlotte froze.

"They were half-clothed." She spiraled into anguish again.

"I didn't know what to do so I ran out the door. I paced and walked and tried to make sense of the information and thought of Delphia."

Charlotte groaned. "Priya—"

"I went to her, hoping she could help me. She told me that today I would truly learn how to pleasure a man in a way that would capture him eternally." Tears dripped upon her dress.

"The meetings were typically she and I, sitting in her grand house among finer things than I've ever known. She pulled out a wooden stick, rubbed smooth as a stone by God only knows what."

Dear God.

"She instructed me to...do atrocious things, pretending as if it were a man. When I thought the lesson had ended, I thanked her for her time. I'd already decided I was in too deep and wouldn't be returning but she stopped me. John was a lost cause, anyway." She moaned. "And with Amir." Tears ran down her face. "She grabbed my wrist and wouldn't let go."

"So Madame Delphia did this to you?"

"No. Just listen." Priya clenched her fists.

"She took me to a room in her house, blindfolded me, and bellowed it was time to practice. I tried to get away, but that was when the beating started."

"'He's paid for you', she hissed. 'You'll learn your place—and learn how to service a man.' I don't know how many were in that room, but someone forced me to my knees. They were laughing, Lottie! Laughing at my pain. I was crying and screaming, and then she grabbed my throat." She moved her hair to reveal the finger-shaped bruises forming on her neck.

"You'll not scream, and don't you dare cry...little whore," she sneered.

She wrapped her arms around herself, holding back an onslaught of more tears.

"She forced my mouth upon him, Lottie. He grabbed me by the head and slammed me onto him, over and over. I couldn't breathe. Couldn't get away."

Bile rose within Charlotte's throat.

"I did the only thing I knew to stop it, Lottie. I had to get out of there.

You have to believe me. But now they will surely kill me for what I have done!"

"What did you do, Priya?"

"I bit him."

She choked on her own shock, ignoring the insistent flames rising to her ears.

"Bit? You bit him? You bit him where?" Fear gripped her as she suspected the answer.

"You know where. I bit so hard, Lottie, I tasted his blood. God forgive me! I have sinned so deeply and now they will come!"

Priya cried. "And Sarah—"

Ben appeared in the door, flushed and out of breath clutching the wet cloth he was sent for.

"My God, Miss Priya. I have the cloth. How can I help you? I'll call a carriage and we can take you anywhere you need to go."

"I can't stay here any longer. They'll come for me. And what of my parents? If they see me in this state, they will know what I have done."

Absorbed again into tearful disarray, Priya clutched her middle and doubled over.

"I saw him, Lottie. As I wrenched away from his grasp, I saw the man whose blood filled my mouth."

Ben paled.

"That is why I know they'll come for me. I bit him, Lottie. The mayor! I bit into Mayor Richard Payne."

"How did you escape?"

"I don't know. After he screamed, a number of people came running and, in the commotion, I slipped out the door. I ran the whole way here. It was closer than home, and I remembered what you spoke of yesterday about meeting with Ben."

She chanced a look at him, yet Ben stood white as a ghost. His lips opened and closed, as if he wanted to speak but could find no words.

Priya needed assistance. An idea sprang to mind. "Come stay with us. Papa and Nelly would be delighted to have you and we can keep you safe."

Priya peered through her tears. "They will come looking for me. I'll not bring them to your family, Lottie."

What could they do? "Ben, could you call a carriage? You could stay at the Morris House on Society Hill for now. They have two night watch guards posted on either side of the street. The constable is staying there as well."

Ben nodded. "You can stay there at no cost to you. I'll pay for it myself. We can speak to my Papa and find a way out of this, a way to protect you from whatever wrath may come."

"Ben, it was Delphia. She was taking 'lessons' from her."

"Dear God."

"Isn't she a friend of your Papa's? I can't imagine that would go over well. Or with John."

Priya cried. "Oh God, John!"

"Worry not about him. Right now we need to get you safe. I'll send a note with the driver, explaining that you're staying at Morris House as my guest, and you may stay there until you wish to go elsewhere. How would that be?" Ben spoke to her softly.

"I thank you, kind Ben. I don't know what else to do or I wouldn't put you out."

Ben nodded. "It's no trouble at all, Miss Priya. We won't let them find you. Shall I alert the constable?"

Priya gasped. "No! No one must know. You know better than anyone how they hold all the power. I need to get away. I can't stay here."

Charlotte reached for her hand. "Priya, I will come with you." Her friend would need someone to comfort her right now.

She shook her head. "No. I'll go alone. I'll be safe at the Morris House. None will know I'm there. You can't get involved, Lottie. I just want to be alone."

Charlotte frowned. "But I'm already involved, as I've seen you here today."

"Run to my mother and tell her what happened. Don't tell her who, and don't tell her where I was or why I was there. Tell her I've run away from a bit of trouble and will be in touch as soon as possible."

"Priya, I don't like this. Let me take you home." Charlotte begged. "Come stay at my house. Please."

"And bring them to you? Absolutely not. The Mayor and Delphia will come for me. It's not a matter of if, but when."

"I could accompany her to the Morris House and make sure she gets to her room safely?" Ben asked.

Sweet Ben. He needn't do this, but she knew he did it out of a kind heart.

Priya peered at her with pleading eyes. "I'll be all right. Tell my mother not to worry."

Ben nodded. "I'll send for the carriage."

Ben exited the room again and Priya turned to her, voice hardly more than a whisper.

"There's something else you should know. Please don't tell him, for I'm sure he's not involved, but there was one more person in the room that I didn't mention. The room where they took me. I saw her in the corner, watching... dressed in black."

She breathed in deeply. "Go on."

"It was the hostess from the Franklin dinner. Bethshua Franklin."

The Nineteenth
Chapter

# Melody of Malice

*"Sleep—eternal—for dirt was now her bed. Three can keep a secret if two
are dead"*

*-Harry Meanwell*

o medicine could yet diminish the violent natural inclinations felt deep within the soul. The dark, unsettling thoughts that sheltered in the deepest recesses of the mind were, at last, euphorically, sensationally, released. After the intoxicating, erotic thrill he experienced from that last execution of justice, he knew this night had the potential to fulfill him in new ways.

In the words of de Sade, Nothing quite encourages as does one's first unpunished crime.

The two kills prior had thrilled him. And the here and now presented the perfect opportunity. The thought of dripping crimson and the whoosh of her last breath shouldn't excite him—but it did.

She was alone...and needed to atone for her sins. The harlot.

The Morris House sent out a quick word that she had arrived. Of course they would, the innkeeper was among them. She was hidden and safe within one of their rooms. Mayor Payne required justice for her twisted act of defiance earlier, and thus he was sent to claim the kill. Killing two ravens with one stone, as some would say. She would die as the harlot...no further opportunities to play with evil beyond her reach. Her selfish, burning desire to lift out of her current social standing through matters of a sexual nature showed a clear distrust of the voice of reason. She knew the nighttime devilry Delphia dabbled in. How ignorant to think she would not be called upon to repay her debts. Another death required of him. One step closer to safety.

He approached the Morris House by foot. No need existed as a reason to conceal himself, as most of the staff were already asleep, and the keeper knew that he would come. It had taken some time to prepare the basement, but finally the time had come.

'Twas time to exact their revenge.

He met him outside, to the left of the house in the unlit alleyway. The keeper was a cantankerous, twisted man, with an unkempt grey beard, too many missing teeth, and stringy hair with enough grease to light a flame. He was the perfect accessory for unsavory deeds in the night. No doubt he cohorted with them as a means to meet his own desires. His stench alone would keep anything slick between the legs at bay, but not Delphia's girls—they had no choice. The promise of a pretty woman wrapped around him, thrusting with lust, even if feigned, often kept his mouth shut.

But even with that promise, he wouldn't be taking any chances tonight.

"Evening Sir." God...the filth upon his hands.

"Ebenezer. Good Evening." He kept his voice low, no need to raise suspicion. "I trust my room is prepared?"

"Oh yes, yes." Ebenezer licked his cracked lips in anticipation. Putrid filth.

"I have a gift for you, as a thank-you for your assistance tonight and for your eternal silence concerning my involvement."

He shoved a wad of currency into the filthy bastard's outstretched hand. Peasant.

"Not a word. Ebenezer. Or the next time I visit, it will be for you. Do I make myself clear?"

Ebenezer was counting, no doubt straining to use arithmetic and calculate how many romps he could buy with his spoils. "Of course. Of course. She waits for you on the table. Nary a word shall come from me."

***

On the table she did wait. Her ankles and wrists were tied to the four corners, binding her in a most restrictive way. A cloth stifled the screams that she attempted, as instructed. The tattered strips of cloth that were clearly once a beautiful dress had all but fallen away. It was an impossibility that greasy Ebenezer accomplished this himself with his gnarled and weak hands. He had to have had help.

Dim candle light flickered in the damp, wet basement. They needed to make improvements to the rooms below Society Hill. The catacombs were kept up nicely, thus the rooms should be, too.

Perhaps their increased usage of the catacombs contributed to it. Ten years, he was told. Ten years ago was the last time Philadelphia played host to the horrors of the night. He was but an agent, a crusader, sent to confuse and upset the light.

As he stepped out of the shadows, he saw the recognition cross her face. Priya's change was immediate, pure dread transitioned into relief as she relaxed against her bonds and cried.

Poor girl. She thinks her savior has come. Her expression did, however, test the mettle of his cause. Pray his visceral resolve stand yet rigid even presented against her swollen, already battered face. Such ruin on a once beautiful form.

A moment remained to turn away and betray the path. But then he would betray them, and that was not a choice he was willing to make. His loyalties were strong, and unfortunately, not with her, though she might have thought they were.

"Good Evening, Miss Priya." She tried to speak behind the gag, but unknown to her, they'd already spoken their last conversation. To prevent her from screaming, he had to keep the binding in her mouth, particularly since she remained wide awake.

She wouldn't be, for long.

"I believe you got into a spot of trouble today, is that correct, Miss Priya? Meddled in things you know nothing of? Delphia mentioned she was giving you lessons...how eager you were."

When at one time he had stolen a glance at her fair, slender frame, his eyes revealed the truth now. She was but a painted whore, eager to capture societal gain through any means possible. She did not harbor feelings of love... but instead deception. She sought to use her looks and sex for personal gain. Her love had been a farce.

He crouched low and placed his lips on her soft but tear-stained cheek. She looked confused. Of course she would be. He ran a finger down the length of her arm, from fingertip to shoulder. So tender. So supple.

She tried to speak his name around the cloth wedged tightly between her lips. Lips that a short time ago longed to please.

An astonishing number of men only wet their cocks with the juices of women like Priya. Young. Slender. Flirtatious. Devastatingly beautiful. But he knew the truth about life. With time, the face grows lank and wrinkled, then the neck, and then the breasts, but the plump and wet in-between would always stay the same. He'd had many women much older than she, and they came with experience and notable skill. Their husbands paid them no mind, so his length was theirs to please.

Lust blazed anew at the sight of Priya's pert flesh, revealed by her torn dress. How these sensations hardened him now. A bonus to the task of death. Her pleading gaze and loss of hope certainly did nothing to quell these fascinating new urges.

"I want to show you an instrument, Miss Priya. You'll like it, I think. It sings as a songbird, sharing a beautiful melody that tonight will provide an ambience for your demise."

The gag dampened her screams.

"The only trouble, my lustful little kitten, is that to play it, I'm in need of a liquidus component."

She pulled against her restraints and one small, chestnut nipple slipped out.

Dear God. How he'd like to bite that nipple.

He took the glass, a broken bowl from the transport of the armonica, and let it glide across her skin. Droplets of blood soon followed.

He wanted to lick her. Taste her. Fuck her. Why hadn't he tried her before?

Though her swollen, blackened eye was grotesque, the bruises on her neck held a curiously erotic appeal.

When his skin touched hers, animal vigor tightened his breeches.

Such a pity that she had to die tonight.

With each touch of his hand, each glide upon skin, she came closer to experiencing the rapturous caress of Death.

He needed to take her before that release.

Death was a mercy, a gateway to the great beyond, but forced pleasure was a whole new sin to explore. He would find out how far he could sink into the darkness.

Blood pounded in his ears with need, whether from true lust or bloodlust, he'd no idea. Nor, he realized, did he care. In the end, both pleasures would bloom.

Mayor Payne had no concern for the manner in which she was dealt with; his sole focus was ensuring that it occurred. He could have his way with her before he ended her.

She struggled against her bonds once more, which served to further displace her once beautiful dress.

"If you wished to whore, you only needed to ask. Shall I provide for you all that which you desire?" He laced his words with malice, mocking her.

He drank in the illicit curves of her breasts and the brunette tuft betwixt her luscious thighs.

How it would feel to drop his breeches and press against her sex. To meet her with his throbbing desire. To thrust inside of her with the force of a forge master's hammer. He thought of how she would scream and struggle. If anything, that only pushed his desire further, draining the last of his humanity with it. He wanted to ravage her with the heedless, reckless abandon of a boar in full rut. To take her and break her, hands tightening around her throat with each thrust.

He imagined her fading...slowly struggling less and less.

Desire overcame him and he thrust his fingers into her sex, to better prepare her for him. So tight, so slick, she would envelope him fully.

He removed his fingers to find them bloody. This gave him pause.

Still a virgin. Impossible. Especially after all that had transpired. But lessons with Delphia meant...evidently not what he thought.

His throbbing sex shriveled at the sight and what it meant. Had Delphia lied? But Mayor Payne's penis was bit in twain, he'd seen the result himself. From but a sinew of skin it dangled. Never again would he know a woman's pleasure.

Wiping her purity blood from his fingers in disgust, he scowled.

She shuddered.

"You've ruined my mood, but not the lesson."

"I've decided against the worst type of debauchery this night. It seems Delphia led me astray, for I thought you were whoring for her already. Such a pity. I do imagine that together we could have had a wonderful time. Shall we have a lesson, then?" Death was the price of admission. Those he worked for required the demise of the chosen five—the parameters were left up to him.

He twirled the blade between his fingers. "Science to accompany your future music lesson. So much you have learned of late! Isn't that right, darling Priya?"

Her pleading eyes continued to cry. Her struggle had lessened, resigned to her fate, yet the sight of the blade renewed her thrashing with vigor. So spicy, she was.

"Lesson One. There are four types of wounds. There's an abrasion, which I can see from the rope burns on your wrists you are already familiar with. There's a puncture—" he pricked the tip of the knife into her thigh, creating a small hole from which her blood began to flow.

"The two I've craved to try are a laceration and avulsion, though. Do you know what those are, little kitten?"

What little vigor that remained in Priya faded. So, too, did he tire. Time to show her and finally end this little game.

"If I cut deeply, sliding across your skin, you can clearly see the effect called

the laceration." He slit her from hip to knee, two long strips down each leg, preparing for the final step. Her vigor dwindled. Her extremities went limp a little at a time.

"Now all I need to do is connect each line, and pull."

He yanked at her legs, tugging and pulling to create an avulsion in her once soft and supple skin.

"Mayor Payne sends his regards."

He cut her deep, with arterial spurts landing upon his clothes. It only took three liters of blood loss to exit this world. As the fountains grew weaker, he looked at her face, the glassy eyes staring past him. He hadn't even noticed her last breath.

Such a pity. She would miss the song.

Hands slick with blood, he settled at the armonica and began to play. Her blood dripped down, splattering upon the floor. She missed the ambiance of her demise, but he knew with certainty that she had experienced the sweet caress of death. He raised his fingers to his lips.

Copper and salt, like a Fugio cent 'neath the tongue. Every bit as unpleasant as tonight's business.

# Truth is a Terror

**K**nock. Knock. Knock.

"Mr. Scott, it's Ben Franklin." The sound of his voice set her heart aflutter. He had come to tell them where Priya had decided to go.

Papa crossed the room to open the door. Charlotte waited with Nelly, knee bouncing as if to a catchy tune. But there was no music here—only fear. She couldn't escape the intrusive thought that Priya should have known better than to keep the company of Delphia.

"Is Priya here?" Breathless, Ben ran a shaking hand through his hair, brows furrowed.

A pit formed in her stomach. Breathing became arduous.

"Isn't she...at the Morris House? Your carriage took her there last night."

His attention flitted about the room. "She arrived safely...the innkeeper assured me."

A paleness washed over him. She hadn't seen him in much distress before.

"I left her there. She was safe. I checked with the night watch and they were at their posts on either side of the street. I was so sure she had come here."

"Ben, what are you talking about? Where is Priya?"

"She's gone."

"Gone?" Papa straightened in his chair. Nelly gasped.

"Did she leave on her own?" Charlotte asked. Dear God. Any number of horrific events could have happened to her. Surely she knew better than to run.

Ben groaned. "I don't know. I told the keeper of the Morris House to call my carriage the moment Priya asked for it, that it would take her anywhere she wanted to go...but my driver never left this morning. So, I thought I'd go check on her." He clapped his hands together, shifting his weight. "When I arrived at the Morris House, they insisted her room was empty. 'Must have run away in the night,' they mumbled. I was sure she must have come here to seek comfort with friends. Gods be merciful." He sunk into a chair. "Clearly I was wrong."

Papa cleared his throat. Charlotte could smell a bitterness in the air. The biscuits Nelly had made were burning. "And the night watch? They saw nothing?"

"I questioned them before coming here, and nary a man laid eyes upon her last night. They didn't report seeing anything out of the ordinary."

"We have to find her." Charlotte's mouth had gone dry and she could hardly breathe. Delphia got to Priya. She knew it.

Papa leaned close. "Lottie...now is not the time to search the town by yourself. There are dangerous people in control, and not the least also a murderer on the loose. I'll go see what I can find out about her, and pay a visit to Captain Lanivet while I'm at it."

His focus turned to Ben.

"Would you kindly stay here with the girls while I go out and search? Times are troublesome, and even with the watchman I fear for their safety."

Ben rested his elbows on his knees. "Of course. You have my word, no harm shall befall them this day, Mr. Scott."

"Call me Thaddeus." Papa was warming to Ben.

With that exchange, he collected his hat and swept out of the door.

Nelly sat by the fire, silent. Her biscuits were definitely burnt by now. She wrung her hands and kept looking at Ben and then to the floor.

Something troubled her deeply. Ben paced back and forth by the window,

cursing under his breath. When she looked again to Nelly, their eyes met in a brief pass, but Nelly looked away.

Charlotte pressed. "Miss Nelly. Do you know something?"

"Sae no. Plaise don' ast me. I remember a time such as this from afore. It feels tha like." She fidgeted. "If ye know wha' I'm meanin."

Charlotte rose to move closer. "If somehow your knowledge could help Priya, wouldn't you want to do that?" How she managed to speak, she didn't know.

Priya. Poor Priya. What evil had stolen her away?

"Aye, child. But there are things come aboot tha' I've no' remembered for quite some time. Painful things." The internal struggle of whether or not to share the truth was evident in her eyes.

"Miss Nelly, ma'am..." Ben sat beside her. "I beg your help in this. I thought I'd provided safety for Miss Priya and now she is missing. Help me to help her."

Miss Nelly sighed. "No' a word of this to yer father," she looked pointedly at Ben, "...either of ye."

Ben's eyes widened in surprise, but he nodded in agreement.

"Ye say our Priya had a run-in wi' tha mayor?"

They nodded, having spared her Papa and Miss Nelly the details surrounding exactly what that run-in entailed. Best not to tell her.

"Did ye kno tha' before the Governor was elevated to tha' station, he served as tha Mayor of this town? Governor Hellsmith?"

She shuddered at the name. So this is what she would finally learn. Why Papa disliked him and why she inherently knew something was awry. She remembered the trunk. The Rosicrucian Order. Perhaps Nelly would enlighten her.

"Nearly ten year ago, women and men started goin' missing. Always at night, mind ye. For a while, people thought the missin' were hoppin' ships at tha dock, off to find someplace new, but then they started to find them."

"The people?"

Nelly shuddered. "Tha bodies."

Glancing at Ben, Charlotte noticed his face drain of color as Nelly described the gruesome deaths. Though he sat calmly, she saw him fidget with the buttons on his coat, his knuckles white.

"Dead in tha streets. They called in constables from New York and Boston, but never a cause or connection was found. Efter five deaths, tha murders quick stopped." Nelly stared into the fire, her memories ablaze.

"Did they find who did it?" Ben listened to her story with interest...she, less so, because she now had a sad feeling she knew where this headed.

"It was ettled. Planned. Somebody did it on purpose. An' two of the victims, ye never got to truly know, as they were ripped from yer life far too soon."

There it was.

"Mother."

Nelly lowered her eyes, clearly uncomfortable. But that part Charlotte knew. She knew of the string of murders and how her mother was one of the claimed.

"But what of the other? Mother's sister was never found."

"Yer right, child. She wasn'. But wha' ye didn't know was from where yer Aunt Abitha was taken."

She'd scarcely thought about it, and Papa didn't speak of any details. He rarely would. They both tried their hardest to block that time out of mind.

Nelly stared straight into her soul, burrowing deep as a maggot into flesh. "Yer Aunt Abitha disappeared from the Hellsmith home," she raised her eyebrows, "as at tha time, she was tha lady of tha house. Yer Aunt Abitha was married to tha mayor, who then elevated himself. He's been the Governor ever since."

Charlotte recognized this as her opportunity. "Did the Governor find out that Aunt Abitha dabbled among the Rosicrucians, perhaps?" The color drained from Nelly's face. "That she and Mother dabbled in witchcraft?"

Ben raised his eyebrows, but said nothing.

Nelly eyed both of them, lowering her voice to just above a whisper.

"He beat her, Lottie. It was brutal. Merciless. Yer mother and Papa both knew it and tried to help her escape. Their order was good. Their ways were good. The Rosicrucians had nothing to do with this, I am sure."

Charlotte forced a swallow.

"Abitha intended to leave, like Priya, when quick like she was gone. No note. No farewell. No sign of her since. It was but a wee week later when—" Nelly halted.

A stone settled in Charlotte's throat. She lurched at the sudden wave of a memory, crashing upon her with such force, she thought surely she would die.

Blood.

Her mother sprawled across the floor.

Murder.

Charlotte wrapped her arms around herself, crouching down and cupping her knees.

"That's when I found her," she whispered.

Ben closed his eyes. At least now he knew.

He crouched down and wrapped an arm around her. The warm pressure brought her comfort, but not a lot.

She peered into the grey, speckled eyes that somehow brought her peace. Among despair, she felt the fires of purpose stir within her.

"We must go find her."

"Your Aunt?"

"No. My aunt was a witch. I mean Priya."

Ben set his lips to a thin, sad frown. "I promised your Papa I would stay here and keep you both safe while he was gone. I have given my word."

Nelly reached for her. "Charlotte, I promise ye. The Rosicrucians are not at fault here."

The pounding in her ears returned. Fear be damned, she was going to find her friend. Their witchcraft would not take another.

"Stay here if you wish, but I am headed to the square. I'll start there and ask around if anyone has seen her. I'll not raise suspicion. If you'd like to keep me safe, then you'll have to join me."

Ben rose. Though hesitation flickered across his face, he set his jaw and gave a firm nod. "I will stay by your side," he vowed solemnly. Charlotte saw the courage building within him and felt heartened. "And what of Nelly?" he said.

Nelly shifted her apron. "Thay's a watchman outside. I'll be fine. Go wi' her and bring Priya home to us." She wrung her hands in her lap.

"But...I strongly urge ye both to be wary of Governor Hellsmith and Mayor Payne. Tha men who sit upon tha council are not as saintly as they profess to be. Mark my words, and heed caution. I can sense it in my bones. Those men, no' tha order, had somethin' to do with this."

Charlotte shuddered. If only Nelly knew.

# A Pinch of Protection

They had to find Priya. Or, at the very least, a whisper of where she might have gone. Surely she wouldn't run away alone knowing the dangers that followed.

"We needn't be out here." Ben flitted his attention nervously around them. Fallen leaves crunched with each step he took. No doubt his legs, accustomed to carriage rides and frivolity, were tired from the walk to the square. She didn't care.

Charlotte scowled. "We shouldn't have let her stay alone. I trusted you that she would be safe there. She trusted you, and now she's gone." Charlotte flinched at the venom that dripped from her own words, but he had failed her.

"Charlotte, I thought she would be. And we do not yet know that she isn't safe. Perhaps she is? Perhaps she ran off to find her family for comfort?"

She narrowed her eyes at him. She didn't want to be angry, but frustration burst forth anyway. "This is Delphia's fault, and Mayor Payne. Why does your family consort with such vile, pontifical people anyway? Surely they don't approve of such matters." Charlotte calmed her racing heart. "Delphia's business is not a secret."

Breathe. Simply breathe.

"Charlotte, it's just the way circumstances are. Families of similar—" He stopped, eyes wide with instant regret.

"Of similar what?" She rounded on him, unsure of his meaning.

"Oh." Her cheeks flushed. Of course. "Similar...'financial standing' is that it? No need to engage among the peasants?" She huffed. Her biting words rolled off the tongue with alarming speed.

Ben's shoulders slumped, looking like a child chastised for something beyond his control..

"Of course not, Charlotte. I thought you, of all people, would understand." Hands stuffed in his pockets, he avoided her gaze. "I am not as they are."

She wilted as a peony crushed underfoot on the path.

Of course he wasn't. Somehow, within the deepest recesses of her heart, she held the certainty that Ben Franklin was a virtuous man. She could feel it.

Her anger stemmed from Priya's predicament, not from him.

The tension in her shoulders ceased; the weight of a thousand words lifted.

"I'm sorry, Ben. I know you're not. I'm worried...I'm frustrated."

She chanced a glance up at him, praying he would look at her this time.

"I'm scared."

Her knees grew weak as she stared straight into his speckled, storm cloud eyes. Ben wrapped his strong arms around her for the second time that day, and this time, in public. How forward he was. She instantly felt his warmth spread to her body, a blazing sunbeam greeting her skin. It enveloped her. Rejuvenated her.

She never wished to let go.

"I know you are, and I am too. She's going to be all right." He set his thin lips with a look of determination. "We will find her."

As they walked along the shops, peering in each window, she couldn't help but feel a trickle of hope with each step. They hadn't gotten to Priya; she was off replacing a dress or having a meal. Surely.

But deep within, she feared a different truth.

'Twas an odd feeling to be standing in the square, surrounded by the hustle and bustle of townspeople without a care in the world. They were purchasing apples, trading squash from the harvest, and finding thicker cloth in preparation for the cold winter soon to reach them. These people hadn't a need for concern. Yet Charlotte stood among them, so sure that her best friend would come home, but also trembling with fear of her demise.

To make matters worse, across the street with a commanding presence that suffocated her senses and further darkened her day, Governor Hellsmith stood in deep conversation with Delphia. They were laughing. 'Twas a roaring thunder to match the storm that arrived with him. Only evil would laugh at a time like this.

Damn Rosicrucians.

Charlotte turned again to Ben, having spotted the Apothecary run by his brother Thomas. She grabbed his arm and paused, remembering the satchel of herbs still safely hidden in her pocket. Mother's secret. It would only take a moment.

She met his eyes, batting her own. "Would you care to visit the coffeehouse across the way while I pop in the millinery shops? If Priya went to find a new dress, she would have stopped there." Charlotte hoped her words were convincing. She would check the millinery shops, that was sure, but first she wanted to inquire with Thomas. Ben needn't know.

"Of course, darling. I'll meet you outside, after." Though clearly reluctant to leave her side, Ben squeezed her hand and ventured across the street, embarking on a mission she believed to be futile.

She made her way to the hand-carved and gilt wooden mortar and pestle secured above the door. It was easily recognizable, even to those unable to read. Charlotte opened the door and breathed in the intoxicating scent of lavender, sage, lemongrass, and rosemary.

Oh dear. Charlotte pinched her nose. A variety of less appealing smells washed over her, no doubt from the dung shelves along the wall. There was the waste of dogs, goats, pigeons, peacocks, men, women, and a hog. There were five varieties of urine and over ten bottles filled with blood, or

so said their labels. There were jars of severed penises of stags and bulls, along with discarded toenail clippings (to induce vomiting). Even the rarest of medications sat among the jars, powdered mummy from Egypt. Papa preferred a lesser approach to medicine, so thankfully she had never ingested any such items.

Charlotte heard a woman's voice towards the back of the shop, so she hurried forward to spark the attention of Thomas Franklin. Mother's herbs grew heavy in her pocket, their presence weighted with secrets. She held hope that he could enlighten her on their purpose.

"Ahh, Charlotte." His smile didn't reach his shadowed, sunken eyes. Poor Thomas. How he managed to work at all after the loss of his Elizabeth escaped her, but no doubt Philadelphia had a great need for their most in-demand apothecary. He rested his weight upon the main counter, studying her. "What brings you in today?"

She produced the satchel of herbs, eyes darting about the room. "Hello, Thomas. I was hoping you could tell me what these are? I stumbled upon them and wondered if they were of any use...in cooking...or maybe as a salve?" Her hands were shaking, surely he would notice.

Thomas opened the herbs and pinched the smallest portion in between two fingers, bringing it to his nose. He raised his eyebrows. "Oh my! What an interesting treat you've brought with you today." He placed the satchel back in her outstretched hand. "Dried mugwort. Commonly used to repel insects from gardens, or so I've been told. We have a hard time importing any of this type across the sea." The corner of his mouth quirked. "And you say you stumbled upon this?"

Charlotte sighed, relief flooding her troubled heart. "Yes, it was locked away in an old box of a family member...nothing too exciting, I'm afraid."

Thomas leaned in, glancing around and whispering as if to a lover. "There are...other, lesser known uses of mugwort, too, Miss Charlotte." Oh dear.

Thomas's lips nearly touched her ear. "Some say it is an herb..." he whispered, "with magical qualities, used to protect travelers from evil spirits or wild animals."

Charlotte tightened her lips, inhaling and clasping her shaking hands together. She carefully selected her next words so as not to raise suspicion.

"Hmmm. How interesting." She plastered a smile on her face, knuckles nearly white. "Luckily my kin held no such fancies for magical usage." She forced a laugh. "Repelling insects, it is!"

A bell chimed near the back door, the same used by those who came seeking a cure for their sickness.

Thomas turned to go. "I wish I could stay and chat, Miss Charlotte!" He spoke while walking backwards to the door. "But it was lovely to see you again!"

Charlotte turned to make her way out the front, to check the millinery shops next door for Priya when a woman materialized beside her, much to her surprise.

Good Lord.

It was Sarah, Ben's sister who she had met at the dinner. The same woman who had spoken with Priya at Elizabeth's funeral.

Sarah smirked at her, leaning over the counter with far too much bosom in full view. "Hello, Miss Charlotte."

Charlotte nodded. Something about the sneer on Sarah's face told her she needed to leave. Now. But Priya had mentioned her by name at the library.

"Hello Sarah. Have you seen my friend Priya? She doesn't seem to be anywhere today." Maybe she would help her.

Sarah's lips twisted into a sly smile.

She knows something.

Charlotte leaned closer to the counter, lowering her voice. "Where is she, Sarah?"

Sarah peered at her and fluttered her eyelashes. "You're getting very close to our Benjamin these days, aren't you?"

Our John. Our Benjamin. These Society Hill types were frightfully

possessive.

Charlotte locked eyes with her. Determined. "We enjoy each other's company, yes. I wouldn't suggest anything serious at this time, but I am delighted when he calls."

So, she had ignored her question.

Sarah narrowed her eyes. "I'll get right to it, then. I'm onto you, and soon he will be too. You left-handed types have a way of weaseling into the hearts of men with greater standing than your own."

Charlotte froze. Surely she wasn't suggesting...

"You see him as an opportunity." Sarah produced a delicate lace fan, the curls swaying around her face with each wave, "and rest assured, he is absolutely that."

Heat rose in Charlotte's cheeks. "I—that is not..."

Sarah clasped the fan tightly and thrust it into Charlotte's face, narrowly missing the tip of her nose. "You're not to pursue him any further."

Charlotte stepped back, fire rising in her throat. She steeled herself. "You are mistaken, Miss Sarah." She stuffed Mother's satchel back into her pocket and hurried toward the front door.

So much for warding off evil.

Sarah glided out of the shop. Oh how she needed to find Priya.

# *Whispered Words*

**J**ust outside the Apothecary and beyond the crowd's flow, Charlotte waited. Sounds of the street permeated her being. The tinkle of bells when doors opened with the promise of new patrons, the clopping of horse hooves on cobblestone, laughter between friends, lovers, the loud bargaining among buyers of all sorts of things, splashes in puddles, shrieking, the methodical chop-chop-chop from the butcher's shop—it was almost too much.

Her friend was missing and though Charlotte had scoured the area, she hadn't even the slightest hint of a trail.

Not that it was a surprise. Not really. Wouldn't Priya be in hiding? Perhaps it was a fool's errand to search for Priya herself, but it was all she could do. She at least wanted to find her before Delphia's men did.

And too, Sarah's words had sliced through her as a dagger and poisoned her thoughts, but Ben knew Charlotte wasn't after his wealth. She hadn't been the one to pursue him. Priya had practically dragged her to the Franklin home, but then after... no. The feelings between her and Ben had blossomed naturally.

The millinery shops held no new information on the whereabouts of her friend, and a great deal of time had passed since they'd parted. Ben must be looking for her by now. She mulled through seemingly disconnected clues. The murders. The mayor. Sarah. Priya's untimely disappearance. Rosicrucian witches...and Mother. Somehow this all felt connected, yet none of it was. They must find her—and find answers. The few straws she grasped in desperation slipped through her fingers.

When she was twirled about from behind and wrapped in a strong embrace, Charlotte nearly fought back. But it was his warmth, his arms, that held her, squeezing tight and melting away heightened state. Unlike others with their cold and slight cocoon of indifference, within Ben's embrace...she was safe.

Ben pulled back, smiling. "Hello, darling."

She couldn't muster one in return. She wanted to. Attempted to... but couldn't. Not with her heart so heavy. "I didn't find her."

Ben's smile fell. "Damn. I'd hoped your luck was better than mine. I searched through all of the shops on the western side. Not a word nor a trace of her trail could I find."

He held out an arm and slowly, locking eyes with him, Charlotte encircled hers within his. "Then we continue to search."

He patted her hand, nodding. "Of course. We will find her."

Together they trudged up the street in silence, Ben's view ever searching through the crowd.

He halted, pivoting to meet her gaze as his hands firmly grasped her arms.

"Darling, we mustn't allow this to trouble us so. Priya is smart and capable. If we can't find her," he paused, "perhaps it's because she doesn't want to be found by anyone. Including us." He squeezed her arms, sliding his soft hands down to hold hers.

And what if he was correct in this assumption? But he couldn't be. Priya had come to them for help. She needed them. Then...and now.

"I can feel it in my heart, Ben. Priya wouldn't have left without telling me. There's something wrong."

Ben wasn't looking at her, but across the street, eyes wide as the banks of the Delaware River.

She turned to catch a glimpse of what had stolen his attention, but Ben reached for her, catching her face in his long fingers and caressing her cheek.

"What is it?" Her breaths came quickly now. "Do you see her?" She turned again when Ben caught her arm this time.

Lightning shot through her from his tight grip.

She wrenched from his grasp. "Ow! Ben! That hurt."

"I—erm. So sorry, darling."

She turned to see what had startled him so. Across the street and beyond the crowd, Christ Church stood at the high point of town.

Ben released a slow breath. "I thought I might have, but I cannot be sure," he said.

She squinted to see…but there, on the front steps, before the stark white visage of their chapel with its towering steeple, stood Minister Horvath.

Charlotte leaned in closer to look upon him. "It's the minister, and… he's talking to someone." Her heart thumped in her chest. "A woman."

When she focused on the doorway, Charlotte saw them—the town midwife, Mary, and two others with their backs turned.

She whispered in his ear. "Do you know them?"

Just then, as if summoned by her notion, the woman in question turned to the side, her silhouette clear among the shadows of the door.

Dear God. Charlotte had only just spoken with her, yet Ben didn't know it.

"Ben! That's Sarah!"

Charlotte glanced at Ben. His eyes were narrowed like a snake's, ready to strike. But why? She looked back at Sarah and noticed her rubbing her stomach as if she were with child.

"Ben, I just saw her a moment ago!" Wait. If she told him of their meeting, then she'd have to divulge her ulterior motives for searching in Thomas's shop.

Best not to mention that part, lest the confirmation of Mother's herbs be revealed. Doubt had vanished, leaving only certainty in its wake.

She prodded him forward, shoving misgivings aside. "Let's go and speak with her." Clearly he didn't want to, but she wanted to confront Sarah about

Priya again and having Ben at her side would be the only way. He needn't know she'd already tried. Perhaps questions coming from him would be entertained with more grace than she had been allowed.

A man with hair the color of warm chocolate, stood beside Sarah. Charlotte couldn't decipher his features.

Ben spoke in hushed tones. "No. Not now, seeing the two of them together, my suspicions run wild."

As did hers. "I wonder who the Papa is." It slipped from her mouth before she could stop it. The kindling of a fire threatened to rise in her throat and ignite her fear, but she held it at bay.

Ben grabbed her hand and brought it to his lips. He closed his eyes. "I shudder to think."

Surely Samuel...it couldn't be.

Just as she intended to rip away from the curious sight and return to their search, another figure, this time larger, stepped out of the doorway and into the daylight.

Madam Delphia.

Charlotte gasped, blurred thoughts whirring together, the stones of hope crashing around her in a landslide of uncertainty.

"Ben! It's Delphia! She knows. They know." She whirled at him. "You must confront them. Find us answers. Priya's life—"

Her words fell dead as Sarah's searing gaze caught her own.

Ben tensed. "No. I cannot make excuses for their friendship with Delphia, but I don't want to involve them any further in this. They probably don't even know Priya's missing."

Sarah did. And obviously so does Delphia. Cheeks burning, she turned to him again. "If you—"

Ben wreathed her hands with his again, his gaze softening. "Charlotte, I am with you in this. I am. We will find her. But, I fear that Sarah and Samuel would be of no assistance to us."

"Ben, I've asked her. Sarah wouldn't answer my questions about Priya. She

knows something. I can feel it."

Ben continued, stepping in front of her view. "They would tell us, Charlotte." He bowed his head. "Think not less of me when it seems I am surrounded by the poor decisions of others."

How troubled he sounded.

"I---Ben...," her hammering heart skipped a beat.

"Ben!" Another voice.

No.

"There you are!" John Priestly appeared with Amir hastening behind him. "Have you seen Priya? We were supposed to meet for breakfast this morning, but she never arrived."

Caught off guard, she took in the ghastly sight that was John. She hadn't seen him since Elizabeth Franklin's funeral. His eyes were shadowed and sunken with wisps of hair covering his unshaven face. John's whiskey-laden breath invaded her senses with each word, almost choking her with its pungent, sour smell. Amir stood beside him. As unsettling as John's unkempt appearance was, Amir's frantic, pleading expression chilled her heart.

"Amir, she's not here," Ben said. His face fell as Ben added, "We haven't seen her, but we've heard she's missing."

He was so casual about it...almost too casual. Why hide it? Unless...

Amir wordlessly caught her eye, studying her reaction. He of all people would know that Priya would seek her out above everyone if she needed help. She knew that they could trust him. In this moment, regardless of whatever happened between him and John, they both hoped for the same thing—for Priya to return home unscathed.

But John had close ties with Delphia too, she remembered. Perhaps she could have told him what had happened with the mayor. The tension between Amir and John was as thick as molasses in December. Did Amir know of Priya's faux pas and what followed? Did John?

Ben had noticed the tension too, which must be what kept him from speaking openly. Was he concerned John was involved in some way? Surely

not.

"When did you see her last, Lottie?" Amir pressed. Desperation burned in his eyes and filtered through his words. "Please, tell us what you know. Anything might help."

John spun away, nearly falling to the ground in a drunken pirouette as he cried, "Yes, please, Charlotte. Amir can't bear the thought that his sweet, innocent sister might have run away in the night."

Ben tensed, straightening his shoulders and standing to his full height. "John, get a grip on yourself. You'll never be of help in your current state." His words were laced with venom.

"Where was she, Charlotte?" Amir asked again more forcefully, taking a step forward.

Ben raised his hands defensively and stepped between them, protecting her. "Everyone stay calm. Amir, we're searching. If we happen to find Priya before you do, I can assure you that I will send word."

John grunted from the wall he leaned on. He was relieving himself, right on the street. For shame. What a lowly state for a highbrow man to be in.

Charlotte steeled herself and offered words of comfort to Amir. She placed a hand on his arm. "We will find her. One of us will. I promise you that."

Amir reached for her, softly, tears welling behind his terrified eyes. "What if she left because of me? Because of—" He glanced at John, before shaking his head.

So, John hadn't told him. That is, if he even knew the full truth himself. She fought the urge to reveal the truth, but Priya had been explicitly clear she didn't want her family to know of her disgrace.

Charlotte settled her lips into a thin line, wordlessly telling him he need not say anymore of the affair. She attempted a smile, albeit small and insincere. Amir offered his own, hardly twitching the corners of his mouth.

Standing among them once more, John was absent of concern or care, muddled in the fog of drink. Ben stood grim, eyes narrowed at his drunk friend.

John had forgotten to button his trousers. Charlotte blushed and turned

to Amir. "I saw her just yesterday. At that point, she had no plans to run away, I assure you." She glanced at Ben. How much was safe to reveal? "I fear her absence might have been persuaded by others." Amir's eyes widened. John's darkened.

Amir nodded. "Time is of the essence, we must find her before—"

Charlotte squeezed his hand reassuringly. He nodded, and with swift determination, John Priestly and Amir set out once more into the square.

She glanced at Ben. "Well that was strange. Are you suspicious of John? Why were you so reticent?" He didn't know of the affair. She hadn't told him.

Ben watched the pair disappear into the crowd with a narrowed view and a furrowed brow. "I'm not sure. Something's not right with John. I'm not a fan of when he swims among the burning rocks. It's like he becomes someone else entirely. When he's like this, there's no reasoning with him. He makes a fool of himself and those he's around."

John did reek of whiskey.

Ben sighed. "I fear...well. I'm not sure what to think at the moment." He raised his eyebrows. "But I believe it best we hold everyone, including John, at an arm's distance until Priya is found."

Charlotte nodded. "I understand." Her mind swam. Perhaps she should mention Delphia once more to underline the point.

Ben continued, walking forward again. She glanced back at Christ Church but the fellowship of mysterious intentions was gone.

"What if they have something to do with it?" She chose her words carefully. "Sarah," she peered at him, "and Samuel?"

Ben paused, closing his eyes. "And what exactly leads you to that assumption, my dear?"

She stopped. A man walking behind them nearly ran into her. She turned to Ben. "You saw them. Consorting with that...that devil woman." She threw up her hands, only slightly noticing that her raised voice drew the attention of a few passersby.

"Charlotte." His low growl of warning did nothing to quash her anger.

"There's something evil going on here. And they're in on it! Sarah ignored my questions about Priya when I saw her in the shop! She knows, Ben." Ben tilted his head, only slightly, but said nothing in response. "Delphia got her into this mess. And now she's discussing it with Sarah and Samuel...what the hell is going on?" Charlotte clenched her fists, surprised at the sudden rage that filled her. Rage at the questions surrounding her that remained unanswered. Rage that her friend had chosen so poorly and now suffered the consequences. Rage that among this bleak world of troubles and trials that for once, she just wanted a break from the fire.

Damn these people. "Just because they're your family doesn't mean they can't be involved in something wicked! You high society types...always protecting your own."

Ben stared at her. Calmly. There was a sadness blooming in his eyes which stole their kind luster. She hadn't meant to speak so harshly, but right now, blazing molten iron poured out of her. Ben just happened to be standing close enough to get burned.

"Darling. Listen to me. Wealth does not equate to villinary. We know of Delphia's interests with her girls, but just because she was engaged in conversation at the church, with the minister of all people, does not mean they were discussing your friend."

"I thought you might consider her your friend, too." Charlotte seethed.

Ben nodded. "Yes, of course." He grasped her hands once more. "Think rationally, darling. Do you really think the minister would participate in such matters? In the persecution of a young woman in trouble?"

Charlotte paused, cooling with his words. He was right. "Well, no."

"Right. Now imagine that we went to them with such lofty accusations of involvement when in fact they were likely discussing something else entirely?"

Her shoulders dropped. Yes. Yes, of course. "They would certainly be less enthused in helping us."

Ben smiled. "There's my girl. We must think with our heads, not only our hearts."

Charlotte nodded. With the flare of outrage burned out, only the weight

of remorse for her outburst remained.

"And now, based on what we just witnessed out of John…don't his actions give you more pause than either Sarah's or the minister's, for heaven's sake?"

She nodded again, hardly lifting her eyes. "Yes."

"Come." Ben turned and started back the way they'd come. "I know just the thing to cheer you up."

He led her back inside Thomas's apothecary shop, dung smells and all. This feeble attempt at cheering her wouldn't work, Ben just hadn't realized it yet.

"Brother! How good of you to come." Charlotte stepped from behind one of the large shelves and into view. "Ah! There she is. Have you forgotten something, Miss Charlotte? I thought we'd finished our business."

Ben cocked his head but said nothing. She'd told him she'd only gone to the millinery shops, yet obviously he noted the anomaly.

Ben leaned on the counter, stroking his chiseled chin in thought. "Thomas, I've a need. Miss Charlotte is having somewhat of a rough day. A sad day."

Thomas furrowed his brow.

Ben continued. "Would you happen to have any of those fresh cut flowers you usually keep on hand? In the back? The lovely pink ones?"

Thomas's eyes grew wide. "Are you certain? Such decisions must be fully considered—" He paused with a portentous, almost stern gaze at his brother.

"My lady deserves something enchanting to brighten her day, Thomas. Now, if you would be so kind, we're in a bit of a hurry. You understand." Ben's cold stare never faltered, only building in intensity.

"As you wish." Thomas feigned a smile before vanishing into the back.

The curious exchange concerned her. Ben could buy her flowers or anything else if he had a mind. Perhaps…Thomas didn't approve? She thought of Sarah's words, of being labeled as one of those "left-handed types." Her shoulders sank, weighted with worry and a slight pinch of shame. Who was she to delight a man of such prestige as Ben Franklin? They must all believe it.

Perhaps he would emerge with larkspur or jasmine. Ranunculus or even a common tulip would suffice, but she feared he would emerge with none of those blooms. How mindless she was, concerned about flowers while Priya was still out there. Missing.

Ben winked at her as they waited. Charlotte's cheeks flushed. Perhaps they could spare a bit of time. Maybe he could elicit a smile from her after all.

The way he could wash away her misgivings with a simple gesture was unnerving, but well appreciated.

Thomas returned with an armful of beautiful, pink conical flowers that flared at the ends. They looked like the flowing skirts of a dancing maiden mid-twirl. They were, as Priya so often put it, divine. Charlotte reached for the blooms, but hesitated as she noticed the odd glance Thomas cast toward Ben. For Heaven's sake, she wished he would at least attempt to mask his apprehension.

Taking the bouquet with a boldness that was foreign to her, Charlotte buried her face in the blooms. Its scent was sweet. She looked up at him and grinned. Their luscious smell intoxicated her, almost too much, in fact. The pleasant aroma was quite strong and a foggy sensation muddled her thoughts.

Charlotte remembered her manners, too late in her current state, and curtsied toward Thomas, nodding her thanks. As she and Ben wordlessly exited the shop, Charlotte couldn't help but wonder where she'd seen these blooms before. They were so familiar. "I can't place the name of them. What are they called?"

Ben grinned from ear to ear. "These are some of my absolute favorite flowers. I do hope they bring you joy on this trying day, darling."

"I love them." Charlotte said, highly conscious of her sudden use of that weighted word. She stumbled on an uneven stone and Ben steadied her.

Love.

Once home, she would have to find the Language of Flowers and decipher their meaning. Her heart beat faster at the thought of what they could signify.

They'd only taken a few steps outside when Charlotte heard a sultry voice behind them.

"Oh Charlotte, here with our Ben once again? Of course you are. Any

excuse to be seen with a man of proper social stature."

Her heart plummeted as she whirled around to see...Holy Hell.

It was Sarah, again, this time only accompanied by Samuel. They were standing with hands tightly joined and lips drawn thin.

"We saw you watching us, Charlotte." Sarah leaned in closer, her voice a sinister whisper. The familiar scent of tuberose wafted over them, its dense, salty aroma reminding Charlotte of the sweet egg yolk and milk custard dessert with burnt sugar crust. Creme Brulee. Nelly planted white tuberose flowers at home because they all enjoyed the rich perfume, and Sarah reminded her of it. But now, her haughty presence poisoned that pleasant memory.

Sarah slid closer. She and Samuel stood, side by side, Sarah's head tilted at a dangerous angle. "You saw us talking with the minister and Delphia. Don't you wish to know what we were talking about?" She placed her fingers delicately upon her own stomach. "Ask your questions! Ask again about your harlot friend." She spat the words as venom. Charlotte's pulse quickened at the venom in Sarah's words, each one a pinprick down her spine. The world rocked around her as if she were standing on a ship at sea.

No.

A paperboy sauntered down the street, shouldering a basket full to the brim with his news. "Extra! Extra! Woman gone missing! Read all about it!"

"What news?" Charlotte reached for the papers. She desperately needed to get away, anything to avoid that twisted glower. The promise of new information, any information, captivated her.


**PENNSYLVANIA GAZETTE**

*Missing Persons Listing: Priya Lanivet. Age 23. If Found, Please Alert Authorities.*


Charlotte's hands trembled, the still-wet ink from the papers sticking in smudges to her clammy fingers, as she saw Priya's name in stark black and white. She read the words as if in a dream, wishing they could bring her closer

to answers for her friend. Her beating heart threatened to burst from her chest. She turned to the boy and reached for the flowers he held, hoping their sweet aroma could settle her senses and ground her. She could add them to the blooms from the shop and make a bouquet. But wait.

Red Begonias. Dark Thoughts.

Yellow Carnations. Disdain.

Purple Lavender. Mistrust.

She knew Ben was still talking, acutely aware of the soft rise and fall of his voice, but the words were distant. Floating. She was floating.

"Charlotte!"

She turned. She and Ben were alone. He examined her, his eyes tight and worried.

Charlotte searched the street, but Sarah and Samuel were gone. "Where did they go?" she asked him.

Ben furrowed his brow. "Where did who go?"

Charlotte frowned, frantically searching. "Umm...your brother and sister? The paperboy? Where did they go?"

Ben grabbed her by the shoulders, turning her attention fully on himself. That concerned look on his face. She knew what it was, and fear crept in. He surely thought her manic.

Ben frowned again. "John and Amir were here, only a moment ago. Is that who you mean?" He spoke slowly with his brow still furrowed.

What on God's green earth? "Sarah? And Samuel? They were right behind us!" She thought of Sarah ignoring her question in the shop. "They know something about Priya, I know it!" Surely they were there. She had seen them here. Right?

She raised her hand to show him the paper with Priya's name upon it, but found her grasp empty, devoid of any evidence.

This couldn't be.

His brow furrowed yet again, deeper this time. "Charlotte...we saw John.

And Amir. Maybe you saw Sarah and Samuel in the crowd?

"No. We saw them. At the church. Then here!" Her breathing was heavy now and her fists clenched.

Ben's perfect, pencil thin mouth dropped open. His concern evolved into shock.

She had surely seen them. Yet the familiar spirit of doubt crawled into her mind as a creeping fog floating across a still-wet ground. Hadn't they been there?

But she'd believed the paper had been real, too.

Charlotte paused, forcing an unconvincing smile. Her lips prickled at the forced gesture. Regardless, they had to find Priya. "Perhaps I thought I saw them in the crowd. I must have gotten lost in my thoughts again."

Maybe she had. Ben clearly hadn't seen them. She needed more sleep.

"Let's get you home, Charlotte. It's been a trying day for all of us. Priya clearly isn't here. We can check the edges of the forest as we come closer to your home." He reached for her hand. "And then I'll try the Morris House again and see if she's returned."

"Yes, yes. That sounds reasonable."

Home. Yes...that would make her feel better.

# CRIMSON COBBLESTONES

# Kissed by a Rose

The final rays of sunset faded, painting the autumn leaves in rosy golds, ambers, and deep purples. The streets emptied as families hurried home to safety come nightfall. Charlotte wished she could do the same, but she had to find Priya.

Where the hell was she?

Charlotte and Ben walked in silence toward the forest at the edge of town, both lost in thought.

It was a comfort to have Ben walk her home, even after her outburst. Something about his calm demeanor brought her peace, especially if she was having visions again. During her last journey from the town center to Quarry Street and 3rd, she had suffered a fright she was none too eager to experience again.

For that was when she had last encountered the woman in black.

A familiar cloud of dread hung about her, joy snuffed out as a candle's flame. She wrapped her arm in his, clenching tighter. His warmth kept that meager spark alight.

She must not think of crossing paths with the woman in black. She was better prepared this time. She wasn't alone. She wasn't afraid.

Yet, she was.

Charlotte suspected this woman in black to be of the order that had

163

conspired to kill Mother. Perhaps a fellow witch, if that's what they were, or something worse. Such details remained unclear.

Echoing her fears, the sky above darkened into a cold navy, with a misty fog rising between the houses. Whether it was God or some unknown in the universe—a higher power was having a laugh at her.

Still...they walked further into the fog and the consuming shadows of night, taking steps she had so often taken alone when she was unafraid. It was a path that typically brought peace in a world full of heavy shadows. Lately she couldn't shake the feeling of danger, nor turn her thoughts from memories of Mother. And Mother's sister. Still, there were no answers regarding the fate of her aunt. Had she been murdered too?

Perhaps the Rosicrucians were striking again. What heinous activities were afoot at this very moment?

As she and Ben rounded the corner, passing the late baker's shop, Charlotte thought of the biscuits, of the familiar smells of muffins and bread that no longer wafted through the air, greeting her with cheer on Saturday mornings. The house of Gayle Williams sat silent—his bakery turned cold.

As cold as he was now.

Time enough had not passed for someone to feel comfortable taking it over. She wouldn't feel comfortable going there again. Not for a long time.

Ben's hand squeezed tight around hers. They were alone. He missed a step and she looked at where he stared.

Bloodstained cobblestones.

It was the stain of Gayle Williams' blood. She urged her legs to move faster, but darkness lingered, thick and visceral, as if she could taste it on her own tongue. The misty fog rolled in thicker and she wished only to be home.

A few steps forward. Get past his house.

A few steps forward. Not far from home.

But with each passing doorway, she knew they drew near to a place she feared even more....the home of the woman in black.

She spotted the roses, some dead, others dying. The crinkled blooms

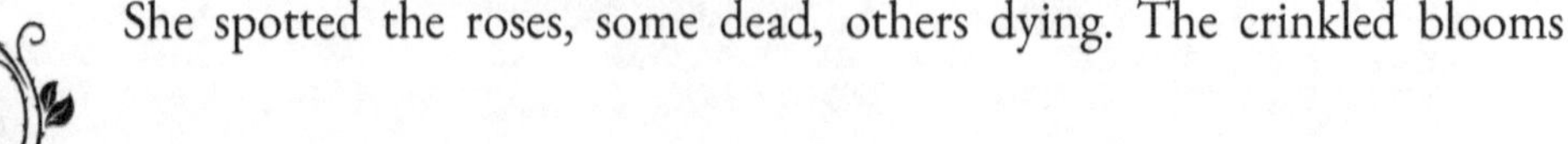

mirrored her own withered fortitude. The winding vines and unkempt grass of that overgrown garden did nothing to ease her discomfort. There was a staleness here. As though time itself lay dormant, awaiting its own demise.

"Who lives---" Ben whispered.

"Shhh! You don't want her to hear us." Charlotte quickened her pace and dragged him along.

Get past it. She must get past it.

Against any will or sensibility, she glanced up to the imposing home. If only she hadn't.

With a veil black as midnight and trailing to the ground, on the front steps stood the horrific, unmistakable nightmare of the woman in black.

Charlotte.

She wrenched her hand from Ben's grasp and urged her legs to carry her down the street, heart hammering, masking the sounds of Ben's protests. She looked behind, searching for him, when the ground reached up to snag her ankles.

Damn!

The sharp bite of her knee slamming against stone was excruciating. She couldn't see, couldn't hear. For a moment, panic consumed her, leaving no room for anything else. When her vision cleared, she noticed her hands were smeared with blood, gravel stuck to her skin that she couldn't feel.

The woman in black glided across the path, advancing, as an ominous wind across the open plain.

"Charlotte, listen to me!" The faint rasp of a voice had gathered in strength. The veiled woman came for her.

Ben grasped her blood slick hand and hauled her to her feet.

The woman in black lunged. "No! Charlotte!"

As she ran with the thundering rush of blood in her ears, one thought obscured all else...how did she know her name?

They reached the edge of the dark, foreboding forest. Though this path

provided an ample shortcut to her home, the twisted tendrils of branches, reaching for her with every step, encouraged her fear. She hadn't wanted to go this way, but Ben suggested Priya might have taken it to stay off the main road. She searched for a scrap of cloth, a footprint, anything that might tell her that Priya had come this way. Dread crept over her as a tangible force, a slithering serpent writhing and constricting her breath. As the last of light faded between the trees, Charlotte slowed to nurse the stitch in her side. Ben followed on her heels, no doubt confused as to why the woman in black terrified her.

And truthfully, she was unsure herself.

"Are you all right?" Ben reached for her. "You fell. Let me see your hands. Your knee! At this rate, you'll be nothing but bloody rags."

Charlotte cradled her bleeding palms. "It's...nothing. A tiny scrape." Why had she run? Her chest was on fire.

What a fool she was. She needed to look for Priya here.

Ben cupped her hands in his, careful to face her palms upward, only wrapping his thumbs around her fragile wrists. "Tell me you're all right."

"I'm fine." She didn't know if it was adrenaline or infatuation, but her skin tingled at his mere touch. Regardless of the woman in black, Ben, again, proved her rock against the storm.

He wrapped her close in his warm arms. "Charlotte, I worry for you. I want you to feel safe."

She stared intently at him and drank in every detail of his chiseled face, those falcon's eyes. Even now, caught in the fear of the moment, the edges of his lips turned comfortingly upward. He was so close to her, his chest rising and falling with each breath.

"But you have no cause to worry for me, Ben. I'm nothing to you. Only a friend."

She could hardly believe the words had flown out of her mouth. What was she saying? Her heart thundered, but whether it was from the run or from heightened sensations—she didn't know.

He grabbed her shoulders, leaning in so close she could feel his warm

breath on her face.

"The desire I feel is not for that of a friend."

Charlotte's breath caught as Ben's hand cradled her chin, his face inches from her own. Her pulse thrummed wildly at the feeling of his fingers tipping her lips toward his. He brought his lips to her. They were soft. Exquisite. Full of a tenderness she could never imagine tiring of. His hand clutched her waist, pulling her hips to meet his.

The stirs of emotion from the unsettling woods were quickly supplanted by an intimate tingle between her thighs. Charlotte yearned with burning desire as his lips parted, coaxing hers to respond in kind. She had not known of the use of tongue, but now could imagine it no other way. She tasted him. Wanted him. This man stole her breath. She clung to him, afraid she might melt away completely. This was passion– raw and visceral in a way she had neither experienced nor imagined.

A twig snapped, and as quick as the flame had ignited, her euphoria quelled.

Ben pulled away, peering into the trees. She thought of Sarah and Samuel. Surely it was not them again. Perhaps it was Priya. She needed to keep her wits about her.

His gaze narrowed, glaring at something in the distance. Something had captured his attention more than her lips. An unbidden pang of jealousy rattled at the edge of her thoughts.

Was that...surely not.

Through the trees among the shadows, perched delicately on a mound of moss beneath a blackthorn tree, sat his Aunt Bethshua. She was dressed in black, gathering the pokeweeds and foxglove that surrounded her.

How odd that a lady of her stature would sit on the forest floor at the edge of town. What on God's green earth was she doing out here among the dampened underbrush?

The fog was thick now, like the white sheet one spreads over the deceased. Charlotte was surprised Ben had noticed Aunt Beth at all. But they needed to continue their search for Priya. Hopefully, Aunt Beth hadn't seen their

passionate kiss.

A black raven fluttered from the trees with a shrill caw. Charlotte gasped. Beth's black eyes met hers, rooting her feet to the ground as if she were one of the trees. The whites of her eyes were obscured so that only swirling ink orbs pooled within her sockets as if the woman had none at all.

This can't be real. The sight before her was impossible.

"Aunt Beth!" Ben called out.

No.

A smile spread across Ben's face. This can't be happening. Surely the sight of his aunt's fathomless eye sockets would disturb him, as it did her.

Perhaps he hadn't seen.

Aunt Beth turned to them, her words dripping with the warmth of hot honey added to a steaming tea, and just as soothing.

"Ahhhh, dear nephew! Come and join me in collecting herbs!" When Charlotte looked at his aunt again, her countenance calmed but not by her own doing. The forest prickled with an irresistible sense of tranquility. Aunt Beth's eyes had returned to the same probing blue she remembered from the dinner party. Perhaps the orbs were of her imagination. Her fears.

Surely not. She knew what she'd seen.

Ben tugged her toward Aunt Beth. She tripped again on a gnarled root, lifted from the ground as an escape from its prison of soil. A faint urge, a need, to escape tugged at her. It was hardly recognizable in the back of her mind. But she wouldn't run. Not this time.

"Hello Aunt B. We've been searching for Charlotte's friend, Priya Lanivet," Ben said. "You haven't seen her come this way, have you?"

Aunt Beth reached for Ben with both arms. "Ahh, Darling. Surely you don't mean that little tart who's been gallivanting around town with our John?" She pursed her painted lips. "I should think not."

Charlotte stilled. Don't make a face. Don't let her see.

Ben helped his aunt rise from the forest floor. "She's a nice girl, Aunt Beth."

Though Ben smiled warmly at his aunt, Charlotte noticed his shoulders tense, his words growing more clipped and terse.

"I couldn't help but notice how familiar you and Miss—" Beth said, surveying the mud on the front of Charlotte's dress, "oh dear. I've forgotten your name."

A flush rose on Ben's neck as he avoided his aunt's gaze. Charlotte sensed his discomfort at her implicit accusation.

"Charlotte."

"Oh yes! Miss Charlotte." She turned to Ben again. "How familiar you and Miss Charlotte seemed to be."

She had seen them kiss.

"You should bring Miss Charlotte around for tea. I would love to get to know her in a more appropriate setting." Whether it was a smirk or a smile plastered on Bethshua's face, Charlotte couldn't tell.

Ben squeezed her hand. "We would love that, wouldn't we, Charlotte?"

"Your hospitality is endless, Madame," Charlotte said. She didn't know what to call her. My lady? Madame? She wanted to turn tail and race the rest of the way home, but her muscles wouldn't respond.

Ben spoke again. "Do you require assistance in bringing your gatherings home?"

Charlotte screamed within. We do not want to go with her!

Aunt Beth snapped her ruthless gaze up to meet them.

Dear God...could she be gifted with a talent to hear thoughts? Was Bethshua yet another Rosicrucian witch?

"No, no, dear. That's quite all right. The chaise should be along at any moment to collect me. I sent them on an errand. No need to linger. However, if you'll stop by later, I have a gift for you in celebration of your return."

Ben chuckled. "Aunt B, you spoil me."

"It was nice to see you, Ma'am," Charlotte said with a quick curtsy. Maybe ma'am? No, that still wasn't right.

Bethshua Franklin raised one delicate brow, the smirk playing about her lips again.

"See you at tea, my dears."

# Whiskey Whispers

Charlotte rubbed her sweaty palms on her dress. If Ben noticed, he was too chivalrous to mention it. His presence did nothing to lessen the sensation of being watched. Evil might lurk behind any given tree. Shivering, more from fear than cold, Charlotte clenched Ben's arm, his warmth a measure of safety in an evolving world of cruelty and corruption.

Generally, she enjoyed the tranquility that came from living far from Philadelphia's center, but now she yearned for the benefits living around people offered. There was safety in numbers with a murderer on the loose.

"I'm sorry it's so dark," she said.

It was a coping mechanism. Nervous words brought life to dead silences. The rustle of fallen leaves and snapped twigs under their footsteps scratched at what little composure she had left.

Ben raised an eyebrow. "Surely, you don't presume to apologize for the natural cycle of the sun and moon?" He laughed, the sound echoing around them. "Darkness falls without regard for mortal preparations. It is how we react to it that determines the outcome."

"If you say so." Charlotte's foot caught at the edge of her dress. Only Ben's natural grace saved her from yet another fall; a guardian at heart. Quick to save her from any stumble, physical or social.

His need to protect her released a swarm of moths in her stomach. She turned, hoping to salvage the awkward situation with her own attempt at wit. "Darkness breeds fear…an unknown where imaginations run wild." She glanced around. "But the reality of it is worse by far."

Her thoughts turned to Priya again, and their failure to find her.

Ben frowned. "Should we revel in the imagined demons of the dark, consumed by our fears, or seek that which brings us comfort?"

Charlotte stepped over a fallen branch. "A fair point. Comfort can still exist within those shadows, yet solace has its own fleeting nature." She sighed. "But our current darkness is real. Priya missing is real. An embrace may bring comfort, yet a knife in the back proves its folly." She bit her lip. How dour were her thoughts and words tonight.

An owl hooted in the distance, startling them both.

Ben raised empty palms. "There is no knife here, only affection and succor."

Charlotte couldn't help but smile. But her joy was short-lived.

Guilt turned her attention to the path below. "I'm worried about Priya. Having you is such a blessing, but what does she have? Who does she have? If she's alone or among threatening company… my mind races with dreadful possibilities."

Ben slowed his pace and spoke again, softly. "Do not anticipate trouble, or worry about what may never happen. It's a wasted endeavor." Her hand warmed as he squeezed it. "Keep in the sunlight, even if the sunlight only lives within your heart."

Charlotte smiled, quickening her step to finally escape from the trees. "The light of home is such a dear treasure. Imagine if we could carry its comfort with us when we traveled." She bit her lip. This must sound strange to the ears of another.

Ben studied the crooked and worn posts of their fence now. Curiosity swirled around him, or so it seemed to her. He was so full of ideas and wonderment, she could scarcely predict what he would do or say next.

And what about her? The sudden realization washed over Charlotte

that it was highly probable that Ben's intuition had allowed him to read her accurately. It surely made it easy for him to know her. To truly understand her.

"Would you happen to have a glass bottle inside?" Ben asked.

Raising an eyebrow, she searched his face for the hint of a joke. There was none. "I'm sure Miss Nelly would."

Ben rubbed his hands together, a mischievous glint sparkling in his eyes. "If she does, and you could spare a lit candle—I may have an idea. You've inspired me."

Crash. The front door slammed open, ripping Charlotte from the momentary harbor of curiosity. Amir stormed out, striding past, without a look or word.

"Amir! Stop!" she called but he stalked past the fence posts toward the path through the woods.

"I'm finished with him!" Amir yelled.

She glanced at Ben.

"I'll tend to him. Head inside, I'll join you in a moment," he said.

She grasped her wrist and pulled at her bracelet, a feeble attempt to stop her hands from shaking. She watched as Ben strode after Amir. He could settle him. Something moved within the shadows of the trees. A figure. A person. Maybe nothing at all. A twig snapped and Charlotte flinched, straining to see what lurked in the forest. But there was nothing.

Only silence.

Charlotte wrapped her arms around herself, calming her breaths. Nothing was there. It was only the dark. Ben would be back soon. She stepped closer to the warm safety of her home.

When she crossed the door, she saw Papa, seated by the fire and deep in heated discussion with none other than...John Priestly.

Papa raised his arms to welcome her, but the tension baking in the room was of a thick, palatable nature. "Lottie. God be praised you're home. The night has taken a chill and mischief abounds." He glanced at John before looking past her, as if expecting to see someone else. "Have you found Priya? It

would right many wrongs if so."

Her eyes passed from Papa and landed on John Priestly. He was disheveled, his shirt untucked, sweat dripping from his wrinkled brow. "If only that were the case." She crossed the room, embracing Papa. "What happened with Amir?"

"They've been on the search for Priya as you have and thought she might be here." He lowered his voice. "I believe Amir is enraged by the sodden state of your friend here." He motioned toward Mr. Priestly.

John's eyes were bloodshot and his face gaunt with a dribble of vomit crusting his chin. Generally, his pristine hair was combed and oiled, but now was a tousled mop. He looked even worse than before, which she previously thought impossible for one so meticulous about his appearance.

John gritted his teeth then dry heaved over a bucket, glaring at her. "You weren't very forthcoming with information."

A familiar fire rose in her throat. Stay calm. Keep in the sunlight, as Ben said.

Ben. He'd been the one holding back, not her.

Charlotte steeled her breath before speaking. She understood that he was taken with emotion, yet she was, too, and if John were drunk—his actions could prove to be of an unpredictable nature. "John, we could smell the whiskey under your breath. It was concerning to say the least. Amir is up to his ears at the moment as are we. Ben felt—"

John wilted. "Say no more." His bloodshot eyes narrowed. "Ben knows of my habits better than I do sometimes. Whiskey whispers of danger, so I understand your... hesitation." He scooped a bottle up from the floor. "But that was not the case this time."

She fumed. "While we were out searching, scouring the town to find Priya, you were God knows where getting drunk! How was that supposed to help your search?"

John bowed low, wobbling as he did so. "My apologies, Miss. 'Twas but a nip of the bottle to calm an unsettled heart." He stared at the floor, taking in the well-worn path in the wood, no doubt. "And Amir hates the stuff. At

times, he won't even look at me when—"

Another retching heave cut him off.

She kept her expression neutral, taking deep breaths to mask the full extent of her anger at him, but could not stop the rise of heat in her cheeks. Taking care not to meet Papa's watchful eye, she said, "And as for Amir, don't get me started on what the two of you have been up to behind Priya's back. That's her brother, John. How could you fight with him now, in the midst of her disappearance?"

John spoke again, slurring his words now. "Sheeee's really left, then." Tears welled behind his sunken eyes. "Swept away to God knows where." He stood to clutch at Charlotte's dress, and she could smell the whiskey on his breath, even through the rancid vomit. "I care for her, Charlotte. Truly, I do. I messed it up, but I care for her. And Amir...He means so much to me. They both do."

Papa stood. John released her dress, stumbled back, and sank into the chair, immediately slumping over. Whether it was from sorrow or drunkenness, Charlotte didn't know. She could sense his emotions, and something lingered other than sadness.

Regret, perhaps.

Papa moved closer. "I couldn't find her either, Lottie." They watched as John dissolved into tears. Papa turned back to him. "Calm yourself. I searched the whole of town and surrounding roads. None among the night watch saw her. They assumed that she stole away under the shroud of darkness."

The candle. Ben should have returned by now.

"Do we have a glass bottle and a candle?"

"Here ye are, dear child." Nelly greeted her with her favorite smile and John's bottle, deftly stolen. "He won' be needin' any more this evening. Perhaps ye can put it to good use. Take ye a candle from tha windowsill, we've plenty more."

"Thank you!" Charlotte stepped around a sobbing John Priestly and snatched up a candle. "Ben went after Amir. I'll see if he's returned with him."

She should be crying for her friend too, but strangely, the tears didn't

come. Something troubled her heart and held back the flood of emotion that she knew ought to be there for Priya. This morning she had been so sure that Priya was taken...taken, perhaps, by Delphia. But now a small, almost hopeful, voice within her questioned if Priya had fled on her own out of embarrassment. Or shame. Or even anger at John.

Maybe John was right that she had run away. It was a sobering thought—one Charlotte wasn't proud of.

Charlotte hurried outside, thankful for the cool bite of the night air on her heated skin. Ben stood there, disheveled and leaning against the fence post, trying to catch his breath. He forced a small, tight-lipped smile.

He was alone.

"I lost Amir. He wasn't far ahead of me and even though I called for him repeatedly, he wouldn't turn around. I suppose he made his way back to town."

"John is inside. Drunk as a skunk."

Ben clenched his fists. "Dammit. He knows better. Every time he turns to ale, it's never enough. And at a time like this—"

"I know." Charlotte moved closer to him, circling her arms around his waist, careful not to clink the candle holder and wide-brimmed bottle together.

"What's this?" Ben surveyed the items in her hands.

Charlotte cocked her head. "The candle...and glass. You said—"

"Ahh! Yes!" he brightened, "I have a solution to help you stay in the light." He reached for the bottle and affixed it to the top of the fence post with the handle.

Ben reached for the candle. "When one of you is gone until nightfall, whoever remains could light a candle, set it in the glass...," he placed it inside, "and then you will have a light for the path, protected from the wind." He grinned. "You could even set out multiples, providing for a well-lit street."

Charlotte smiled at his cleverness. Among the darkness, Ben truly did bring her light. "I'm impressed, Mr. Franklin." The flicker of flames flashed across his smooth chin. She stared at his lips.

Maybe she could forget about John for a minute, too.

Ben pulled her closer by the waist. "Am I sensing a thank-you for the lantern, Miss Scott?"

Her friend was missing. She shouldn't be feeling like this.

But he was so handsome.

"Kiss me, Mr. Franklin."

Though their bodies didn't touch, she could feel the heat between them. The warmth was spreading, from her navel to her chest.

Surely he noticed how her bosom rose and fell with each breath.

Ben's lips were temptingly close to her now. Soft, pink, luscious lips that she wanted to kiss her...and never part from. His hands, lightly playing about her hips, set her soul on fire. She wanted him to touch her.

Anywhere.

Everywhere.

Charlotte parted her lips, ready for the ecstasy that traveled from their kiss down to the tingle between her thighs. He pulled her to him, pressing their delicacies against each other. His hands held firmly to her lower back and her skin prickled at his touch. Good God, the two of them, together like this—but it felt right. The layers of clothing between them were such a burden. She wanted to feel his warm skin upon hers.

If it weren't for his strong hands holding her to him, Charlotte would surely have melted as his lips came for her...again and again, claiming her as his own. They were living together, breathing together. Her senses overwhelmed, she wanted to strip bare, right in the front garden, and have him take her in every way.

She would give it to him. She would give him anything.

Ben broke the connection, leaving her breathless. Senseless. He met her lips once more with a kiss...a slow, sensual exploration of each other's mouths.

He moaned into her neck. At the front of his hips she felt a hardness pressed against her.

How sinful they were.

But it didn't matter. She stared into those gray, speckled eyes that she had come to love.

Love?

Before she could wrap her mind around her intrusive thoughts, a sudden crash pierced the night. The lantern, now shattered into fragments, lay on the ground.

A graveled voice sliced her to the bone. "How dare you."

Amir?

The cold voice extinguished her joy. Standing in the garden, was the last person she wanted to see... Dirch Johnson.

"Excuse me, sir?"

Dirch sauntered towards them, each stomp upon the ground the sound of impending danger. "Charlotte is spoken for."

Charlotte staggered backwards, her heated passion smothered by disgust "I absolutely am not." Dirch surely wasn't that delusional.

Ben stepped forward, positioning himself between her and Dirch as a shield. "Mr. Johnson, I beg your pardon, but I believe you are confused." There was a cold, menacing warning beneath his words.

Dirch lumbered out of the darkness and into the moonlight, a bottle held low as if a club. He circled around them, she and Ben turning to meet each step. The smell of whiskey nearly choked her.

"Thaddeus and I agreed. I would take over the shop," he stumbled, "and Charlotte would become my wife." Dirch squinted his eyes as thin as blacksmithed steel, shifting his weight back, preparing to strike. "It's the way things are. It will be so and you've no say in the matter." He tapped his bottle on the fence post.

Ben held her tight against him. "Dirch, I believe you are disguised. A drunken fool."

Charlotte trembled. "Papa wouldn't agree to this. Not if he knew..."

Dirch straightened, smirking as he did. "Knew what? That you... wanted it?" He spat at her.

She gasped. That wasn't the truth. She didn't want him. Maybe at first but...

The bottle of whiskey slipped from Dirch's grasp and spilled on the ground.

Ben cocked his head.

"No." Charlotte could only utter a whisper, and even so, she forced it through her lips.

Ben froze. "What is he talking about?"

"Oh she hasn't told you? Your virginal prize isn't so...pure." Dirch smirked, "Mr. Franklin."

Charlotte squirmed. "Dirch. Stop it."

He lunged at her. Charlotte dodged his grasping hands. "You wanted me."

"I didn't." Her voice was hardly more than a breath this time.

"You are no longer welcome here. I suggest you leave immediately." Ben's words dripped with menace.

The sight of him dried her mouth. She clutched her throat.

"I will take—what is mine." Dirch shoved Ben to the dirt. Charlotte screamed as he grabbed her by the arm, dragging her beside him. With a burst of strength, she wrenched from his grasp, shoving him away.

Ben rose to his feet, his movements sluggish, as if he were moving through water. She watched the two men scuffle, everything floating around her. as if viewing their fight from above, in a dream.

I will take what is mine. The words plastered upon their home echoed in the deepest chasms of her mind. He'd painted them the night he attacked.

Charlotte gasped aloud, the blood draining from her face as the truth slammed into her - Dirch's menacing words the night they were attacked, his obsession, it all led to one horrible conclusion.

Realization tore through her. It wasn't just them. Elizabeth had turned him down years ago. The baker wouldn't hire him. He frequently visited Delphia's girls.

Dirch Johnson was the killer.

The front door of her home flew open and Papa came running to their aid, John Priestly trailing behind him.

Dirch tackled Ben and slammed him to the ground, landing blow after blow, beating him into the grass. Ben's eyes blazed with the burning fires of rage, his teeth clenched as he grabbed Dirch by the collar and threw him off. Sweat, spit, blood dripped from both of them. Ben lunged for Dirch, punching him, over and over, the sick slap of his fists meeting skin turning her stomach. Ditch was hurt, that was clear, but Ben kept going.

"What the hell is going on here?" Papa shouted.

Dirch flung a handful of dirt and rocks into Ben's eyes. "Unhand me you devil!" Blood poured from his nose and mouth.

Ben leapt to his feet, fists clenched. "If you ever touch her again. If you dare train your twisted eyes upon her or anyone in this home...I swear to god above—"

Dirch swung for him again, weaker now, fists flying in a frenzy, hardly touching Ben.

"Ben! What the hell." John Priestly threw himself between them.

"ENOUGH!" Papa and John hauled the two men apart. They struggled, but eventually settled in the cold wet grass. Dirch was injured, but a low-class lad such as he was used to scuffles. Memories of Dirch's fighting flitted through her mind.

She cringed at the sight of her love. She knew the candlelight concealed even more, yet he stood resolute, ready to defend her and her family with reckless disregard for his own safety

Charlotte bristled. "Papa. Dirch is the man who came to our door. He attacked our home. He uttered the words written on our wall!" She pointed at Dirch as he glared with a twisted snarl. He wriggled in John's grasp.

Papa's eyes widened, still taking in the scene before him.

Dirch spat at her feet. "You harlot. I knew as soon as I saw you with that high-class piece of meat, you'd forgotten where you came from. Who you

belonged to."

"She belongs to none but herself." Papa knelt in front of Dirch, knife pointed so close to his face Charlotte expected it to draw blood.

"If I ever..." Papa brandished his knife to drive the point home, "have the displeasure of hearing you speak of my daughter in that manner again, I will cut your tongue from your throat and nail it to your forehead then gouge the eyes from your skull."

Charlotte froze, stunned by the vicious threat that poured from her gentle father's mouth. Unease stirred in her gut at this darkened shift in his calm character. She had never heard him speak with such violent fury.

"If you come within steps of her presence, I will slice the bottoms of your feet and stand you in a fire—is that clear?" Papa breathed heavily now.

Dirch stared at Papa through narrowed eyes. His mouth dribbled with spit and sweat poured profusely down his furious face.

"Damn. You." He spat in Papa's eyes.

Calmly, much more so than she expected, Papa wiped the spittle from his face and cleaned his hand on Dirch's shirt. He righted himself, brushing out the wrinkles on his sleeves and straightening his coat. "Ben, grab some chains. John... send word to the constable. We have found their killer."

Something about the way Papa looked at Dirch Johnson sent a tremble coursing through her body.

Ben nodded. "Yes, Sir. The chains for now, and then the night watch can throw him in a cell."

# Ends in Shame

*"To mock the master, one make's their bed. For now, in wrath, he'll wind up dead"*

*-Alice Addertongue*

Reputation is a powerful, yet fickle tool. As a skeleton key, it opens doors closed to others, both physical and metaphorical. It takes a public record of many good deeds to painstakingly craft a likable reputation; however, a single poor decision can shatter it beyond repair as a teapot against stone. Once ruined, it would forevermore suffer from appraising eyes. Glares and stares questioning the cracks, assuming that it will fail again. Fortunately, it is only the known deeds which are weighed. If one...or in this case, two or three unscrupulous actions occur without witness in the dark of night, a strong foundation holds true.

The man in the crimson cloak looked down at his victim, bound and gagged. The fool. If ever a death was unquestionably, undeniably, unexpectedly deserved—this was the one. It had taken every ounce of self-control not to simply beat him to death the moment it was safe to do so. Nay, patience is ever a virtue and the recompense would be sweeter, more luxurious this way. Nothing more or less than that which was earned through word and deed.

Such a fool this man had been. He was a wheelwright's apprentice with a chance of marriage to an extraordinary young woman far beyond his own worth, all squandered through piss poor actions and foolishness. Ignorance could be overlooked, but willfully threatening something more precious than

his own pathetic existence? Unacceptable.

This man's...nay, this beast's recklessness was a danger to far more than he understood; more than he could ever comprehend. The girl was critical for what was planned. This odious weed must be ripped out by the root. His demise would fulfill a two-fold purpose this night. Perhaps that made him more valuable than previously considered.

"Alas—it doesn't matter." He wandered closer to the prey.

Leather straps with iron fasteners bound both wrists and ankles. A fifth and sixth lashed the forehead and waist of this naked cretin. Though his hands and feet were already purple, the man in the crimson cloak tightened them further to whet an insatiable desire for punishment.

"Whatever is begun in anger ends in shame...or in this case, in blood." He trailed a finger along Dirch's arm. "Your anger brought you to this end, Mr. Johnson. You've chosen to act as a rabid dog and as such, you shall face the consequences. You will suffer and suffer again, Mr. Johnson."

Dirch struggled against the bonds, speech even more unintelligible than before the gag. Still, it was better this way.

Years before coming to its dilapidated state, the site of this grisly ritual had been a haven for the sick and poor, serving as a hospital for those found lurking the streets of Philadelphia. Once, it had been a place of healing. Tonight, there would be no kindness and no healing—only cruelty and death. Again, as with Miss Lanivet, his prize would be awarded upon their demise. Strapped to a board as long as a death box, Mr. Johnson would pay penance for his crimes. Luckily, a handful of pine shillings goes a long way among the peasants. Regardless of his other...less redeeming qualities, the filthy inn keep, Ebenezer, had mastered the art of scurrying between shadows, moving undetected in the night. Many an unpleasant deed could be covered in the night when those that held the shackles were on your side. The innkeep had his uses.

In the quest for knowledge, the pursuit of one's highest level of existence and potential, his work had crossed into the arts, the sciences, life efficiencies, and medicine. The man in the crimson cloak lifted a hinged rod into the faint light. It was yet another magnificent creation modified by his own hand. The

future would appreciate his genius even if the present did not.

"Are you familiar with this instrument, Mr. Johnson?"

Smoldering, rageful eyes glared back. Those were the eyes of someone willing to murder. The man in crimson knew them well, as he'd seen them in the mirror earlier this night. However, there was more. A sparkle of truth in this critical moment, beyond fear, beyond dread. The bastard was utterly terrified.

And rightfully so.

"This is a catheter." He held the simple device aloft so it glinted in the candle light. "Men cursed with kidney stones suffer to insert silver rods into themselves, relieving pain from urinary retention. However, obvious complications arise from sliding hard metal within the penis. I'm sure even you can imagine what agony could be inflicted." Dirch writhed with wide eyes, struggling to be heard, unable to fight back as would be his unrefined, brutish way if given such opportunity.

Not tonight...not ever again.

He laughed. "I know! Doesn't release from pain seem such a wondrous luxury here and now? Your release will come, but first the pain."

It is said that men have but enough blood for one head to function properly at a time. Either one makes decisions with his brain or his cock and generally there's a balance. However, men such as Dirch thought only from below. A catheter seemed a wildly appropriate device for this evening. Every repugnant, low brow thought that issued forth in this man's life would now be replaced with something more tangible.

Doubtless, Dirch feared what might happen to his favorite toy; however, there was something well beyond simple mutilation in order.

Smirking down upon Dirch, the man in the crimson cloak tilted his head to the side. "I wracked my brain for a solution. There must be a way to avoid such catastrophic accidents. Punctures, ruptures, I could only imagine. As always," he smiled, "the solution came to me. Bringing flexibility to the instrument would allow for twists and turns while traveling the urethra. No more punctures leading to infection and inflammation. By using a series of

segmented metal rings to mimic the carapace of a centipede—" He stared at him. "No matter, this is beyond you. I've a prototype here."

Dirch thrashed impotently, wetting himself in the process.

"Shall we try it out together? In the pursuit of knowledge?" He hadn't imagined excitement at the thought of being so near Mr. Johnson's member, though it was not for the thing itself, but the thrill of experimentation.

He glanced down and sighed. "Ah...perhaps I overestimated the necessary length and width. No matter, the device will compensate. Rest assured the next iteration will be thinner. You will not enjoy this nearly as much as I will."

This night was intended for pain. Pain for this pathetic excuse of a man.

Dirch had crossed him. Perhaps not directly, but that would be no stay of execution. It is a bold man who acts in place of others. Since the first death, his sadistic cravings had intensified. As the hungry crave sustenance and the weary desire rest, these wants have morphed to needs. Too long they had been suppressed and now the feelings ached to thrive.

He was amused by the fact that it was unimpressive, seeming to withdraw like the head of a frightened turtle.

"Before we begin, I want to experiment with something I learned in reading the works of Hippolytus De Marsiliis." His heart quickened. This was penance for the pig. "'Tis a pain inflicted by water."

Thankfully, his instructions for preparation were well kept. They had ensured that everything was in place to accomplish his twisted desires, and with such quick notice. He would have to congratulate them on their efforts.

Of course, they wanted him to succeed.

To join them.

Two large wooden buckets filled to the brim with water from the Delaware River hung overhead. In the bucket placed at the head of the table, he dunked a cloth and placed it upon the edge, allowing for a slow, cool drip of water to land square on Mr. Johnson's forehead.

Drip.

He chuckled. "It doesn't seem like much now, but eventually you'll come

to loathe that small drip."

Dirch stared above confused, frantically searching as the water fell to greet his sweaty brow.

Drip.

He needn't bother. Tonight, there would be no means of escape. The only release would be in the inevitable grasp of death's icy fingers.

The restraints that bound him held, but only just. With such a brutish man beneath their hold, the man in the crimson cloak needed to work efficiently.

But not too quickly—the fool must suffer.

Drip.

Slowly, carefully, he slid the articulated silver deeper within. A small release of urine signaled it was far enough, yet he forced it further. He only needed access to the bladder, but this would make it near impossible to retrieve. There would be no rejecting this length.

Dirch fought valiantly, but to no avail. He even managed a scream around his gag. Whether from shock or pain or the fear that comes with having a metal rod forcibly placed inside one's sex...the man once so proud of his own strength went limp. He'd been warned victims occasionally did this. A way of the mind to shut out the overwhelming horror, protecting itself from the moment and the memories to follow by shutting down.

Perhaps he had given up, but the man in the crimson cloak hoped not, for that would diminish the fun of it. Knowing what he did, he'd prepared. Naturally.

A dab of pure ammonia on his upper lip would rip him from that stronghold.

"This is no time for rest, Mr. Johnson, we're only just beginning."

In order for this to work, he needed to siphon water from the second bucket above and connect it to the catheter. Only god knew what bacteria this water contained...an added bonus...but Dirch's bladder would burst long before any infection could settle.

This was undeniably, unavoidably, absolutely...going to hurt.

He tilted his head and met Dirch's bulging, trickling eyes with his own predatory glare. "The average man expels nearly two coffee cups full of urine each time he voids. This bucket holds at least ten times that. You should feel the fullness soon."

Sweat poured from Dirch's face now, mixed, of course, with the occasional agonizing drip from the water above. Water and tears fell down his face and the gagging cloth did little to mute his screaming now.

It, in time with the metronome drip, drip, drip, was a symphony of delight. Again, he enjoyed the melody of malice that surrounded him in this humid hospital room. It was the sound of success. The rhythm of vengeance. And the tune of victory.

Perhaps he would compose an arrangement to match, something of low tones and delicately balanced fugues. But there would be time for that later. There would be so much time to milk every drop of pleasure. He had all the time in the world.

He pulled The Pennsylvania Gazette from his coat pocket. While time usually passed at a swift and costly pace, tonight it appeared that she would glide through it with a languid waltz, while Dirch either hemorrhaged or succumbed to blood poisoning. That could possibly take days if the shock of trauma didn't steal him first.

He, too, would wait until greeted again with the sweet serenity of Dirch's eternal silence.

Drip.

Until then, there were only the exquisite screams and the persistent drops of water.

# Windswept Worries

With Nelly away visiting it fell on Charlotte to take out the washing. She didn't mind chores, in fact the cool morning breeze whipping her hair and kissing her cheeks brought with it pleasant memories of her youth. She would laugh and run through the sheets on such a day as this. Linens became capes or veils, even da Vinci's parachute on occasion. Her own creativity was the only limit to what the world could be. Those were easier days.

The time for such fantasies had passed with age. As Paul penned in Corinthians, "When I was a child, I spake as a child, I understood as a child, I thought as a child: but when I became a man, I put away childish things." She sighed as grey clouds announced themselves with a rolling rumble. Even a child would have understood that if she dallied long, the thunderous pride of lions would storm all over her linens. It simply would not do.

Delicate wooden pegs, each hand carved by Papa, offered another glimpse into precious times with Mother. Her soft hands, untouched by the calluses of hard labor, pinned each sopping bit of cloth to the line while her lips offered laughter and clever prompts. She'd always encouraged Charlotte's fantasies, regardless of how absurd. But the thought of Mother's hands no longer offered comfort. Now they were skeletal hands buried below six feet of earth attached to the corpse of a dead woman. Mother's empty sockets stared into the dark death box for eternity. Had she seen the one who'd ended it all?

Murder.

Unbidden, a flash of macabre reality slammed against her heart. A pool of blood, Mother sprawled at its center with mouth agape. The once bright sparkle of life transmogrified into a grotesque, milky film.

Charlotte clung to the line. No. Not like this. She didn't want to think of Mother like this. Remember Papa. Nelly. Pleasant days from before.

She could never remember Mother without blood stained shadows creeping about the corners.

Then came the flames, burning up her throat and into her ears with the speed of an unyielding wildfire. Her heartbeat quickened with every breath, thumping madly within her chest, and with every heave she tried to stop it. Charlotte pulled the first and only linen she hung to meet her face. The damp, well-worn cloth brought a small comfort, so she held it there for a time. She inhaled the smell of soap and bleach...breathing in, breathing out. Let it cleanse the horrid thoughts as if they were dirt and dust.

Time slipped by as her head pounded and she collected her senses. She slipped off her shoes, seeking calmness from the earth, as Mother had taught her. The darkness could claim her in an instant. She wasn't sure how long she had been standing with her face in the linen, the soft grass tickling her toes, but the thunder was getting louder, and closer. The first gentle patter of rain blended with her tears, the former growing in strength as the latter subsided.

No time for the sheets to dry. It was time to go inside.

When she turned to head back, a tall, hooded figure draped in crimson red blocked her path inside.

Standing.

Watching.

Waiting.

Death had come to take her to the beyond. Perhaps she could join Mother again.

Her muscles seized, rendering her as a statue. Unable to breathe. Unable to move. An eerie hiss slithered from beneath the hood.

Charlotte.

This was not Death. This was one of the Rosicrucian witches.

Lightning flashed and the figure lunged. Charlotte ran to the side of the house as fast as she could, legs pumping like never before.

She turned. The figure crept across the yard, stalking closer, crouched low, closing in upon its prey. Her.

Long arms reached for her. Get to the front door.

She turned to race around the corner. Where were they now?

Thud.

Charlotte's foot slammed into something heavy, something stiff... and damp. She fell to the ground, linens flying, catching the wind and landing with a sickening squelch in the mud. She raced to collect them. The one who chased her was nowhere in view. She reached behind her for a sheet, but instead grasped something large. Beneath her eyes, sprawled in the grass as a doll tossed aside, lay the tangled remains of a body she once knew.

Charlotte froze, waiting for the glazed over eyes to move, or the pale, blue lips to speak, but they didn't.

Bile rose in her throat as she clutched at her middle, the unwilling force of sickness crawling up her throat and spilling onto the grass. His shirt was unbuttoned revealing a bloated stomach stained with the blues and yellows of significant bruising, his breeches, below the knee. Good God.

Thunder rumbled as she backed away from him, the rain peppering her cheeks, mixing with tears. This couldn't be happening. Another heave, dry this time, wracked her middle and tore through her throat.

"Papa!"

Sweep the floorboards. Wash the cupboards. Dust the latches. Charlotte concentrated on her cleaning.

"I've no idea why he's at our door! He was taken away in chains. Just last night. You know it to be true." Papa's stern voice echoed from the other room.

"I'm obligated to question all involved, Thaddeus. That is something you are well aware of, my friend."

Sweep the floorboards. Wash the cupboards. Constable Cobb sounded angry.

"Thaddeus, tell me again what happened last night. Spare not a detail. This looks bad. Very bad for you."

Sweep the floorboards. Wash the—.

"Dammit, Robert, you know the details. Dirch attacked my Charlotte. He was here, yes, and got into a scuffle with young Benjamin Franklin. I was tending to that sorry John Priestly in his sodden state. We pulled them off of each other. Then put him in chains. That's the end of it."

"But, you must understand, Thaddeus, that gives you motive."

Dear God. The constable was right. Sweep. Sweep. Sweep. Papa was enraged with Dirch last night. She'd never seen him in such a fury. A murderous rage...

She paused. Constable Cobb's shaking voice met her ears once more. "You need to tell me. If it was you, this can be explained and you'll serve your time for the one. But you know how this will look. One murder, all the murders. To them it could be the same."

"I'll not have you stand in my house and accuse me of MURDER!"

Sweep. Sweep. Sweep. It was nearing evening now. They'd taken Dirch's body from their lawn this afternoon. She'd watched them as they went. Stiff as a board. Rigor mortis, they'd said. Sweep. Sweep. Sweep.

Oh Papa. Don't let it be true.

"The investigation goes nowhere. I'm no closer to finding the culprit than when I first arrived. There's no way this death can be connected to the others, as it's on your own property. If you won't cooperate, I'll be forced to take additional measures to get to the bottom of this. Help me help you, friend." Constable Cobb was stern now.

"Friend?" Papa scoffed. "He wasn't murdered here." Sweep. Sweep. Sweep. Oh Papa.

Sweep. Sweep. Sweep. The door behind her creaked open. Dust from the sweeping flew into her mouth and she didn't even care.

The constable entered the room. "Uhhh, Thaddeus?"

Charlotte froze with the sudden realization that she held the broom out at the waist, sweeping the cupboard instead of the floor.

Papa stomped into the dark room where she listened. The moment he saw her, he halted, eyes wide and a look of concern crossing his face.

"Lottie, darling, what are you doing? Are you all right?"

She set the broom down. "Umm. Yes, Papa. Yes. Simply cleaning out cobwebs." She forced a smile, but it pained her. "We don't need any spiders."

The body didn't look like Dirch. Not anymore. She was shaking, clinging to the broom for support.

Papa glanced at his friend. "Robert? Could you give us a minute?"

The constable glared. "This isn't over, Thaddeus."

Papa nodded. "Give me some time. If you truly consider me a friend, let me tend to my daughter. I give my word that I'll be here when you return."

The fire climbed to her ears. If Papa was capable of murdering Dirch–then it was possible he could have murdered Mother.

# Riddles and Remembrance

Even the treat of extra cream in her coffee could not dispel the grey shroud that clung to Charlotte's thoughts, couldn't touch the miasma of a crushing void. She was without sensation, numb, going about her chores out of routine rather than necessity. Papa busied himself at their newly fashioned metal fireplace meant for cooking that his friends in town called a stove.

"Cheer up, dear one." Papa smiled, but it was a cheap facade.

She tried to smile. She did. But the darkness encircled her thoroughly. "Papa." She swallowed, choking down the sip. "Priya was desperate for help. She came to me in her time of need and I fear I've failed her. I need to do something. What if she's bound wherever Dirch left her?"

Dirch. A simple mark discovered on Dirch's body had kept the constable at bay. Evidently the same mark was found on Elizabeth Franklin, and Papa had a solid alibi. But she couldn't let go of her thoughts, her worries that he had been involved in Dirch's death, though she didn't dare ask him directly. She knew he wouldn't lie to her and wasn't certain she wanted to hear the truth.

Papa sighed. "As cruel as Dirch turned out to be, I'm not quite convinced he is responsible for Priya's disappearance."

"Why not?"

Unless he was a member of that Rosicrucian Order. She still believed they were behind the other disappearances. And maybe they got to Dirch

195

too. Clearly Delphia was one of them, and with Dirch's connections to her... it only made sense. She glanced at Papa. Or maybe Dirch's murder was of a different kind.

She wasn't sure how to feel about that.

"Frankly, Lottie, a lone maiden stands a better chance of hiding alone."

She rose to look out the window, seeking a signal of hope from the heavens. Even a sliver of sunshine would lift her spirits and burn through her darkness, but she was greeted only by the thick overlay of dismal clouds. They were full to bursting, no doubt bringing with them a dreadful storm to mirror her own turmoil.

Papa continued. "With the watch on the lookout, I can't imagine anyone being so brazen as to strike again. At least, not so soon." He smiled, a feeble attempt to fill her with confidence. "For now, Priya is likely safe and on her way to refuge." He busied himself with the makings of breakfast. "And if Dirch was this murderer of the town, then he won't have the chance to claim any more souls."

"But what if–what if Dirch already...?" She couldn't finish the thought.

Papa slammed a cast iron skillet back on top of the stove with more force than he surely intended. He sighed. "I'm sorry, Lottie. Even the memory of that foul vagrant makes my blood boil. I'm sorry to have put you in that position. I was wrong. I truly thought him a righteous man until—."

Charlotte tensed. "I believe the sight of Ben set Dirch to rage that night. That's why he attacked."

Papa nodded. "Jealousy has been known to twist a man's heart."

"I'm thankful we both now know that he is not the man to whom my heart shall belong." Charlotte managed a smile, if forced.

Papa placed a bowl of porridge and fresh berries on the table in front of her. Hopefully, she would be able to taste it. Nelly was still away, thankfully, visiting family. Away from this mess. On these days Papa had made it a tradition to serve her breakfast himself. It was something he had always done for Mother.

Mother.

"When did your heart know, Papa?"

Papa paused for a moment, spoon halfway between bowl and mouth. He knew she meant Mother. He set aside his spoon, absently reaching for the maple syrup he usually despised instead. Perhaps it was a subliminal desire to sweeten the bitterness of their predicament or to match the sweet memories of his late wife. She would never know, and perhaps he didn't himself.

"From the first moment I met her, Lottie."

Sweet berry juices had just enough tartness to tickle her tongue—and helped her feel alive. "Was it a lover's meeting? In which you knew the first time you laid eyes upon her?"

"Actually, and don't mistake my meaning here," he lifted his eyes to her, "but no. It was not love at first sight."

Oh really.

"Her beauty astounded me, absolutely." A soft smile played about his lips as his expression glazed over in memory. "Blazing red hair, sapphire eyes, porcelain skin, smooth and unblemished as fresh cream, glowed with a hint of blush on her high cheekbones whenever she grew impassioned....your mother was the most beautiful woman I had ever seen and that remains true to this day." He glanced at the floor. "But it was her mind that captivated my soul."

She leaned in. Papa spoke of Mother so rarely, she didn't want to miss a word of it.

"She was deep in conversation with the fisherman by the docks the first time I saw her." Papa smiled with the absent wave of memory. "That woman's sharp tongue could flay a man quicker than a bolt of lightning. Her wit and cleverness proved a bottomless well."

It warmed her heart to see him smile.

"Those men were trying to bargain with her over nearly rancid fish, and she wasn't having any part in it." Papa's eyes held a mischievous glint she had only so rarely seen.

"I drew closer, thinking they were trying to take advantage of her, but to

my astonishment, it was she who held the upper hand!" His chuckle blossomed into a full, belly laugh. "She challenged the fisherman to a battle of wits! If they could solve her riddle—she would pay the full price. If they couldn't, she would take a fresher catch without charge."

Papa sighed and looked down at the table and picked at the wooden knots.

"I'd never seen anything like it. The fishermen were entertained by her riddle, as was I. She'd have a fresh fish from me as well, were I to have the misfortune of challenging her."

Charlotte leaned in further. "Do you remember the riddle, Papa ?"

"Of course, dear one."

Alive as you but without breath,

As cold in my life as in my death;

Never a thirst though I always drink,

Dressed in mail but never a clink.

Who am I?

"Hmmm." How curious. Charlotte searched her thoughts. "Dressed in mail but never a clink...was it a soldier of some sort?"

Papa sat back in his chair, crossing his arms with a satisfied grin. "Nay. Try again."

"Alive as you, but without breath." This was a tough one. Alive but didn't breathe. Plants?

She would have to speak with precision or Papa would poke fun. If Mother knew it, so could she. Never a thirst, though I always drink.

Charlotte laughed. "Ha! I have it!"

Papa raised his eyebrows in surprise.

"It's a fish! They breathe underwater and have scales like chainmail. How clever."

Papa grinned. "Your mother walked away with free fish that day, and I walked away with a taken heart." He wrapped Charlotte's hands in his. "I

knew at that moment that I needed her to be mine. I would do anything to win her over."

She beheld her Papa . This was the face of a man washed in memory. One of tortured pain mixed with the warmth from happier times—it was a face that she loved so dear, and now worried for even more.

Papa continued. "My only hope is that your husband will feel that same way for you, my Lottie. If this has taught me anything…it's that I need to look below the surface as well when speaking with your suitors."

She rolled her eyes. "Oh, because there are so many, Papa."

He raised his eyebrows. "Ben suits you well, dear one. Wealth and fanciful speaking have a way of hiding what truth lies below, yet I can't help but believe that Ben is more than proper raising and a silver tongue. He cares for you at more than a surface level. Were I blind, I could still hear it in his words. More importantly," he narrowed his eyes, "perhaps most importantly, I see the change he brings in you. Your step is lighter, your cheeks rosier with laughter, and you are left with a glow after each meeting."

Charlotte blushed, frozen by his admission of approval. "We shall see, Papa."

A sharp knock sounded upon the door. She glanced at Papa, searching for worry or alarm in his eyes, but there was none.

He rose to greet their visitor. She waited, straining to hear who it was. Thudded footsteps led back to their table and she turned to see him.

As if summoned by the very mention of his name, now in her home, stood the one person she'd been hoping to see.

Ben.

"Good morning, my beautiful rose!" He pulled a bouquet of flowers from behind his back, a sheepish grin playing about his lips. "I've come to collect you."

Charlotte paused. "Collect?" She looked from Ben to Papa. "Where are we going?"

"To…brunch? Remember? Aunt Beth invited us to brunch at her house."

Charlotte's stomach dropped, her throat tightening as she racked her mind for any memory of agreeing to brunch. How could she have forgotten? Panic fluttered in her chest at the thought of maintaining pleasantries and a facade of normalcy when her world was collapsing around her. As she stared into Ben's crestfallen eyes, guilt twisted in her gut at the idea of letting him down and spoiling his cheerful plans. The urge to confess her turmoil and beg his patience nearly spilled out, but the risk of appearing deranged clenched her jaw shut.

"I...um...well, I hadn't remembered that was today. We've had a lot going on around here—"

"Yes, yes, I've heard." Ben set the flowers upon the table. Papa busied himself by pouring water into a vase for them. "The perfect reason to get you out of this house and take your mind off recent events." The bruises on his face were faint, hardly visible. Perhaps they were covered by powder.

But she wasn't sure if she was up to brunch with anyone today. She inhaled slowly, considering the thought then blew out her breath. Ben drew his eyebrows together. "Perhaps we can send word ahead that you've fallen ill?"

Even she knew this was a weak excuse.

"Or you're caring for your Papa or something?" Ben attempted his best smile.

But, to Charlotte, the thought of lying wasn't enticing.

She gathered his hands within hers. "No. Give me a few moments. I will gather myself together and we can go." She stepped closer. "I'm so sorry. I do need to get out of this house."

In a sudden realization, she became aware that Papa was still present as he spoke up from beside her. "Yes. I agree. The merriment will do you some good, Lottie."

"Then it's settled!" Ben nodded at Papa, "Thank you, Sir," and headed for the door.

"I'll wait for you in the carriage. But don't be too long!" Ben winked at her and whisked away.

One thing was for sure. Even among the strife and unanswered questions that surrounded her, her worry had all but melted away. Ben's presence seemed to do that.

She rushed to her bedroom. Charlotte felt so alive with the opportunity to spend the day with him she was actually sweating. This would never do. She filled the water basin and added perfume, the cold water greeting her fingers as any icy pool, but she had no time to heat it. Now, she must find the powder for her teeth.

There it was. A simple scrub, and it tasted of cinnamon. No time to paint her face, but alas, she preferred the natural look anyway. Now for the dress, her shoes, but no wig--her hair would have to hang limp, as it usually did.

It wouldn't be prudent to keep him waiting any longer. Nelly would be aghast that she kept him waiting at all.

It was time for their brunch with Aunt Beth.

# Paintings and Passion

The intimacy that a private one-horse chaise provided proved to be an intoxicating affair. With each bump in the road Charlotte scooted closer, pressing herself against him. Ben ran his hand up her back, into her hair, and squeezed with just enough strength to make her swoon.

She tingled at his touch, and crossed her legs as her mound pulsed. Such thoughts were immoral. They were sinful. But his lips were so smooth.

With his other hand, he took hers and placed it upon his breeches. Beneath the expensive linen she felt his bulge. Ben was stiff and throbbing. He pulsated with need just as she did.

They couldn't do this. Not here. Not now.

But oh how she wanted to.

Charlotte wasn't sure if Godly influences kept her from it, or if it was the threat of a child. But then again, she wanted him to touch her underneath her skirts. To feel the passion between them that burned within her.

He loved her. She knew it. She loved him. She knew that as well.

Nay had it been spoken, but she could feel it in her heart.

He pulled her in for a slow, tantalizing kiss, his familiar scent of leather and spiced liqueur washing over her. He parted her lips with his tongue, softly biting down on her lower lip. She could hardly catch breath before his lips grazed her shoulders, trailed up her neck, and settled upon her ear. She didn't know that men would kiss the ear, but the way he gently sucked on her lobe hardened her nipples.

Each jolt pulled them closer. Ben moaned against her lips.

With an abrupt jolt, the chaise came to a halt. She pulled away, lest his driver might see them entangled.

There, standing tall and domineering among the grand mansions of Society Hill, stood the Franklin home belonging now to Aunt Beth. It hadn't been long ago since she had trod upon these front steps with a pit in her stomach, joining Priya for dinner with the Franklin family. As she stared at the long white columns, reaching to heaven above, the dinner seemed an eternity ago.

Now Priya was missing, there was a serial killer among them, and somehow Ben had noticed her.

An eternity, indeed.

Braving the rain, she ran the walkway, up the steps and onto the blissful safety of the sprawling front porch. Ben splashed mere steps behind her as the storm mercilessly raged around them.

Curious, though, that the door lay open. Especially during a storm.

Ben stepped onto the threshold and looked at her with a slight shrug. "Perhaps the storm unsettled the door?"

No one was there to greet them. Surely Aunt Beth had remembered their invitation? She couldn't blame her if she hadn't, for she had forgotten about it herself.

The entrance looked empty. No doorman, no whispers of conversation, no delectable scents of berries and scones wafting through the air. There weren't any signs of an impending brunch that she could see.

Charlotte paused. "Maybe we should go."

Ben remained unfazed. "Mmmm. Not yet. Perhaps they're in the back making preparations or closing windows in the storm.

No signs of servants. No light inside of any kind. Something about this didn't feel right.

Thunder rumbled as sheets of rain poured down around them, rolling

through her chest as the drums of nature's war.

"Let's at least get out of this blasted storm."

The wind slapped damp hair across her face. If he felt safe, then so did she.

Charlotte nodded. "All right. I'll follow you in."

Ben opened the door further with an ominous creek that she could still somehow hear over the claps of thunder and lightning. They stepped inside as two drowned rats seeking shelter.

He led her past the glorious paintings and sculptures of the entrance to the dining room down the hall. She'd never seen such sweeping canvases and carved marble this close. Please God let their wet footsteps do no damage to the soft carpets.

Ben led her to a cream-colored chair with a tall back and lions' feet on the capriole legs. "Here, sit down. I'll run to find drying linens." She settled between its wings and rested her hands on the outswept arms. Then, Charlotte was alone.

The dining room was as cold as a corpse. There were no flowers blooming within the vases at the center of the table, nor people to care for them. In fact, nothing in sight offered her a glimmer of hope.

She was an intruder, coming to sit among someone else's riches as her clothes dripped rain all over the expensive floors.

Ben's voice echoed from down the hall. "Aunt Beth! It's Ben! I've come with Charlotte…"

She could hear the open and close of doors as he checked each room downstairs.

She glanced at the walls of the dining room.

Odd. She didn't remember that painting before. Charlotte stepped closer to examine a canvas that stretched nearly from the ceiling to the carpeted floor. She surely would have noticed if it had been hanging there before. It would have been impossible not to.

A shiver crawled from the base of her spine all the way to the nape of her neck. It wasn't from the cold, but from what depictions her vision was met

with in the painted scene. Twisted, menacing, grotesque monsters of creation swirled in a pit. Skeletal women, mutilated children, and fanged men with wings all with limbs entwined together were suspended in eternal agony. Where limbs left spaces, she noticed snakes. Some with two heads and others with three. Among the monsters, tortured persons with clear, pained expressions of anguish attempted to escape. Bile rose within her throat. Surrounding the pit, a wall of thick thorns stood between the mangled bodies and cloaked figures.

Hooded robes.

The Rosicrucians.

Surely not.

Ben gracefully returned with an armful of dry cloth. "There's a fire in the sitting room."

How on earth was he so calm?

She strained to force her words out, whispering in his ear. "Have you seen this painting before?"

Ben glanced to the wall and shrugged

"Edmund, Aunt Beth's late husband, had an unusual fascination in depictions of Hell. By heaven we understand a state of happiness in infinite degree, and endless in duration." He turned to her, grabbing her hands. "But by that same token, if we are to linger eternal in Hell, then suffering in a state of agony we shall see."

As always, Ben brought with him the voice of reason and a sense of peace. He settled her tortured thoughts, but still she didn't wish to look upon it.

He must have seen how she averted her eyes.

"See this, right above the painting?" He crossed the room to stand beside it. "It's the tapestry Aunt Beth hangs to cover it when hosting guests. As this painting was Edmund's, she says she finds comfort in his possessions, and thus allows it to remain upon the wall." He raised his eyebrows and shrugged in apology.

Charlotte nodded, the motion deliberate and unhurried. "Perhaps I'm unused to such elevated taste." She wasn't sure what to say about it.

She glanced around the quiet room again. "You're sure she was expecting us? Where is everyone? This home hasn't a soul within it."

Ben smiled. "Charlotte. You're freezing. Come, sit by the fire." He reached out his hand. "I'm sure she's gone to the marketplace. The roads will have muddied by now, and they won't chance the carriages getting stuck within the storm. Regardless of what may keep her, I feel confident that we are alone until this storm passes."

Odd. But she trusted him.

Charlotte followed Ben to the fire. The warmth its crackling flames provided would surely feel nice on her soaked dress and chilled skin. Someone had to have lit the fire.

He placed a chair near the fireplace and bent into a deep bow. "After you, m'lady."

A coy smile played about his lips.

She couldn't help but grin. "Thank you, kind sir. Such a gentleman you are."

He chuckled.

She held her hands toward the glorious flames, the heat penetrating her ice-cold skin and relieving the slight numbness of her fingers. Ben kneeled beside her and clasped her hands in his. He blew hot air onto their hands. Her skin tingled where he had placed his lips.

Ben stared at her with those smoldering pewter eyes. "Let me warm you."

She paused. The way he looked at her was the way she had imagined it in her secret dreams. Sinful dreams.

His gaze was filled with intent. With need. With lust.

She leaned down, becoming acutely aware of the snugness of her dress against her bodice, leaving little to the imagination. She cupped his neck in her hands, leaning closer until they were nearly nose to nose. His breath was warm upon her face. The fire crackled. Hot. Burning.

Just like they were.

He brushed his lips against hers, teasing them with each soft kiss he placed upon them. They were alone. The storm was heavy. Her breath began to match it.

"My dear. Your petticoat would dry much better beside the fire."

She tensed. Now was the moment. Was she a sinner? Or was she a lover?

The way she felt in this moment couldn't possibly be considered a sin. Her heart was his. But her purity was her own. She could choose whom to share it with.

He sensed her caution.

"I'm sorry." He caressed her arms. "If I am too forward, please tell me so."

Such a gentleman. But of course she was nervous.

"I want to share this with you. But please know, I've never—"

Confusion crossed his face. "But, I thought—"

For Heaven's sake. He was thinking about the comment from Dirch.

Heat rushed to her cheeks. "My flower...remains." This was mortifying. "Dirch merely tried. We batted eyes and exchanged a few words until one day he forced me up against the shop and tried to take it beyond my comfort. It went no further, but from that day I knew."

A flicker of anger ignited in his eyes, yet it yielded to an overwhelming sadness. He softened. "We go as far as you want to go, my dear. I am yours." He brought her hands to his lips and kissed them. "You are mine. Forever from this day we shall be, but only if you so choose it."

So many thoughts. His life. Her life. Their families. The unknown. The town would have much to discuss. Papa might not approve. This was all happening so fast.

He rose to light the candles on a table near the window. She faintly recalled that someone had mentioned the late husband of Aunt Beth was a beeswax candlemaker.

"I—" Ben kneeled in front of her once more. He pursed his lips then opened them again. "Tell me you love me."

"Ben Franklin, I love you."

"Charlotte Scott." His grey eyes pierced her soul. "I desperately, passionately, eternally—love you, too." With each word he trailed a kiss up her arm, coming to rest inches from her face.

The heat from the fire paled in comparison to the flames in her heart.

As intensely as the flames licked the logs upon the fire, Ben kissed her speechless lips. He urged her to stand, then untied her petticoats from the waist. His lips never parted from hers. She could hardly breathe, and yet, she didn't want to. She felt a wetness between her thighs and found herself touching him. She squeezed his firm, strong shoulders, pulled at the small hairs on the back of his neck, and caressed the skin of his chest. She leaned forward to kiss him there, as he had already unbuttoned his shirt. As he assisted her in removing the stay, a sense of exposure washed over her, leaving her clad solely in her shift and stockings.

Ben's shirt was open now, a trail of hair leading into his breeches.

Seeing his skin, so close, so warm.

They stood toe to toe, exploring and touching and teasing each other until she pulsated once more.

He gently pressed her shoulders, guiding her to sit in the chair.

Ben knelt before her, his hands moving unhurriedly from her shoulders to her waist, trailing down to her ankles and back up along her legs, sliding beneath the fabric of her shift. He rested his hands upon her knees.

"Do you trust me?" He whispered.

How could she speak right now?

"I...do." She was breathless. Weightless.

Ben grinned.

An unexpected gasp escaped her lips as he took both hands and parted her legs, trailing his lips up her thighs.

My God, what did this man intend?

His hands scooted her bottom forward on the chair, with the back of her knees now resting on his shoulders. His lips had traveled to the tuft between her thighs. She felt his nose upon her mound, his lips upon her sex. His tongue

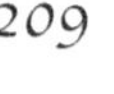

licked in ways she never knew possible. Thank God the storm continued to rage outside, because if anyone came home, they would surely hear her gasps of pleasure. She couldn't help but release them.

He flicked his tongue. Over and over, deep inside her slick, steamy fold.

This wasn't a sin. This was ecstasy in its purest, primal form.

She never wanted it to end.

Her legs were twitching, her toes were curling...Charlotte found herself holding her breath. When she thought she could hardly take anymore, he plunged his tongue lower, licking wider. She clutched his head and held tighter to him. His arms wrapped around her thighs and spread her legs even more.

It was too much. God this was too much. She needed release and had no idea when it would come.

Her body stiffened. Pulsating waves of rapturous release shook her to the core. Never had she felt a euphoric bliss such as this. And all from his tongue. She was utterly amazed.

Her body collapsed into the chair. Slight tremors continued to shake in her legs as she was exhausted of all energy.

He wiped his face and came to kiss her. She knew there was more to the pleasures of the flesh, but my God how could she go on?

"Can you stand?" He nuzzled his face into her hair, kissing her on top of her head.

Charlotte's breath escaped her, stolen away as her purity this night. But not stolen, really, as she had freely shared it with him. Breathless, she answered him. "I...think so."

Ben smirked. "Excellent."

He led her to the table with the candles. The fire burned, but lower now. The rain continued to batter the window panes, but it had also slowed. He placed himself behind her and leaned her body over the wood. His soft linen pant legs tickled the backs of her calves. She rested her weight upon the table, nearly laying down. Her juices were slick between her legs. Her mound still tingled from release.

Ben's belt buckle clanged upon the floor. She felt his stiffness slide up and down against her. Dear God—how she wanted him inside.

She felt the tip of his length linger just outside of her, sliding in her wetness. He leaned down, blew out the candles, and whispered in her ear. "My love, please tell me if it hurts. I will stop if you need me to."

Please don't stop, Charlotte thought. "I love you."

Ben rubbed her back. "And I love you."

He slid inside her throbbing mound, slowly, gently. She couldn't have imagined how it would feel with him inside her. So full. So complete.

Yes, there was pain. But the pain was minimal compared to the pleasure. Her legs still shook from the wonders of his tongue.

He started moving. In. Out. Sliding back and forth while clutching at her hips. He lifted her shift to expose her back.

"Do you trust me?" Again, he asked her.

Charlotte struggled to find words. "I do! Oh God, yes, I do!"

He seized one of the extinguished candles, and in an instant, she felt the scorching wax drip onto her back. It tingled and burned, but not in a bad way. Good God what would he do next?

Ben plunged inside of her, faster and faster.

"Charlotte Scott. You are...forever...mine." With one final grunt he slammed into her. This one hurt, yet she could feel him throb inside her. He clutched at her hips and steadied them both. She dared not move. He was emptying his seed.

When the trembles ceased, Ben knelt, kissed her back, and helped her stand to face him. He caressed her cheek and greeted her with the sweetest kiss she'd ever known.

"I love you." He placed a delicate kiss upon her forehead. "Now that I've spoken it once, I'll say it a thousand, thousand, times."

And Charlotte knew it, and she loved him too. Ben Franklin had her heart, her mind, her body, her soul. Forever.

The Twenty-<br>Ninth Chapter

# Invocations and Conjurations

Though the empty house was cold, a warmth radiated through her body, permeating her every thought. As she moved, her swollen bits were a constant reminder of what had transpired—and she celebrated it.

Charlotte was liberated. Free. In control of her own body, for once. At this moment there was no darkness, no killer, no worry. No memories to haunt her, nor persons to plague her. She soaked in each moment of bliss, wishing for it to never end.

Ben stood by the window, his shirt back on but still unbuttoned. She slid her arms underneath, melting into his warm embrace, allowing the two of them to become one.

"They will surely return soon." She wanted to be gone when they did.

Ben chuckled. "Yes, I look for them, too."

He had helped her peel the wax from her back and wash the remnants of their deeds away. Having him wash her was nearly as intimate as the deed itself.

"So, your uncle made candles?" She gestured to their lavish surroundings. "He must have made quite a few…"

Ben laughed as he buttoned his shirt. "The Franklin fortune comes from ownership of land." He settled his gaze upon her. "Business ventures are merely a hobby for some."

213

She hated herself for it, but she couldn't deny that the thought of finances had crossed her mind. Ben finished with his shirt and pulled up his trousers. "Would you like to see the candle room upstairs?"

He was fully dressed now. As was she.

She smiled at him. "Why, yes. Yes, I think I would." The smell of intimacy still lingered in the air. "You're sure she wouldn't mind? I do still feel odd to be here, in her home, without her."

He ran his fingers through her disheveled hair. "Charlotte...she's family. Soon enough she will become your family, too."

She was breathless. Weightless. Floating in the clouds. She rested her chin on his chest, staring at the man she loved.

He led her up the stairs, to the landing above which overlooked the grand entrance. Luckily, no muddy or wet footprints revealed their earlier intrusion. She couldn't imagine what kept the house empty for this long.

Two gargantuan columns stretched from floor to ceiling beside the door, and two more beside the landing where they stood. What it must be like to live in a home like this. It was impossible to dream of.

Charlotte stepped through the hall, admiring the artwork and busts that lined it, peeking into each bedroom. Perhaps she was looking for something. She didn't know.

Ben stopped at a black door to the right, across from which hung a tapestry of merriment. Perhaps it hid another grotesque painting. The rain pattered down upon the roof above them, filling the silent household with welcomed noise.

"This...is where Uncle Edmund made his beeswax candles."

She entered the room and froze from the shock of it. From floor to ceiling, covering all four walls and piled upon tables, were as many candles as she had ever seen. If every candle she had ever lit within her lifetime, or seen among the shops and homes she had visited were placed within this room, there still wouldn't be enough to compete with what lay before her eyes.

"Uncle Edmund's candles were popular in town because he liked to add

214

herbs or other elements to the wax as it dried." He reached for a candle with small beads placed inside. "These are cranberry candles. Best lit during the holiday season for added cheer." He flashed a grin at her. "The candle we used earlier was beeswax with rosemary." Her cheeks burned, but she smiled.

"Oh, and this! These were very popular. Aunt Beth still uses them often." He held out two tapers with a honeycomb design on the side. When she looked at the bottom, a miniature honeybee had been stamped into it.

She idly ran her fingers among the carved designs of the larger candles and felt subtle indentions. Upon further inspection, she noticed a name.

"Who is... Timothy Scarborough?" She absently chose another, and another. "Mary Watters? Theodore Matthews? Who are these people?"

Ben shook his head with a shrug. "I'm certain I've no idea."

As she considered each candle, she noted they all bore names. Each a different one, it seemed. Curious. Perhaps Edmund had stamped them with the name of those for which they'd been intended. Popular indeed. She stared at the incredible number of them. What fortune sat idle in this room with so many customers?

The tapestry again caught her eye. Curiosity overwhelmed her every thought. But, when she lifted the tapestry expecting a painting, Charlotte was greeted by a door instead.

A door painted in streaked crimson.

"Where could this possibly lead?" The hair of her arms prickled. A door hidden behind a large tapestry was surely no place for the wandering eye.

Ben hesitated, then shrugged. "I don't know. I've never seen it before." He looked at her. "Shall we venture to find out?" The mischievous glint had returned to his eyes.

"Typically...Mr. Franklin." She gave him an exaggerated look. "I would not presume to gallivant around someone's home at my own free will." He snorted. "However, we were invited...and she isn't here."

Her heart thumped in her chest. She grabbed his hand. "Just a quick peek."

Ben laughed and encircled her waist with his arms. "Only a moment. We

mustn't be discovered."

When they went through the crimson door, what lay beyond the other side, visible only by the candle in Ben's hand, astonished her senses and stole her breath. Aunt Bethshua was a practitioner of the occult.

Somehow, the walls were colored in black...covered in skins and skeletons. Ben lit the candles near the door, casting an eerie light on the rest of the small, cobwebbed room. Jars of dried herbs filled shelves upon the wall. Skulls lie piled in the corner. Dear merciful God in Heaven. There looked to be human skulls among them.

The evil one stared down at them from a painting upon the wall. A wash bin filled with red. Dear God. It was surely blood.

The fire. It came for her now. They must be of the Rosicrucian Order.

Her throat. The pressure. Ben's family. This was evil.

The hot sting of tears surprised her. "Ben, please, we shouldn't be here... we have to go." He stood beside the table, where a drawing of a five-pointed star adorned its surface. Charlotte noticed all color drain from Ben's face as his eyes darted wildly around the macabre scene before them. His hands trembled and slick sweat glistened on his brow as he struggled to make sense of it all.

"Charlotte. There are writings." He gestured to small scraps of paper, some half-burned, lying in a bowl. There were six papers, and scrawled upon each she saw:

The First, The Fool, The Harlot, The Enemy, The Lover, The Servant.

Ben fiddled with his hands. Uncomfortable. But she would be, too, if she had found out her aunt was a heretic. His mouth opened and closed wordlessly, no sound escaping as he desperately grasped for some explanation, for some reason this nightmarish altar didn't confirm his worst fears.

And on the candles, carved with a knife, she took in the sight of the names.

Gayle Williams. Elizabeth Franklin. *Priya Lanivet.*

"We must go to Constable Cobb. At once."

In a tumultuous surge, the weight of understanding crashed against her mind, leaving her reeling in its wake. Dear God. The prior room. Thousands of candles. Thousands of names. Thousands of murders—pray no.

The room spun, its edges darkened and swirled. What Hell of a home had he entered?

# Damsel Discovered

Charlotte broke the cold silence as they sat uncomfortably on the ride back to her house. "Haven't you anything to say?" She knew it wasn't fair, but anger filled her heart and she found that it was mostly toward him. He had brought her to that home. They were his family. For Ben to not know of his family's dalliances with the dark was an impossibility. He had to. Thank God Aunt Beth had missed their brunch. She wouldn't be able to look at that dark woman the same again.

She should have known at dinner when the devil entered their conversation.

Ben focused on her and sighed.

"I once knew a man who advised me to speak not but what may benefit others or yourself; avoid trifling conversation."

That did not settle her restless thoughts.

"It would benefit my soul to hear that you had no knowledge of Aunt Beth's consecrations with the devil."

Surely he did.

He turned to her. "I knew it not."

"But you had seen her paintings."

He shook his head. "Those were Uncle Edmund's."

"Oh, so the devil's work is a family affair then?"

Where the words came from, she wasn't aware. He surely heard the tremor in her voice.

He frowned and suddenly became interested in the floor of the chaise.

She knew she shouldn't be cross. He hadn't conjured anything or been anything but wonderful to her.

He loved her. Earlier this day he'd brought her bliss beyond all she'd ever known.

"I'm sorry." She scooted closer. "Seeing Priya's name among Gayle and Elizabeth, whom we both know to be murdered, has my heart torn to pieces." The tears threatened to well again. "She's gone."

Perhaps she felt guilt. Her friend was missing, almost certainly dead, and she was skipping about, headed to brunch and lying with a man in an apparent witch's mansion.

It was all so absurd.

She looked up at him with an unfamiliar fierce blaze stirring in her belly. "I'm afraid your aunt had something to do with Priya's death."

He sighed. "I admit that a room devoted to darkness unknown is worthy of suspicion...but just because she has the names of the victims written upon paper, does not mean she was the one to swing the ax." He pondered. "I'm not so sure that Aunt Beth could physically wield an axe anyway."

Charlotte stared at him. "But she can wield her words...and her wealth." She sighed. "She's clearly involved in witchcraft!"

Ben raised an eyebrow. "So, you think she's the grandmaster behind the slayings?"

"I'm merely suggesting it is a possibility." Charlotte gathered his fingers in hers. "You'll speak to the constable with me, won't you?"

He raised one hand and tucked stray strands of hair behind her ear. She loved when he stroked her cheek with his thumb. His touch brought with it a tingle to her skin.

"Of course I will." He moved in slowly. She braced, but instantly relaxed. This was her Ben. From now on and for always.

But Aunt Beth couldn't be ignored.

"Does anyone else in your family practice this witchcraft?" She thought of Sarah. And Samuel. They were strange.

He raised his eyebrows as if thinking of it for the first time. "If they did, that would be news to me. I can't imagine it though. Aunt B has always had a mysterious air about her...even when I was a child."

Charlotte pursed her lips. "Perhaps the constable will have news to share in the direction of justice?" Ben helped her step down out of the chaise. The ground was muddy, which was unsurprising considering the great storm that had passed.

Storms used to bring her darkness, but after today...

When her home came into view, Nelly swung open the front door and raced up the path towards them. She surely had only just made it home.

"Lottie! Darlin' yer Papa has gone to the Morris House. The constable's there. Go. Quick like. Amir sent word!"

Charlotte gasped. "Have they found her? Priya? Is she safe?"

"Go, child. Go now."

The keeper of the Morris House shuffled out from behind the front desk. The stench of him stifled her. She looked at Ben and saw his lips set to a thin line...he wasn't breathing.

The keeper licked his cracked lips and scratched his brow. Flakes of dead skin fell to his shoulders. "Good evening, Mr. Franklin." She watched as his eyes drank her in from boot to bodice, violating her. "...Miss Scott."

Ben grasped her hand in his. In public!

He gave a slight nod. "Ebenezer."

"What can I do for you and the misses?" He looked between them and down at their joined hands before cracking into a devious smile. "A room, then? How long will you be needin'?"

She noticed his gnarled hands reach for his belt. Bile rose in her throat.

"Ebenezer, that will be unnecessary. We've a need to speak with Constable Cobb, and had hoped to find him here." Ben produced two coins from his pocket, brandishing them at the keeper.

Ebenezer's eyes widened. "Yes sir." He shuffled past and beckoned them to follow. "Your Papa is here as well, Miss."

Ebenezer stopped outside of a first-floor room. "They're in here. Best to knock."

Ben flipped him the coins and turned to the door.

Knock. Knock. Knock. "Constable Cobb? Mr. Scott? Are you in there?"

She heard the shuffles behind the door.

"Oh thank Heavens! Oh good gracious. I thought—" Papa burst from the room and wrapped her in his arms. "Never mind what I thought. Where have you been?"

"Where have I been? Ben came to collect me for brunch, remember?"

Papa faltered. "Oh. Yes. Yes, that's right." He wiped the sweat from his brow.

Ben closed the door behind them. "What's going on here? What news of Priya?"

Constable Cobb gestured to the small reading chair. "I think it best you sit." He bit his lip, apprehension in his eyes. "There's something we must tell you."

Charlotte lowered into a chair. "There's something we need to tell you, too."

Papa rubbed a hand over his unshaven whiskers. "Lottie, they found Priya."

"She was here the whole time." Constable Cobb added in his stern, but slightly shaking voice.

All air escaped from her lungs. Ben raised his brow. "That's wonderful news! So, she only wished to hide...after what she went through...that's completely understandable."

But the two men weren't smiling.

Charlotte tensed. "Is she safe?" She searched their faces. Neither rejoiced. Neither moved.

Oh no.

"Papa." Her vision blurred. Ben stood behind and squeezed her shoulders.

"They found her body."

Here came the fire. Indistinguishable voices swirled around her.

"...so sorry"

"She didn't suffer—"

"Her parents—"

"Before anyone discovered her....it was the smell—"

Charlotte's soul was numb.

She couldn't wrap her mind around the broken bits of sound coming from Papa and the constable, as though accepting the truth would make it real.

She couldn't see.

Couldn't breathe.

There would be no climbing back out of the dark hole within which she fell.

"What of Delphia? And the mayor? Should not justice seek the souls responsible?" Ben held her now. She could feel his quickened breath.

"You know of Mayor Payne's power, Mr. Franklin." Constable Cobb paced back and forth within the room. "We've no solid proof that he committed this act, nor that Delphia pulled the strings either."

Strings.

"Bethshua." She whispered her name, hardly wishing to speak it.

"What was that, Lottie?"

Charlotte forced out the words. "Bethsua Franklin," her ember of anger was growing, "is a witch. She wrote down her name...all of their names. In candles." She opened her wet eyes to look at Ben.

His lips were tightly sealed.

"The names...of those...she's killed." Constable Cobb opened his notebook and scrawled. "You've seen these signs of witchcraft, have you?"

"No." Ben let her go. "We witnessed a hidden room in the home of the late Edmund Franklin...my uncle...but we didn't actively see Aunt B performing any witchery."

The constable nodded. "An audacious claim to make...'tis true."

Charlotte yelled. "She spoke of the devil! At dinner!" Her hands were shaking now. "She keeps artwork of the evil one in her home!"

"Again, Uncle Edmund's painting—" How dare he.

She fumed. "But those consulting with the devil cannot be ignored."

"I'm confused as to how Priya and the other murders are connected in all of this?" Papa sat in the other chair.

Charlotte focused her attention on him. Through gritted teeth she muttered, "And what of the Rosicrucian Order...Papa?"

The color drained from his face like blood from a stuck pig. He didn't answer.

Constable Cobb consulted his writings.

Finally, he spoke. "So far we have four deaths to account for."

Constable Cobb muttered again. "Gayle Williams. The generally well-liked baker with the nasty habit of trying to stick his cock where it didn't belong..." His cheeks flushed red as a pickled beet as he realized what he'd spoken out loud. "Apologies, ma'am."

Charlotte huffed. "It's all right. Please continue."

"Elizabeth Franklin. Wife to Thomas Franklin, the apothecary. Generous philanthropist and occasional midwife. Discovered in her own basement."

"Beth would have had access to the home." She wasn't going to drop it. She knew it in her heart. Beth was a Rosicrucian, probably a friend of Mother's, and she was responsible for these deaths. Ben passed her a withered look.

"Priya. Unmarried. Employed by Madame Delphia."

Curious. How the constable could have known that detail escaped her.

"...injured the mayor and was found dead at Morris House."

Those all make sense. Perhaps Elizabeth and Beth had a row, Gayle Williams tried to have sex with her, and she clearly didn't like Priya because of John.

"Yet Gayle Williams was killed with an ax." Ben started a pace of his own. The sound of his voice only deepened her rage. "There is more than one person at work here."

Charlotte threw up her hands. "Exactly! Mayor Payne, Bethshua Franklin, and somehow Delphia is involved. She's probably a witch herself! She knew about it at least." Charlotte wiped the remaining tears from her cheeks. "And Dirch!"

"Since they wouldn't want to get their hands dirty, no doubt they've hired help. A vagrant. A miscreant." Constable Cobb lifted a finger to his lips. "And among all of this...the crime scenes were clean. Save for bodily fluids discovered on Elizabeth."

"The what—" Papa gasped. Appalled. As was she.

Constable Cobb waved a dismissive hand. "Never mind the particulars, but I can assure you there was a man at her death."

Dear God.

Ben protested again, color rising in his cheeks with a hint of narrowed eyes. "Which couldn't have been Aunt B." Charlotte glared at him. He raised both hands as though it settled the matter.

She turned to the constable. "And what of Dirch?"

Constable Cobb fidgeted with his handkerchief. He took a deep breath before his response.

His attention flitted between them as he frowned.

"Dirch held the same markings as all that have been discovered. A cloven hoof. And Fire."

Papa furrowed his brow, placing his rough hands in his lap. "Go on..."

The constable continued, frowning. "I'm sorry to have accused you, Thaddeus, but seeing as he was on your property...an investigation had to be made."

Papa nodded. "Yet, you know I wouldn't have murdered sweet Priya."

The constable nodded. "Aye. I never honestly believed...you're a man of integrity, Thaddeus. Everyone knows that."

In an instant, the memory flooded back to her.

"In the witch's lair at Beth Franklin's house, we saw strips of paper that I imagine to be of importance. You said there were five deaths thus far...right?"

The constable nodded.

Charlotte continued. "There were six strips of paper. What if the killer, or killers, aren't choosing at random? What if they are trying to kill six people—for a reason?"

The constable nodded, scrawling in his notebook again. "Then we must prevent the sixth from happening."

"I'll call a meeting of the council." Papa squeezed her tight and headed for the door. "Ben, will you stay here for the meeting? I'd like your witness on the witchery you saw at your Aunt's house."

He turned back to face her. "Charlotte...dear one...do not visit that home again."

Charlotte nodded. She hadn't planned on it anyway. "But what of the mayor? We haven't ruled out his connection in this."

The constable answered. "We must all be careful. We present the facts—"

"But—"

"The facts, Lottie." Papa gazed at her, sorrow and sympathy swirling in his eyes. "We will bring justice, dear one."

"Then I'm staying too." She wouldn't hear it otherwise.

Papa raised his eyebrows. "You're sure about that?"

Her heart said yes. The moths in her stomach said no.

She steeled herself. "Unquestionably. None on the council can be trusted, in my opinion, save for Minister Horvath. This meeting will serve only to increase security in the streets."

Constable Cobb let out a slow breath. "We haven't enough proof to make any formal accusations or arrests of the perpetrators, but we do have enough cause to heighten the night watch on the streets. A killer of many is among us, thus, in this our darkest hour, we must keep a watchful eye."

# When the Council Calls

**M**essengers traveled far and wide across the town to assemble the pompous, macaroni men of the greater Philadelphia council. Money speaks, wealth whispers...and these men were all but silent. They were the great spiders lurking among the tangled political webs spanning Philadelphia and England. She felt these most recent victims were but flies snared in some of those very webs.

It could be witchcraft. The work of the devil. But the reasons behind it remained unknown, and yet she still wondered if their help would lead to any solutions.

Among the business owners and wealthy merchants that arrived, she felt a stillness of the heart upon seeing Minister Horvath. They needed God among them now, more than ever.

Did God frown upon her for her earlier fornications this day? In her heart, she was committed. Confused, what with his family and all, but committed. Ben sat with her in the lobby as the peacocks arrived in their carriages.

He took her hands in his. "Please take what I am about to say with good intention and know that behind it lies a kind and loving heart."

Oh dear. How quickly her ears could pound with blood rush. It would almost be astonishing if she weren't so familiar with the feeling.

"Go on, then."

"I caution you against making accusations against Aunt Beth."

Of course he did.

Breathe deep through the nose, out through the mouth.

Good intentions.

Good intentions.

But clearly Aunt Beth and whatever order she was involved in didn't have any good intentions.

"I understand that she is your aunt...and that we haven't yet witnessed her black magic...but suspicions need to be raised when persons have been murdered and she knew their names."

Ben opened his mouth, but she wasn't finished.

"How could she have known of Priya if not complicit in her death? Hmm?" Charlotte faced him with her hands upon her hips.

His lips closed, yet eyes widened.

"A fair point. You make a fair point, darling." He shifted to face her. "What I wish to express is...that we know there is wickedness about. Whether one or perhaps many are responsible, I want you to think about the men in that room."

He continued. "Governor Hellsmith...whom we know had something to do with the disappearance of your kin. Rufus Spencer...Delphia's husband," he looked at her pointedly, "surely that point is clear. I highly doubt the Mayor will be in attendance as he is still recovering. And then there's my father, the brother of your accused."

"But--"

"Charlotte, listen to me...hear me clearly. My Papa is close with Aunt B. They see each other nearly every day. I'm not saying we don't keep a watchful eye, and I'm not saying she isn't guilty of involvement. I would like to think if Papa suspected any wickedness from her, that he would come forth. I'm merely suggesting a delay in formal accusation—that's all."

She pursed her lips. They needed evidence.

"Surely your Papa wouldn't approve of such dalliances with the devil?"

He scowled. "Of course not. Papa is a Godly man."

"What of Minister Horvath? If she dances among the devil, she might command darkness we know not of...we may need his help for protection."

Dear God.

Her dreams, the shadows, the hooded figures.

Was this Bethshua Franklin? Come to claim her as the next prize? Best not to mention the dreams. She wasn't entirely convinced about what she saw anyway.

"I think it best we lay low. Gather evidence. Hear what the council has to say with the new information and work from there."

"But Papa called them here to specifically address your Aunt."

"No...they're discussing the two most recent murders...requesting an increase of the night watch."

"Papa wanted you to speak on it."

"And speak on it, I will—if so bid. I do not wish for you to become further involved and endanger yourself in this business. If Hellsmith and Rufus and Payne are to blame, then we do not need their view upon us."

His own eyes pleaded now. Perhaps he spoke with reason.

"I...understand your concerns."

"And you'll not draw attention?"

She sighed. "Nay. I will merely set the record straight on Priya's behalf if needed...and wait for proof from Bethshua. But know this—we must further investigate any and all connections they have to an order of magic I fear is among us." She grabbed his hands. "I think they had something to do with the death of my mother, too."

His lips thinned into that small smile she was sure was only for her. "Thank you, my love. My concern is for safety...there is evil among us. Investigate, we will."

The front door slammed open, and with it a roll of thunder reached her ears.

These storms were ever unrelenting in their presence. An ominous sign of

the times.

"Ahhh Benjamin! So nice of you to join us. What calls for an emergency meeting of the council with such little notice? Another murder?" Mr. Franklin senior stepped into the foyer flanked on either side by his sons, Thomas and Samuel. They must be permanent council members now.

"Hello Father. Indeed. Thaddeus Scott has called the council to discuss not one...but two additional murders. One discovered within the very building where we stand."

Samuel's mouth fell open and Mr. Franklin gasped. Thomas merely shuffled his feet and frowned as he looked at the ground.

Oh...that's right. He lost his Elizabeth.

The front door opened to reveal Minister Horvath, the kind but always sweaty man she hoped could bring peace among the council. However, if it were even possible, he was more unkempt than usual, wiping beads of sweat from his reddened face and forehead.

"Good Evening, Ms. Scott...gentlemen." He was breathless. And, astonishingly, smelled of ale.

Charlotte turned to him. "Minister, are you all right?" Something was terribly wrong with him.

His swollen fingers fumbled with his coat buttons. "Why yes...yes of course. I'm only...late. I apologize for being late."

Mr. Franklin and Ben shared a knowing look. The minister tried to walk past them, but stumbled a bit, burping and releasing flatulence with each step.

For shame.

"Where are the washrooms, pray tell?" He burped into his handkerchief.

"Up those stairs." The gruff voice that spoke behind her was startling, but she knew it. Ebenezer stalked behind, always creeping out of earshot. A chill ran down her spine.

Minister Horvath studied the stairs with increasingly bulging eyes, drunkenly calculating the effort they would require. Rubbing his eyes and staring at them again as though it would reduce their number.

It was no wonder, he had to weigh at least as much as a steer. She had always admired him, but his current demeanor of drunkenness was a shocking sight.

He waddled past the stairs in defeat, clinging to the wall.

Thomas rushed to him to lend a hand. "Horvath...are you...have you been drinking?"

"Nay...nay." He flailed about with one gigantic arm. "'Tis medicine! 'Tis only my med-cine."

Such a shocking display. Crushing disappointment wracked her soul. So much for the presence of God among them.

"I believe you may be mistaking the bottle for your medicine, Minister." Thomas gestured for Samuel to assist him, as he was struggling to keep Minister Horvath upright. "Let's get you to a chair, Minister. That's it. Easy does it."

They lowered him upon it with a hard thud. The way it groaned in protest made her question if it would contain his mass for long. His expression of gaseous fumes caused all in the room to cringe.

"Perhaps the piss can wait," he muttered.

Ben didn't care to hide his cringe. Charlotte didn't know how to feel. Minister Horvath was not who she thought.

Papa stood, calling for the attention of all collected. Edward Robinson, the greasy coroner, sat hunched in the corner. He hardly murmured much of anything, yet his watchful gaze still made her uncomfortable. Somehow he possessed a seat upon the council now.

"Two more murders have taken place as of today. My apprentice, Dirch Johnson, and the lovely Priya Lanivet, daughter of Captain Lanivet."

A wave of despair crashed around her again. Poor Priya. Her dearest friend.

Mr. Franklin gasped for the second time that evening. "Does John know? Someone has to tell John! I've not seen him in a fortnight."

John. She hadn't even considered him, as she was too absorbed in her personal grief and trials. For shame.

"We've sent a message to Priestly Manor, yes." Papa peered with unwavering focus upon Mr. Franklin. "Yet, Ms. Priya was staying here at the Morris House on your son Ben's dime—" all eyes turned to them, "as she was on the run."

She started. "Papa—"

Ben squeezed her hand and cleared his throat to address the wide-eyed men. "Miss Priya found herself within a situation she was unsure of how to continue. I offered her safety by covering the cost of her stay at this hotel. None were supposed to know she was here, and it was merely a temporary arrangement before she could settle her issues."

"A chivalrous act, then! Well done, my boy." An eternal optimist, Mr. Franklin was. His heart was kind...and for that she was thankful. Perhaps he didn't know about his sister after all.

"What complications could Ms. Priya possibly have, Thaddeus?" Rufus Spencer, Delphia's spindly husband, sat upright with his ginger hair and thin freckled face. A scowl was hidden under an obscene mustache and large nose. He crossed his legs and placed both hands on his knee. He looked the same as a Madame, lips pursed, daring their husband to speak against them. Macaroni indeed.

Papa knew. He knew better than to speak it out loud.

"I believe she might have run into trouble with some of the townsfolk."

Rufus sat back, a smirk resting upon his face. "Unfortunate, that is."

The bastard.

Stifling tension thickened the air and threatened to close Charlotte's throat. Surely one of them possessed a hand fan.

"Constable Cobb. I'd like to hear your take on the murders. What evidence has been gathered? What news do you have?" Thomas Franklin stood by the fireplace, eyebrows raised and eyes open wide. "Have you done anything at all to discover the one who murdered my wife, or the others?"

The constable looked up from his notebook, surveying the room. "Upon review of the circumstances surrounding four murders...I do believe Philadelphia is plagued by a killer of a serial nature. One that seeks to end for

no purpose, other than the act of demise itself." He stood and began to pace.

"Gayle Williams. The baker. Not altogether an unproblematic man, but certainly not a nuisance to the town. He took an axe to the head, under the cover of night." He placed one hand upon his chin, studying his notes. "I questioned if our killer was male or female. Considering the force used to split Mr. William's skull, it would most likely require the strength of a man."

She grimaced.

"Which brings us to the second victim, Elizabeth Franklin." All concentration flew to Thomas, who now stared indefinitely at the floor.

"Discovered by the servants in the basement of your home. Another nighttime intrusion. Taken whilst you slept." The constable lifted his eyes. "And yet you proclaim never to have heard a sound."

Mr. Franklin straightened in his chair. "Constable, I do hope you are not about to accuse a grief-stricken husband."

Thomas paled, his face a sickly shade of green. Tears filled his eyes.

The poor man.

Cobb raised his eyebrows, returning to his notes. "Nay. Nay. Merely making observations." He continued to pace. "Elizabeth had been drained. Emptied from lacerations at the wrists and the neck. Male fluids were found upon her."

It was then that Thomas vomited.

"Good God! Samuel, he doesn't need to hear this. Help your brother into the hall, please." Mr. Franklin was frantic now.

The sullen Samuel rose without a word. He caught her eye before assisting Thomas out the door. Something was off about him. She remembered the market.

Constable Cobb continued. "The third discovery came at the hospital. Dirch Johnson. Former apprentice to wheelwright Thaddeus Scott."

Papa sat in silence.

"Death by catheter of a new design."

Edward Robinson broke his suffocating stare from her long enough to add, "an unusual, intriguing method of death, that one was…filled the bladder to bursting. They did it well."

The constable raised his eyebrows yet again, scrawling away in his notepad. "And the fourth death, Miss Priya Lanivet. Beaten, multiple wounds from a blade, blood loss—"

Charlotte rose. "Priya was beaten before she arrived at the Morris House." Ben squeezed her hand. Harder this time. But she wouldn't stay silent.

Minister Horvath's booming snore echoed from the corner.

Governor Hellsmith, a silent statue up to this point, cleared his throat. "The condition she arrived in is unrelated to her death, I would wager."

Papa stood now. Oh dear.

"And how could you figure that? Does it not seem suspect that she was beaten nearly to death and then brutally murdered? Have you no sense at all or do you choose to ignore the facts in front of you, Hellsmith?"

Hellsmith's demeanor darkened. "Watch yourself, Thaddeus."

Rufus Spencer uncrossed his legs. "The troubles of a harlot are no cause for investigation. She probably had a rough customer."

She wouldn't allow this. "Priya was no whore!"

Governor Hellsmith slams his fist on the table, causing her to jump. "Mind your tongue, girl, lest it be removed," he growled.

Ben grabbed her arm. "It's time to go."

"I beg your pardon, Governor. Why don't you tell the council exactly why Ms. Priya arrived at the Morris House beaten…hmmm?" Papa's face was red and he spit when he spoke. His rage was clear. "And while we're at it…YOU, Mr. Franklin, can enlighten us as to why your sister dabbles in witchcraft and has the names of the dead written in her home."

Charlotte froze.

Mr. Franklin sat in shock, his face draining of all color.

Papa continued. "Did you know that your sister dances with the devil?"

Mr. Franklin spluttered. "Beth? I know her to be of eclectic interests... but...

witchcraft...say no. It is an impossibility. But how?"

Whispers broke out across the room.

"She attends the Sabbath...witches couldn't do that."

"Surely not Bethshua—"

"That is of serious concern—"

"The night watch—"

"The children—"

Constable Cobb rose again, calling attention to the room. Hellsmith stared at Papa with daggers in his eyes.

The constable spoke. "The one we seek prolonged their deaths. Yet...even with the amount of blood found at each scene, there were no footprints, no evidence, no trace of whom it could be."

"Witchcraft!"

"An experienced killer, perhaps?" Charlotte turned to the familiar voice. John Priestly had entered the room. His eyes were red and wet, his face unshaven. He was the very opposite of the dapper gentleman she had seen across the town square not that long ago.

The constable continued. "The killer we seek is male. Of that, I am certain. I suggest an increase to the night watch, posted along as many streets as possible surrounding the town proper. I will formally question a list of suspects—" he glanced at Papa, who still breathed heavily, "Bethshua Franklin included."

All eyes across the room widened. Her heart would surely burst from her chest. Ben guided her toward the door.

"Dancing with the devil is a sin that cannot be ignored." The drunken minister had awoken. "If there be a witch among us, I would wager any involvement in the murders to be true. You say she knew the names of the deceased?"

Papa spoke yet again. "Yes. Prior to public knowledge."

"And how did you learn of this, pray tell?" Mr. Franklin had so many questions behind his eyes.

Papa's gaze flitted to her. "I—"

Ben gently pushed her forward and the door closed behind them. She could not hear what Papa explained.

She whirled to face him. "We must go back in. Papa is alone."

Ben brushed a curl from her face, caressing her cheek as he spoke. "There are many other council members that came today with sense about them. They will listen. You heard the constable...he will interview Aunt Beth and find out what is truly going on." He wrapped his arms around her. "My concern is for you."

Charlotte pulled away. "I'm fine."

"You're playing with fire here...dangerous fire, and I don't wish to see either of us get burned." She stared into his piercing grey eyes. He spoke again. "My chaise is outside. The driver awaits. Let me take you home."

"But Papa..."

"He's a grown man, love. He knows what he is doing."

"I'll not leave without him." He stared at her with sadness in his eyes.

Ben sighed. "What if I stay?" Well. That was an idea.

"Take my carriage, and I'll return to the meeting and stand with Thaddeus. My Papa will have plenty of room for us to ride home with him in our family carriage." He stared into her soul. "Does that settle it?"

Charlotte hesitated, then leaned up to kiss him. "Yes. My heart is settled. Thank you."

# When Lightning Strikes

*"Down the path, alone he went followed by one of pernicious intent"*
-Martha Careful

Thunder boomed; a harbinger of the coming storm as a jagged crack of lightning arced like tendrils of an undead god. It sundered the sky and illuminated a tree which had served as a gallows not so many years past. In simpler times, remnants of simpler, darker ages. It was a fitting place for this one's end.

Rough wind battered his face and billowed his crimson cloak. Rain would soon follow, though it would do nothing to wash away tonight's heinous sins. The night was black as coal ash, hiding his deeds from even the most persistent of eyes. Lightning would be welcome, even necessary, to fuel the carnage to come.

There, just ahead, he spotted a cloak held close around the form of his enemy. The enemy required a sacrifice. The man in the crimson cloak quickened his pace, like a wolf stalking a lost sheep. His pack supported him in spirit only, from the comfort of their homes.

This night, he would exact judgment. Judge, jury, and executioner, he would take the life of one who would bring them harm. This death would serve a series of purposes, to send a message to any who would stand against their will, to fulfill a necessary aspect of the grisly ritual, and to shatter the last

line of defense on the way to his true prize. But, most importantly, it would slake his newfound thirst for blood.

He needn't bother with stealth as the storm would mute all else. No sound of footsteps to give him away. Darkness would shroud his path from the forest to his prey. Licking his teeth, he felt every inch an apex predator and grinned wickedly.

Staring from between the weep of an ancient willow, he sent a black prayer of thanks to the fallen angel who'd been given dominion over the Earth. Surely it was he who'd sent the tempest this night. Perhaps they had turned the prey's footsteps away from safety, too. Instead, the enemy neared the tree which would serve as his cross, just beyond the outskirts of town, far away from any brave enough to patrol.

There was no god in Philadelphia, not anymore.

This petulant fool would have no cover, none to come to his aid, and no hope of escape. It wasn't sporting, but the man in the crimson cloak had never been one to adhere to candor. At this late stage in the wicked game, any advantage was fair play. Love and war be damned, this was the cycle of life and death.

The club was an uninspiring, simple tool, yet it remained just as effective. If given the chance to fight, his prey might struggle. Regardless of age, the enemy had the strength of an honest man's hard work and that was something he had no desire to test. The man in the crimson cloak would need his own strength for dragging the man up the hill.

In the scriptures, their precious savior had two thieves to share his final moments with, but this one would have no such comfort. His last act would be no parable of grace and forgiveness. The man would die surrounded only by laughter; without a single friend. He would know pain beyond pain as he gazed into the eyes of one he'd once trusted.

Rushing from the forest without a drop of hesitation, the man in the crimson cloak brought the club to the back of his skull without the force to kill. As expected, the enemy crumpled. It took every ounce of self-control to not bludgeon this one's face to an unrecognizable paste. No, what sweet cruelties the next minutes held would be far more satisfying.

Wrapping his head in burlap and binding the wrists, the man in the crimson cloak hauled the body upward with surprising ease. Adrenaline throbbed through his being along with lust for slaughter even as icy needles stabbed his flesh.

Atop the hill, the lone tree waited for them. Its dead, gnarled branches looking every bit a twisted crucifix. It was a mockery of this man's misguided faith. Where was his god now? The shepherd, the lord of love, the bastard who watched without care as his flock died every day without lifting a finger. He had never provided protection, not even for his own son. Such nonsense.

Even as he worked, he was proud of the elegance in simple form.

This man was far too large to lift alone, outweighing him by fifty pounds or more, yet, with a simple double pulley, woven between the two branches, he managed to haul his enemy into the air, bound upside down against two planks of thin cedar in the form of an inverted cross. Wind sent him swaying.

Lightning, followed by thunder, marked the moment his enemy woke. Realizing his predicament, he struggled and groaned. Yet, the knots were tight and the rope strong.

The enemy yelled. Muffled. "Untie me, you bastard! Show yourself!"

He would, of course, in due time. For the moment, he was content to relish in the cries as the last necessary steps were completed. Thin strips of wood wound with copper, lashed to the four corners of a large silken handkerchief to form a kite. To that he attached a single strand of unbraided cord.

But something was missing. The tail. It was necessary for stability.

Damn. He must have forgotten it. He tore a strip from the enemy's shirt.

"Reveal yourself, coward! Face me as a man!" the enemy growled.

Even in this lowly state, the man had bravado.

The man in the crimson cloak obliged, jerking away the burlap and squatting, eye level, with his prisoner. His enemy. Their enemy.

Thaddeus Scott.

The outraged look of shock and betrayal was worth every moment of effort.

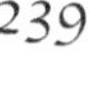

Twisting the bracelet idly between thumb and forefinger, he placed it on Mr. Scott's wrist with the string tied to it.

"You recognize this, yes? Your whore witch of a wife wore it as she died. I thought you'd like to have it back." The man in the crimson cloak chuckled.

The enemy's mouth opened, vulgarities that spewed forth unheard, whipped away by the wind.

In the maelstrom, it took no more effort to control the kite than to get it airborne, even in the pounding rain. But, once flying, it whipped about of its own accord.

He ceased in struggle for only a moment before screaming, "How dare you hold that which is hers? You unimaginable BASTARD! You cowardice, lobcock, unlicked cub! So help me, GOD I will see you burn in HELL!"

"They gave it to me. Thought it might be of some use. And tonight...it shall be."

Thaddeus spat in his face. Incredible, considering the rain.

He'd been correct to avoid direct conflict with this man.

Lightning cracked again. He backed away, confident this would work. The wind whistled, but broke long enough to be heard.

The man in the crimson cloak leaned close. "You should have taken the Franklin carriage home. Your poor choice led you to this end. Unaccompanied. In the dark." He snorted. "With a killer on the loose! Your intuition wanes in your elderly state."

Electricity danced above them in the clouds. The rain slowed, yet the wind remained fierce.

He needed the wind. "Just the same as how your debts led to the demise of another."

Thaddeus fought hard, limbs likely numb without proper blood flow. He screamed and sobbed while thrashing. Right about now, his enemy realized that this would be his last storm.

The man in the crimson cloak doubled over with laughter, even as he moved to a safe distance. "Give your wife our regards, Thaddeus!"

A streak of salvation split the darkened sky. A singular bolt collided with the kite and ran its length toward the enemy. An explosion of light cleaved the mangled tree in two with a deafening crack and the smell of charred flesh. The figure convulsed before slumping.

Thaddeus Scott dangled on the inverted cross, silent and smoldering, swinging with the wind.

This enemy would trouble them no more.

# Goodbye, Ben Franklin

The silky, white gloves had always been uncomfortable. Fitted snug to her hands, the first set had reminded her of Mother.

But now Charlotte had a matching set.

Two pairs of gloves. Two parents. Two beloved souls taken from this earth too soon.

They were gone.

Murdered.

The warm autumn sun did nothing for her. Inside, an icy cold had taken hold. Inside, she too, was dead. Nelly clutched at her hands. Charlotte wasn't sure who was holding up whom at this point. The act of standing at the graveside took more effort than she thought she could muster. John Priestly stood to the other side of Nelly, his head bowed low.

It might be nice to lay in the grave with them.

To rest.

To end.

"But our commonwealth is in heaven, and from it we await a Savior, the Lord Jesus Christ, who will change our lowly body to be like his glorious body, by the power which enables him even to subject all things to himself."

She couldn't look at Minister Horvath. She couldn't look at any of them. Ben stood by her side, stoic and somber. The songs, the scripture, the lowering of Papa into the ground; it all seemed a nightmare she would never wake from.

As the small crowd dispersed, patting her shoulder and touching her hand as they went, still she stared at the grave.

Whoever had done this remained a mystery. But in her heart, she knew. The Rosicrucian witches had surely struck again.

Ben leaned over and whispered in her ear, "The Lord is close to the brokenhearted and saves those who are crushed in spirit." He wrapped his arms around her. She couldn't lift hers in return.

She thought of the council. The Governor. The mayor. Bethshua.

The killers walked among them, yet none that could act took a serious interest in catching them. Constable Cobb was a fool. Hellsmith came for her Papa and somehow Bethshua Franklin was involved.

Charlotte whispered, "Ben. I can't do this."

He turned to her. "Yes, you can. You've been through it before. You've got Nelly and me, and my family will welcome you with more than open arms."

"Your family?" The jolt in her stomach was the first feeling she'd had in days. Since the night they knocked on the door to tell her about Papa and the tree, she remained unchanged.

When they took her to him.

And his flesh. And the smell.

At first she couldn't believe it.

Not Papa. Not her rock. It couldn't be. But now, with the jolt in her belly she started to feel again...and the feeling wasn't pleasant.

"Well. Yes. You and I are one now. You are my family." Even his penetrating stare couldn't seem to bring her warmth.

"Your family," she scoffed. "Your privileged, macaroni family sitting on their high horses on Society Hill?" Charlotte wrenched away from him. "They gallivant about in the largest carriages in town, never having known a struggle. And some keep company with the devil! Through whoring and witchcraft and God only knows what else."

Ben tilted his head, the skin creased around his eyes. "My darling, that's not fair." He reached to grasp her hands yet she pulled them away. "I can't fathom how you're feeling. Your mother...Priya...Thaddeus...it's not fair. It's unquestionably a horrific and tragic chain of events that should never have come to pass." He looked at her with anguish in his eyes.

It was difficult to swallow. How dare he. He didn't know pain. He didn't know suffering. How could he help her?

Rage boiled within her. "You DON'T KNOW!" Everything spun now. In the farthest corners of her mind, much deeper than the anger she now felt, she knew he wanted to help. But she didn't want his help. She didn't want his presence. At this moment, she didn't want him.

Charlotte wanted to be left alone.

The grass of the graveyard still held the morning dew. She trudged through it. Heading somewhere. Heading nowhere.

"Charlotte! You can't leave!" Ben's strides were much longer than hers...he made it to her in hardly three steps.

She wrenched from his grasp again. "Let me be!" She spat the words as a striking serpent.

The words were bitter upon her tongue.

It was then that she saw her.

A specter appeared, dressed in clothing so black it seemed to draw in the pale light, as if it were more of an absence of color. Full veil to the ground, the mysterious woman who plagued her stood beside a dark, painted carriage with beveled glass windows. Even now Charlotte could appreciate the delicate wood carvings that adorned the sides. At the rear, the carriage had a place for her footman, also dressed from head to toe in coal-black cloth.

The carriage door opened. With gnarled hands, not unlike claws, the woman beckoned like death itself. The carriage beyond may have been a death carriage for all the promise it held.

Ben shouted. "Charlotte...NO! Do not get in that carriage! What are you thinking, my love? Has grief stolen your reason?" Ben clutched at his sandy

brown hair, his perfect, chiseled jaw clenched tight.

But wait. Death could not be so lovely. 'Twas not twisted fingers, but a trick of the sunlight.

It didn't matter. She could not summon a care. Death. Life. Either would do. At this moment, dying shared the same draw as an embrace from the departed. Perhaps, if death did indeed claim her this morning, she would again share an embrace with Mother and Papa. Nelly would be left alone, but she would manage.

She whirled around to meet his eyes. "I'm going."

He clenched his hands, as if in prayer. "I beg of you not to."

Charlotte turned and strode toward Death's carriage. "Goodbye, Ben Franklin."

# Familiar and Forgotten

When the door of the blackened carriage closed behind her, the sudden, crushing realization of what she had done knocked the breath from Charlotte's chest. Her cheeks flushed, a bead of sweat dripping down her brow. The crook between her ears and throat was as tight as it had ever been.

Breathe.

Don't cry.

Just breathe.

Sitting across from her in the carriage, she could finally see the weathered face of the woman behind the veil. As they sat in close proximity, an unaccountable shift occurred within her, inexplicably dissolving any remnants of fear. Minimal harm could befall a walking corpse. Death had claimed her family, and now called to her.

The woman lifted her veil. Violet eyes stared at her, framed by wrinkles and a soft expression.

Violet eyes.

Charlotte whispered. "Have you sharpened thy scythe for me? Have you come to carry me to what lies beyond? I hang in the veil betwixt life and death." She sighed. "Shepherd my soul as you will."

But wait, she'd seen these eyes before.

The elderly woman smiled. "Have you put it together, dear child?"

247

The whispers. This voice.

She knew it.

Charlotte concentrated, desperately clawing back into her memories and tried to recall. This was not Death, but one met in life. Charlotte didn't recognize her face, but that wasn't a surprise since it was covered in scars. Deep gashes stretched across the beautiful face of someone she had met before. It was long healed, but the grisly image still shocked her.

"You've grown into a beautiful woman, Lottie." The carriage jostled along the path, the path to the house with the flower gardens, no doubt.

"You've a sharp mind as well." The woman coughed, the raspy voice reminding her of each time she ran. Ran from death. Ran from the unknown.

But now, Charlotte was done running.

"I know you—" She was sure of it. She knew those violet eyes.

"Yes, child. You do." Sunlight poured across her scarred face as she peered out the window. "Or rather...you once knew me."

"You knew my mother—"

Could this be, surely not.

She noticed the ring set upon the woman's wrinkled hand. A red ruby, cut into the shape of a rose.

The sight of the ring induced sudden flashes of memories long forgotten. A childhood she'd repressed.

The rose garden. The cross. Her mother. Their family.

She remembered the fireplace at Christmas and the long white veil of a beautiful new bride with violet eyes.

She stood beside Mother, looking up at the bride. She leaned around her to see the face of the dashing young groom.

Dear God.

The groom was Governor Hellsmith.

A jolt of the carriage slammed her back to reality. To the realization that while she had lost one family member this day, she now gained another. The

woman in black, with the golden rose ring—was Mother's sister, Abitha.

But the Rosicrucians were evil. They dabbled in witchcraft.

Emotion welled within, threatening to leak from the corners of her eyes. This could not be. She had been there all this time.

Something had prevented her aunt from stepping out of the shadows.

Abitha smiled at her, the delicate black lace of her dress in such stark contrast to the white funeral gloves placed gracefully in her lap. She didn't wear them.

"You came to honor Papa." She reached out to grasp hands.

"Yes, yes I did. I was hoping to finally catch a word with you, as each time you've seen me you were taken by fear."

"But the voices. The whispers. You said my name. They were in my head."

"I needed a little help with such a raspy voice, dear one."

Dear one. Charlotte's heart faltered.

"But how could you do that? I've so much to ask." She took in the silver wisps of hair playing about Abitha's scars. "What happened to you?"

"'Tis a chilling tale best served with something warm, I believe." The carriage stopped at the iron gate of the once beautiful manor. "Come inside, dear. Warmed chocolate should suffice."

She thought of the children...of the readings at the library. Of late, she'd hardly seen them at all, and oh how she missed their smiling faces. And now she might never see them again, for she was in the presence of a witch.

The cool Autumn breeze prickled the hairs on the back of her neck. Answers waited behind the tattered manor door. Emotions. Feelings. Her will to live sparked anew. As wine red and burnt orange leaves drifted lazily to the ground, she floated as one of them among the breeze. Perhaps Abitha held the words that could help restore her soul and provide her with answers.

"Yes." Charlotte hardly recognized her own monotone voice. "I think that would be lovely."

***

"Some say that in life, we are bestowed with hidden gifts that enable us to improve our powers of visualization and concentration in order to manifest the life we truly desire. The life that we deserve. That we, as humans, are able to beseech the great powers of the universe through karma, focused thought, and guiding principles to enact our dreams into our current reality," Abitha said.

The faintest memory tickled the back of Charlotte's mind. "Sky above me, earth below me, fire within me." It was a phrase Mother had taught her as a young girl.

Abitha smiled. The sight of it settled her fears and spread warmth through her body as swiftly as the warmed chocolate treat.

"Exactly that, my child. The key to all mysteries and source of illumination lies deep within the self." With a faint clink, Abitha set her teacup upon the grand marble table in the parlour room where they sat. She thought back to the countless times she had passed this darkened home and thought it mostly vacant, and stifled her shock at seeing each attendant as they passed. All were dressed in fine clothing and smiled as they went about their day.

Charlotte's breath caught at the sight of a portrait's painted eyes following her every move, the stern patriarch's gaze cold and unsettling. This wasn't a dark place at all, but still, she felt as if it might be a prison.

This home, which appeared dilapidated on the outside, was curiously filled with the finest ornate furnishings she'd ever seen, even among the Society Hill homes. The musty scent of aged wood and faded velvet wafted over Charlotte as she stepped across the threshold, a stark contrast to the manor's crumbling exterior. Charlotte jumped at an ominous creaking sound from overhead, her eyes darting upwards to find a crystal chandelier swaying ever so slightly, its candles unlit. This was impossible.

"Catherine and I—"

The chocolate in her cup rippled ever so slightly from her shaking hands. None had spoken Mother's name around her in far too long. Abitha paused. She must have noticed her reaction.

"—were raised to follow the Rosicrucian Code of Life. It is a constant endeavor to awaken and express the virtues of the soul that animates you. A

mental, physical, mystical, and spiritual awakening, as it were.”

“But what of God? Surely this is witchcraft. I found Mugwort and relics among Mother’s belongings.” She pondered her upbringing. “The earliest memories I have surround the Sabbath with Mother and Papa. Did she forsake one faith for another?”

Abitha smiled. “Oh no, dear one. The Rosicrucian way of life encourages one to thank the God of their heart each day, requiring no one religion. It encourages a deeper connection to the higher intelligence of your religion of choice, if any. Your Papa, a devout Quaker, if I do recall correctly, appreciated the passion your mother exuded for life. Her endless quest for knowledge. He appreciated her fire and supported her in all endeavors—even if he didn’t fully grasp or take heed of most Rosicrucian teachings.”

“So...it isn’t witchcraft?” Charlotte trembled as she spoke.

Abitha shook her head and smiled. “Nay, child. Perhaps the most devout would view it as so, but the Rosicrucian way offers only peace and enlightenment.”

Charlotte hadn’t expected this type of conversation, but was taken with curiosity.

“And Hellsmith? He, too, followed this spiritual path with you?”

Abitha’s violet eyes flashed.

“Unfortunately, my child, that is what I wish to warn you about.” She stared into the distance, as if remembering a dream. “When Samuel and I courted, I learned of his upbringing in the Rosicrucian Order as well. We shared a common vision. Together we discussed the meaning of life and all the ways we could work to improve it—for us and for the greater good of mankind, serving our fellow neighbor.” She cast her gaze to the floor. “Those first few months were wonderful. Blissful, in fact.”

Charlotte nodded. “But then something changed?”

Abitha met her with a grim stare. “Yes. At one time, his goal of perfecting one’s self was accomplished through good works and service, his tongue untouched with hate or the vile speeches of power. You see, shortly after we married, Samuel positioned himself as the Mayor of Philadelphia. Well-suited

for the role at the time, he was kind, forgiving, and an honest and just man with the well-being of the town consuming his thoughts."

Abitha sighed. "Yet, the lust for power became too great. And that...was when his countenance changed."

Abitha pulled at the sleeve of her black lace dress to reveal scars similar to her face, but covering her arms.

"His fingers dug deep each time I displeased him. No warning. No whiskey under his breath." She snatched the sleeves down. "As his position rose, so did his anger at my lack of enthusiasm. I never wanted to rise by stepping upon what he considered a 'lesser' person, and anyone that wasn't him resided in that 'lesser' camp."

Abitha continued. "He grew hungry with power-lust. He was plagued with an insatiable thirst for control, lording over the town and most of all myself, his unwaveringly devoted wife."

Abitha sat on the lounge beside her, cupping her thin, wrinkled hands around her own.

"Wealth...Power...Success...it changes people. Samuel no longer wished to follow any Rosicrucian teachings as they were too 'binding,' as he saw it. Thus, he broke from our order and began a quest into the darker side of occultism."

A single tear fell from Abitha's eye.

"When I wouldn't join him, the threats against my life began. 'A cleansing' he had called it. And anyone who got in his way would suffer the same fate."

The warmth from the chocolate was all but gone now. Charlotte whispered. "And Mother?"

Abitha squeezed her hands. "Now, I have no proof. But the day he gave me this—" she traced a finger along the gash upon her face, "is the same day he discovered Catherine helping me pack my belongings to leave. And your Papa owed him coin."

Charlotte was shaking now, anger rolling within. "I've always known that evil surrounded him, I felt it."

Abitha looked at her knowingly. "It's your spirit guides, child. They've

warned you away. And best to heed them, and stay far from those that reside on the hill, as well."

Charlotte paused. "Are there others?"

"Nay, I cannot know," Abitha said. "But when one holds as much power as he now does...you can be sure that his reach is long and his influence wide. I firmly believe he was responsible for the murders of Philadelphia that claimed sweet Catherine, and now I fear he has risen to cleanse the city once more."

And while her words still lingered in the air, together they sat in silence.

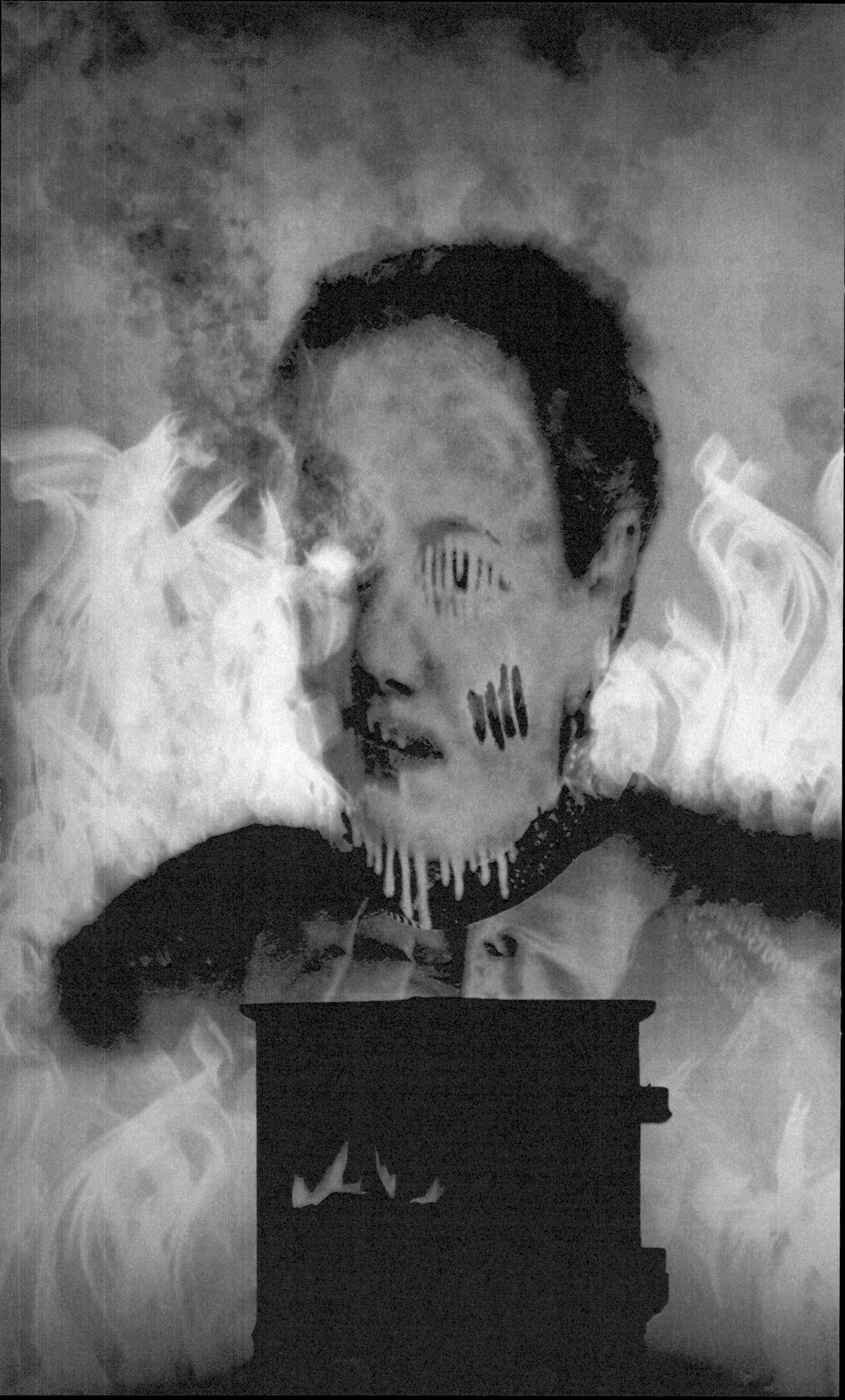

# Kiss the Flame

*"The servant's last, her life burned bright*
*T'was death by fire that blazed this night"*

-Timothy Turnstone

Since the dawn of life, death saunters toward us as a seductress on the prowl. It is an inescapable resolution to the human experience of this realm, but death is not the end. Nay. To pause the journey of the soul as it carries along an earthly corpse is but another step into the beyond. The man in the crimson cloak had once feared god...the wrath... the rules...the restraint one must have to cage the free-reign of their darkest desires. Yet, that fear was no more.

He was his own god now, in service to another, and today he would claim flesh yet again in order to earn what was owed. The frayed rope of time narrowed to a mere thread, and he intended to sever it promptly. The sun lowered, spreading a coruscating crimson hue across the horizon.

Much the same as he spilled blood.

He wondered if the evening would turn into a bloody affair. He hadn't brought any weapons, preferring instead to utilize what could be found at their home. When, yet again, he was provided with a quick opportunity to further meet his goal—he had to rise up and take it. While his work demanded quick and decisive action, choosing the proper moment held great significance. As with the baker, moving with haste would be careless in nature and could spoil the element of surprise.

255

Besides, the excitement of observation now thrilled him, witnessing their final moments from afar. To know that their life, their fragile existence among men, would soon, by his hand, be no more.

In her sorrow, the one he sought had turned to that which she held dear...their family books. Still clothed in her bereavement dress, her face was illuminated by the flickers of fire light. He could clearly see her tears as they dropped upon each page. Pages she and Thaddeus Scott had no doubt read together.

Such an interesting pair. Was it abuse of power? Perhaps her intention was to elevate her status after the death of his wife. Perhaps it was true love. But for him, today was a gift. He would be one step closer to earning his desires and further discovering his darkness, and she would be reunited with her love in whatever Heaven she believed in.

Alas. None of that mattered. He would spend eternity among those he preferred to keep company with, those that protected him, and he didn't get the feeling that their Heaven was that place.

Her face was to the fire, her back toward the door. He was a hawk in the tree, waiting to capture its mouse.

Nelly turned, wiping her bleary eyes on the fine black silk she had worn to the funeral. It was a mistake on her part, as the shielding of her view provided the perfect opportunity for him to slip inside unnoticed. Her sobs covered the creak of the door; her sharp breaths disguised his footsteps as he drew near.

She heaved and sobbed, blowing into her black lace handkerchief. Most likely this was the finest outfit she had ever owned.

He spotted her rolling pin on the table and grabbed it. The tool of a servant...what a fitting end for Miss Nelly, the servant.

He was a demon in the night, coming to claim this soul for his own. Another death to satiate them. Only the steady war drum of his own heated blood pounded in his ears. He was behind her in an instant.

Nelly's skull cracked from the blow and she swooned, hardly able to keep her legs. The stark view of recognition clouded her gaze and he saw a flash of anger in her eyes.

She was no frail bird to die so easily. She was strong. Defiant.

He liked a bit of a challenge. It excited him.

Aroused him.

He wrenched her back by the base of the neck, raising the pin high yet again and prepared it for a secondary blow. Then, the warmth of the fire washed over him.

The stove.

It was of new design, a freestanding, cast iron fireplace.

The fire roared within. Cracking fingers of flame beckoned him forward. They licked the edges of the stove.

It was perfect.

He forced her head down to the flames. She was but a foot from the openings. The aroma of singed hair filled the kitchen.

From behind, with her in such a posture, rounded rump in the air, his breeches tightened.

Such power was intoxicating.

Exhilarating.

He drank in the essence of sin and reveled in it.

It would be little effort to throw back her dress and petticoat. He could be inside her in a matter of moments...but alas, there was no time to enjoy forced penetration this night.

Still, he took note for future pleasures, burning the image into his mind.

It took but a single hard shove, unbalanced and addled as she was from the crack of the pin. Her head and shoulders went into the stove and she shrieked in delicious horror.

Cruel fate had its way with her then. Her thrashing thrilled him.

Nelly scrambled back, but he forced her inside once more. She fought, strength dissipating as her head burned alive. Her screams were invigorating.

The charring flesh on her head reminded him of roasted pork.

The curves of her figure as she fought while he held her there sent a pulse through him.

The fire had spread, but her dress only smoldered past the shoulders.

Her rump presented, still fresh.

It is impossible with two women to know an old one from a young one. In the dark, all cats are grey, thus the pleasure of corporeal enjoyment with an elderly, wrinkled woman is at least equal, and frequently superior, to that of the young. Every well-enjoyed crevice of an old woman is ready to accept a man yet again.

He'd had women older than her, but her efforts in life had kept her figure better than most.

The fire enveloped her torso now. He grasped her arms and pushed her deeper into the flames.

Gods be damned. He would have his way. And after, he would leave the body to burn.

# *Philadelphia on Fire*

Fog floated among the rose bushes of the garden in her dreams like a doused fire. It was at Abitha's where she had laid her head to rest, but even as she stepped among the path, Charlotte knew what was coming. Who she would see.

For it was in her dreams that she often met the shadow of Mother.

Some say that every guilt, every shame, every sinful piece of ourselves that we cast into the abyss of our soul resurrects within the deepest, darkest corners. These shadows, if given the opportunity, can appear with maleficent intentions.

There she was. Fiery curls spilled down the back of her white silk dress. They shifted in the wind ever so slightly. She was twenty paces away, but every step brought with it dread.

This wasn't Mother. This was a shadow. And being awake within her dream, she knew it.

She gingerly stepped forward.

Closer.

Closer.

Mother spun around, only to reveal an inky velvet visard mask, covering her face in the sun. Charlotte's breath caught within her chest. Typically, visards allowed for the wearer to see, through two holes for the eyes and one for the mouth.

She wouldn't be able to speak, as the mask was held within the mouth by a single bead.

Charlotte...

Oh dear.

Her pounding heart encouraged the rush about her ears. Her throat was filled with the ever so familiar fire. Mother was within inches now. Her outstretched hand trembled as she reached to remove the mask.

Her fingers closed around it; the cloth was slick. Wet.

Dear God.

Beneath the mask, the sunken sockets of Mother's gouged eyes pooled with blood.

***

BANG. BANG. BANG.

She awoke with a start. Judging by Abitha's darkened abode, night had fallen. She wasn't sure how long she had slept, but it must have been quite some time.

Odd. Her nose tickled with the faintest smell of smoke.

BANG. BANG.

"This is Constable Richard Cobb. I am searching for Charlotte Scott and need to see her at once!"

She knew not the hour, but none went to answer the door, so she hurriedly rose from the sofa and opened it herself.

She peered outside. "Hello?"

"Charlotte! Oh thank God! Mr. Franklin seemed to think you were here, but we couldn't be sure. We thought—" He stood breathless on the doorstep, covered in sweat.

She took in his clothes, drenched in sweat. "Constable...did you run here?"

He nodded, gasping for air. "I came swiftly. Yes. The others are back at

your house."

Charlotte froze. "My house? Who's at my house? What's going on?" The smoke was thicker outside. Her vision stung from its presence.

"I think it's best you come with me." Constable Cobb held out his hand to her.

"RICHARD. On this, the eve of my Papa's burial service, I demand you explain yourself. Why is there a gathering at my home?"

He looked at her with pleading eyes. "Charlotte. It's on fire."

***

The ring of the fire bell met her ears long before she could see the flames. A rampage of billowing smoke from her childhood home fogged the air and burned her eyes. This could not be. She ran with Richard, closer and closer until the sight of menacing flames were within her view.

A long line of men was stationed from the creek in the forest up to the edges of their property. They had established a bucket brigade, water sloshing from the leather satchels with each pass toward her home.

Through the smoke and dark of night she could hardly make out the faces of those who desperately tried to tame the flames, but it was too late. Towering flames licked at the night sky as they engulfed the entirety of her refuge.

The men standing by the charred front door were frantically yelling for more water. They held soaked cloths to cover their noses. Another stood to the side nursing what looked to be burnt flesh.

Grab the trough from the garden!

There's no use! The house is taken!

The effort to stand was too much. Too great. The weight of this day consumed her.

Perhaps she could summon the strength to meet death at its glorious doorstep. What little resilience for life she had reclaimed in conversation with Abitha had all but disappeared.

Mother...murdered.

Priya...taken.

Papa...gone.

She could reunite with them in a much better place. Perhaps in the Heaven which Mother so often spoke of. It had to be better than this.

For only a moment she would be wrapped in the fire. The thought of pain wasn't enticing, but she wasn't even sure she would be able to feel it now.

She noticed the cobbler. The teacher. The dear postman who had always stopped to chat during his daily routes in town. They were trying their best to save her home.

"Charlotte!" The men by the door turned to face her as she drew near.

"Charlotte move away from here! You'll be burned! STEP BACK!"

It was easy to ignore them.

With each slow step towards the flames she thought of the memories they had shared within the now crumbling walls. Mother's singing. Papa's stories. Warm snug hugs shared with Nelly during storms.

Dear God. She paused.

Where was Nelly?

A firm hand grasped her arm and yanked her back in a violent fashion.

"WHAT ARE YOU DOING?" he shouted.

It was Ben.

Emotion threatened to rise from within her, but even as she looked at him, she wanted it all to end. Could she stay? For him? For life?

"Where is Nelly?" She at least had to know before she could go.

John Priestly, the man with burns, ran to meet them.

"I tried to go inside and save your items, Charlotte. I tried. I'm so sorry. I tried."

Ben was shaken, covered in soot and coughing. "Darling, she's not here. Not that we know of. None have been able to make it inside, but gods grant us the mercy that she wasn't home when it started."

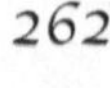

He was panicked. Oddly, much more panicked than she. She had accepted the path that life had presumably chosen to bestow upon her. The message was clear. It was her time to go, too.

"Ben. Let me go."

Maybe Nelly was at her family's house.

"I won't! You stay far from that fire, Charlotte. There's nothing inside that you need. Items can be replaced. You can't. You're staying here."

John looked between the two of them. "They're bringing more water. The fire will subside. We won't leave you, Charlotte. It will be all right."

"Charlotte, I love you. Let me stay with you. We are one, remember? I need you." Ben's stormcloud eyes pleaded. Her resolve faltered.

"And I know you love me, too." His touch was gentle now. "If your promise of love still holds true, come away from the fire."

The smoke was so thick. Her vision blurred.

She turned to him. Her thoughts of demise crumbled to ash, as did everything inside her home.

Nausea crept from her stomach, up into her chest, and settled in her head. When her knees gave way, she welcomed the darkness and its comforting embrace.

# Thank you, Mistress

*"Bathed in blood, they did conspire*
*Insatiable lust, their one desire"*
*-Celia Shortface*

There was the door, streaks of blood having dried from the top to the floor. An illusion, as most thought it was painted by design, but he knew from whence the paint came. The room beyond waited, beckoned him within for what would surely be a thrilling time. Time and life did not allow for private visits with her very often, but when delicious opportunities presented themselves, one must grab hold of the peach and suck on the sweet juices inside.

The man in the crimson cloak turned the key, the pulse of excitement raising him. Light spilled into the corridor where he stood, and then he took in the sight of her...a silhouette of sin, settled in the white, lavish clawfoot tub across the room. Her arms rested on either side and she raised one leg, brandishing her ankle as a coy, sly smile played across her lips. The luscious smell of rust and iron filled his nose.

Tonight, she bathed in blood.

Upon entering, he turned his attention to her surprisingly supple breasts and fine, smooth skin. He was entirely unfazed by the other woman's body haphazardly tossed to the side. The sacrifice lay on her back, throat slit neatly across, eyes of glass forever staring at the ornate carvings on the ceiling above.

He smirked. "You started without me."

"Oh, darling...I couldn't wait. My skin needed refreshing and the servant girl piqued my annoyances one too many times this evening." She dipped her hands in the bloody water and smoothed it up her arms.

Slowly. Sensually.

He pulsed yet again.

"And where, pray tell, did the rest of your blood come from?"

She brought the glass to her lips, it, too, filled with blood.

"I had some left over from before. From our last ritual...before that little fire at the Scott house." Her twisted grin gripped him by the loins.

God, he wanted to ravage her.

"You remember that, don't you darling?"

"I remember the folds of that servant's cunt, and how superb they felt wrapped around my cock, if that's what you're asking." He shot her a coy smile of his own. She pursed her lips. She wanted to play.

He chuckled. "But, that's been at least four weeks' time, perhaps even five...I'm surprised you saved it for this long."

She laughed. "I'm quite capable of resisting my urges."

She gracefully extended a hand toward him and rose from the bath, dripping in blood. He brought her fingers to his lips.

Salty.

Sinful.

Exciting.

"Resist not your urges this day, Bethshua Franklin."

She stepped from the washing tub as he unbuttoned his shirt. These buttons typically come apart with ease, but tonight his hands suffered a tremble. An enticing draw beckoned him towards the most sinful of acts... lewd perversions that fueled his need and led him deeper into the abyss. His need to be inside her. His want for her touch. He always wanted her.

While others could provide a temporary solace for the desperate need to

wet his cock, none could compare to the fierce, tight, rapturous pleasure that she provided him. By the flicker of tens of candles, he massaged the liquid youth into her face.

She was his Kitten, and he was her Master.

She walked her fingers up his bare chest, clutching at the back of his neck to draw him lower. She met him with her lips—her plump, luscious, blood-soaked lips. He'd felt those lips on his cock before and tonight he would feel them again.

One finger trailed back down his chest, with her wet kisses behind it. He pulsed with anticipation.

She dropped to her knees when she reached his waist, pulling his breeches down to the floor. She kissed his thighs, licked at his stones—this devil woman knew how to tease him. Her years of experience did her well.

One bloody hand tightly gripped him, her lips gently suckled below.

"Mmmm. That feels nice, Kitten." He gripped her hair. "You've missed my cock."

He looked down to see her gazing at him. She kissed his length, swirling her tongue just about the tip as she held his stare. She let his cock fall upon her, lifting and gently slapping her face with it.

Gods this woman set him on fire.

She coaxed him into the chair beside the washing tub, her bloody handprints upon his thighs. Her lips parted as she took his fullness in her mouth.

"Take it all, Fuckmeat." He forced her head upon his cock. Her eyes watered, but he knew she liked it. This wasn't their first time. Even they had boundaries.

She gagged and spluttered.

"Good girl." He lifted her from him, stroking her hair as she wiped the excessive spit from around her mouth. She knew rather fiercely that he liked it sloppy. And this time, there was blood.

She went back in, sucking, licking...licking lower until she flicked her tongue upon his arse. She was gifted at pleasing him.

He caressed her cheek. The skin of her face was incredibly soft now. He lifted her to stand, and she bent to grip the edge of the washing tub. "Are you ready, Kitten?"

"Yes, Master. Please."

He dunked his hand in the cup full of crimson, stroking himself for added wetness. The sensational, slow plunge inside nearly caused him to spill his seed.

But no. Not yet. The game had only begun.

He fucked her—hard. In one hand he held her raven black hair and used the other to violently spank her ass. He could see his handprints, raised and red, upon her flesh.

With each moan that escaped him, each euphoric whimper that exuded from her, he inched closer to climax. He moved one foot, repositioning his stance and accidently kicking the corpse beside them.

Oh well.

"Take my seed, whore." He thrust, faster and faster.

In one swift motion she surged forward, slipping free from his cock. She spun around to meet him, bloody hand clasped around his throat. He was so close to release, but he knew this game well.

"Whore, you call me?" He sank to his knees, her hands still on his throat.

"You dare to call me whore?" Her voice was a low whisper. She spat in his face, but he caught the smallest hint of a smile.

His heart still thumped. His breath escaped him. He knew he needed to respond.

"I'm sorry—" he slowed his breathing, "Mistress." He felt himself slipping, switching into the headspace she preferred of him right now.

She stepped in front of him, so close that his face pressed against her sex. She parted her legs.

"Pleasure me." Her nails were razor sharp upon his head.

"NOW!"

"Yes, Mistress. Thank you, Mistress." He parted her lips and began the

dance of his tongue on her pearl. He knew exactly what she liked and where she liked it.

She was the lock and he was the key. They reveled in their sick, twisted, sinful natures together, finding arousal in ways that others needn't understand. She had helped him work towards the wishes he desired. He looked again at the corpse on the floor...her arms splayed outward, head tilted toward him now. He wished she had waited. But alas, it was now as if she were watching him please his Mistress.

"Finish me, fuck boy! Bring me to my power!"

He tore his stare from the corpse of the servant girl. We've both pleased her today, it seemed.

# *Cursed be Thy Name*

The striking clock in the state house tolled. She could hear it all the way here, at Ben's house, on Society Hill.

"Quick! To the square! They've caught her, and she's going to burn!"

Townsfolk rushed past. They were running for the square. It was hardly dinner time, what on God's green earth could have happened?

"She's a witch!"

"Burn her!"

"Bethshua Franklin consorts with the Devil!"

"They found her! Covered in blood. No doubt one of her dark spells!"

"You there! Ma'am!" Charlotte stopped a flustered looking woman that was headed to the square. "What news of Bethshua Franklin?"

The woman dropped her petticoat and righted her cold weather cap. "The night watch discovered her, while making their evening rounds. Saw her through a window they did...covered in blood." The woman shifted her eyes along the street. "They went inside to help her, thinking she'd come into a bit of trouble, you see." She put a handkerchief to her running nose. "But she hadn't! She stood beside a washing tub full of blood. Her servant girl... murdered!"

The woman shuffled away, headed on towards the square. She turned

around and yelled, "Blood Magic it was! She's a witch! Best you leave that Franklin home, child! Perhaps they ALL dance among the Devil."

Dear God. Bethshua was finally headed to burn.

The Franklin family had been nothing short of gracious to her after the loss of her home in the fire. They had distanced themselves from Bethshua and the accusations, but no doubt would still be devastated.

She spent a great deal of time boarding at their home, much to the delight of Ben, and Abitha had her around as often as she liked.

They had settled her. Soothed her. Comforted her out of the darkness which she had given herself to. Even with her grief, and great it still was, Charlotte managed to find the joys that life could offer once more.

But now this.

She threw open the front door. "Mr. Franklin! Mrs. Franklin! Ben!" She saw no one. "Anyone!"

Samuel came running out of the sitting room, Mr. Josiah Franklin close behind.

"What is it, Miss Charlotte?" They looked her over with concern. "Are you hurt?"

Ben ran into view from the back of the house. "My darling, are you all right?"

"It's Beth. They're taking her to the square. They're saying she was found as a murderer, covered in blood."

The blood drained from all three faces. She was correct in her suspicions of Aunt Beth, but now was not the time to say it. Constable Cobb had started his investigation, but hadn't yet gathered the evidence needed to search her house.

She and Ben had tried to lay low after everything that had transpired. To admit their snooping in her home would be to admit to their fornication, and neither wished for that to be revealed.

No other murders had occurred in the weeks since the fire. And yet, even with their silence, the truth still came out.

God had a bewildering way of taking care of them, it would seem.

Mr. Franklin sank into one of the hallway chairs. "This cannot be...the rumors were true." His face fell into his hands. Mrs. Franklin and the sullen sister Sarah, floated into the hall.

"What's the commotion about? Papa? Papa, what troubles you?" Sarah was still mostly silent around her, but Charlotte didn't take it personally. She preferred silence rather than outright malice, of which she'd hardly seen of late.

The Franklin family had been wonderful to her of late. And now, she must be understanding for them.

Through his sobs, Mr. Franklin reached for his wife. "She's been discovered as a witch, Abby! My own sister!"

"Josiah...I haven't the words to say." Mrs. Franklin's eyes were sympathetic but her lips were set thin. "Gather yourself. We must get to town. Perhaps we can reason with them?"

Sarah smirked. "But one that consorts with the devil through witchcraft deserves their fate, do they not? Best not to align ourselves with this."

Sarah's belly was unquestionably rounded now. The average passerby might not know, but the family knew. None dared to speak on it.

Samuel shot her a look. "That's enough, Sarah." He reached for his frock coat. "We must go. Regardless of the cause or the end result, we are her family. We must go." He looked among them. "Now!"

Mr. Franklin spoke again. "Perhaps it is all a misunderstanding?"

"Papa, really?"

Ben rushed around collecting hats, muffs, mittens, and shawls—preparing them for the bitter chill of winter that awaited them outside.

A crowd had gathered in the town square. None had been burned as a witch in twenty years or so. After the ghastly occurrences at Salem, it was nearly unheard of anymore.

"Burn her!"

"Burn the Devil!"

"She's a witch!"

The closer they came to the square, the more clearly she could hear the shouts from the crowd. My God, this was happening so fast. But Bethshua is a witch. She knew about Priya. But she didn't want to see it. She didn't want to watch as Bethshua Franklin burned.

Her hand throbbed from the force with which Ben held it as he led her through the impassioned crowd. They brandished torches, lanterns, pitchforks, and crosses.

"Send her to her Master!"

Members of the night watch led a solemn procession with Bethshua Franklin in the middle. Her wrists were shackled and she was clothed in what looked to be a white linen cloth, yet now it was stained with blood. If the woman on the street was to be believed—it wasn't Bethshua's blood they saw.

What did Ben think about this? She chanced a glance at him.

He stared with thin set lips and sadness in his eyes. He turned to her.

"My heart wishes not to believe what my eyes can clearly see."

Bethshua stood beside the stake. Silent as the grave. Her wide eyes manically darted around at the members of the town.

She was searching. Waiting. She displayed no fear.

Josiah and Abby Franklin gripped each other at the front of the crowd. Men of the Nighwatch placed wood around Beth, concealing the ground upon which she stood.

"Some of this wood be damp...to prolong the burn for Satan's whore!"

She clung to Ben. She hated to see it.

No. This woman killed Priya.

Minister Horvath waddled between the crowd and the pyre. He shared a look with Mr. and Mrs. Franklin, then held his hands, and his bible, high in the air.

"SILENCE!"

The crowd quieted.

"We the people of Philadelphia, in this the year of our Lord 1739, condemn this vile woman for her crimes against God!"

Bethshua narrowed her eyes. No spoken word. No tremble, not even from the cold.

This woman was evil.

The minister continued. "An impetuous daughter of the Devil stands before us."

"She's a witch!"

"Murderer!"

"Burn her for her sins!"

His face was red now, a physical manifestation of his burning rage. Sweat poured from his brow. "May the fires of today cleanse this town of the black scourge of your witchcraft. May it shepherd you to your master in HELL!"

Townsfolk at the front threw dirt upon her. Good God. She was hissing. Spitting. Cursing at them.

How could they have not known?

"Bethshua Folger Franklin...you are charged with murder against your fellow man, by way of conjurations, enchantments, and witchcrafts. How do you answer these charges?"

A slow hiss escaped her sinful mouth and she raised her eyebrows.

"Guilty."

"Murderer! Burn Her! Set the flame! Save us all!"

"But wait!" Constable Cobb ran to the crowd. He was followed by more men, dragging along the innkeeper of the Morris House.

My God.

"We have another! A witch's accomplice! He, too, was with the body. He freely admits his crimes."

Ebenezer stared straight at Bethshua, licking his lips and walking toward

the pyre.

"You willingly burn with her?" Minister Horvath was shocked.

As was Charlotte.

The greasy, putrid innkeeper of Society Hill nodded his head in earnest.

"Take me with you! Guide me to him!"

This didn't make sense. Ebenezer was the man responsible for Papa's death, and the baker's, and Priya's? He had burned her house with Nelly inside?

But why?

It sounded as if he were preparing to meet the devil within the flames.

May God protect us.

Ben held her tightly. "The trouble will be over now, my love." He stared at the murderers unblinkingly. Thomas Franklin had appeared by his side, as had Amir. They must have heard the commotion from the shop.

Tears streamed down Amir's face.

"Murderers—" he whispered.

Thomas was troubled. So was she. A quickened heart and the rush of blood through her veins cemented her in this moment. They were on the edge of death, on the edge of life, on the edge of the end to a terrible time full of death and despair. She wished to leap into the dawn of a new, happy existence. One with Ben in which they could marry and start their own family in safety.

In the task of joining greasy Ebenezer to the fire, the bloodstained cloth covering Bethshua slipped to her waist. She stood, bosom bare, with her head held high in hatred.

The minister shouted. "You see! Look upon her nakedness! The witch contains a mark upon the flesh...an extra nipple! She allows her familiars to suckle evil at the teet!"

She had not noticed before, but Bethshua's skin was shockingly taut for a woman of her years. She was smooth as a perfect peach, untouched by the bruising of age. No wrinkles. No blemishes. Even covered in dirt, blood, and rags—Charlotte could not deny Bethshua's beauty.

Or was this more devilry?

Minister Horvath spat upon her face. "Set her to flame!"

Bethshua stood unmoving as the fire touched the logs, but soon she squirmed—it had to resemble the heat from hell now. The menacing blaze raced up the linen cloth, engulfing her in flames to the waist—that was when Charlotte heard the first scream.

"Fools! All of you!

My Father, who art in Hell, cursed be thy name.

Rise from Hell, we know thee well,

Embrace these words among the flame!"

Bethshua wrenched at her bindings now. Ebenezer's screams ripped into her eardrums, the hairs on her arms standing on end.

"Give us this night, to devour the light;

and veil us as truth twists with lies,

Lead us always to temptation,

And deliver us to the dark,

For thine, God of the Damned,

I reach for your hand

Infused forever with your mark"

A conspiracy of ravens burst forth from the pyre. The shock of it sent a weakness to Charlotte's knees. Ben held her. She trembled.

Minister Horvath removed his handkerchief from his mouth. "DEVIL WOMAN! Witches must burn in the proper manner! First the feet, then the calves, then up to their sinful, whoring thighs and bosoms that turn the attention of Godly men!"

"Come enjoy these whoring legs now, Minister! Ahahahaha!"

Aunt Beth's shrieks and cackles of laughter soon turned into violent, gut-wrenching screams of pain.

She thrashed among the smoke, coughing, hissing, hurling curse words at all among them. Blood mixed with soot and dirt as it ran down her twisted face.

Charlotte wanted to go. She needed to go. No need persisted in observing this any longer.

Yet in an instant, Aunt Beth's voice ceased. Her body sagged forward, the remnants of her hair burned away, revealing a scalp marred by blisters and cracks. Ebenezer had long been still. All among them settled, watching, listening to the silence that surrounded them save for the occasional crack from the fire.

A murmur escaped from the crowd. "Is she...dead?"

Thunder rumbled in the distance. Unusual for a cold, winter's day. The wind whispered softly through Bethshua's crisp, remaining bits of hair. A man of the night watch doused the flaming bodies with a leather bucket of water. They extinguished with a sickening hiss.

She focused on the gruesome sight of what used to be Bethshua Franklin— smoldering eye sockets, flesh peeled back from the skull. The smell of roasted meat lingered in the air. The crowd drew closer, pushing Charlotte and the Franklins with it, to have a look for themselves.

God, please. No closer.

The Lord is my shepherd...The Lord is my shepherd.

"FATHER!"

Aunt Beth sprang to life with an earth-shattering scream. She threw her head back and screeched at the sky.

God protect us!

Black smoke erupted from the witch's chest. Scorched and blackened arms reached for her.

Charlotte closed her eyes. There was no escape.

Ben's warm arms encircled her. He protected her.

Hellacious flames sprang to life once more. She felt the heat upon her face, and opened her eyes to see Aunt Beth engulfed on the pyre.

It lasted for a moment, and then the flames were gone.

Bethshua Franklin had descended to be with her master.

# Brunches and Balls

Mid-morning breakfast on a bright spring day had to be the most exquisite experience, outside of love's embrace, that Charlotte enjoyed these days. The dawn of a new day euphorically arrived with the chirping of birds and frolicking of nature's finest in the parsley green fields outside the window. The sweet scent of honeysuckle wafted in through the open windows, mingling with the savory aroma of sizzling sausages and vanilla-laced porridge.

'Tis such a delight to watch the mother doe lead her fawn among the tall grasses, the dew-kissed blades swaying ever so slightly in the cool morning air. Exultation filled her heart. She looked down at her two latest books—a gift from Ben. Perhaps she would have time to read them today.

Winter's chill had left the velvety darkness of before behind them. Charlotte basked in the warmth of the morning sun streaming across the damask tablecloth, its bright rays setting the crystal glasses and gilded flatware ablaze. A light breeze ruffled the gossamer curtains and carried the trills of birdsong over the gentle clinking of tea cups and murmur of refined ladies in polite conversation.

She and Ben were to be married. Sarah's bump continued to grow, as did their friendship, yet she wouldn't tell Charlotte who the father was. Sarah hid it well, and stayed mostly inside, but Charlotte couldn't help but think of the coming babe as she watched the deer across the way.

"Now Abby...nonsense! The entirety of the gentry will be in attendance, no expense must be spared!" The women of Society Hill giggled and clucked as a gaggle of sweet, socialite hens, fervently planning the Franklin Spring Ball.

How she sat among them, dressed in the finest painted silk shipped in from France, Charlotte could hardly believe. Ben had chosen the color himself. Prussian blue, he had called it.

"I've never attended a masquerade party before." She needn't hide her inexperience. They accepted her now.

"Oh, Lottie...we're going to have so much fun!" Excitement sparkled behind Sarah's eyes. She still wasn't used to it, but as soon as she and Ben were engaged to wed—everything changed between them. Perhaps now Sarah knew that their love was true.

"Well, we'll also need to find masks to match our dresses. Does everyone have their fabrics chosen for the dressmaker?" Mrs. Franklin looked around the room. "Josiah prefers it if we cover that cost for you—"

"Abby, you shan't!" Charlotte protested. "There's no need—"

"We insist!" Her future mother by marriage straightened her back with the whisper of a smile playing about her lips. "With the effort you girls have put into planning this fine affair, it's the least we can do."

What a life Charlotte now lived. Sadness still pained her heart from time to time, and pain lets a person know they are still alive, but to be surrounded with the love of her Aunt Abitha and the Franklin family—she felt happier than she had in a long time. Outside the mullioned windows, the verdant sweep of manicured lawns and bursts of flowers in the height of springtime bloom painted a vivid picture of natural splendor.

Charlotte Franklin. How perfect it sounded.

"Sorry I'm late, girls."

Oh dear. It was Delphia. The sweetbread in her mouth turned abruptly repugnant, the taste becoming foul. She imagined the shock on their powdered faces if she revealed what she really thought of their newest member, the insufferable Delphia whose honeyed words dripped with venom.

"Mr. Spencer had a hard time letting me out of the marriage bed this morning..." she winked at Mrs. Havishem, "if you know what I mean."

Oh, they knew what she meant. The brute hag.

Nothing had come of the accusations of Priya's disappearance in connection with Madam Delphia or the mayor. With the burning of Bethshua and Ebenezer, all discussions of mystery crumbled to ash, much the same as her home...the same as they, themselves.

But she knew it. Inside she knew the truth. Delphia was connected. Though they welcomed her into their gilded circle, she didn't for a moment forget they would turn on her at the first sign of weakness, like a glittering school of jewel-toned fish. Charlotte had never been one to tolerate foolishness, and this boisterous woman posed the ultimate test of patience with her frivolous gossip and posturing.

And then there was the mayor. 'Tis a convenience that he had gone on an extended holiday in Europe, or so they reported, but she was thankful that he hadn't been seen in months.

A peacock spread its feathers and rustled in the distance. Such a beautiful bird. This was a glorious day. She wouldn't let Delphia spoil it for her. So many lessons she had recently learned.

"Would you pass the syrup, Mrs. Delaney? I'd like to add it to my porridge." Charlotte turned her attention back to the flock.

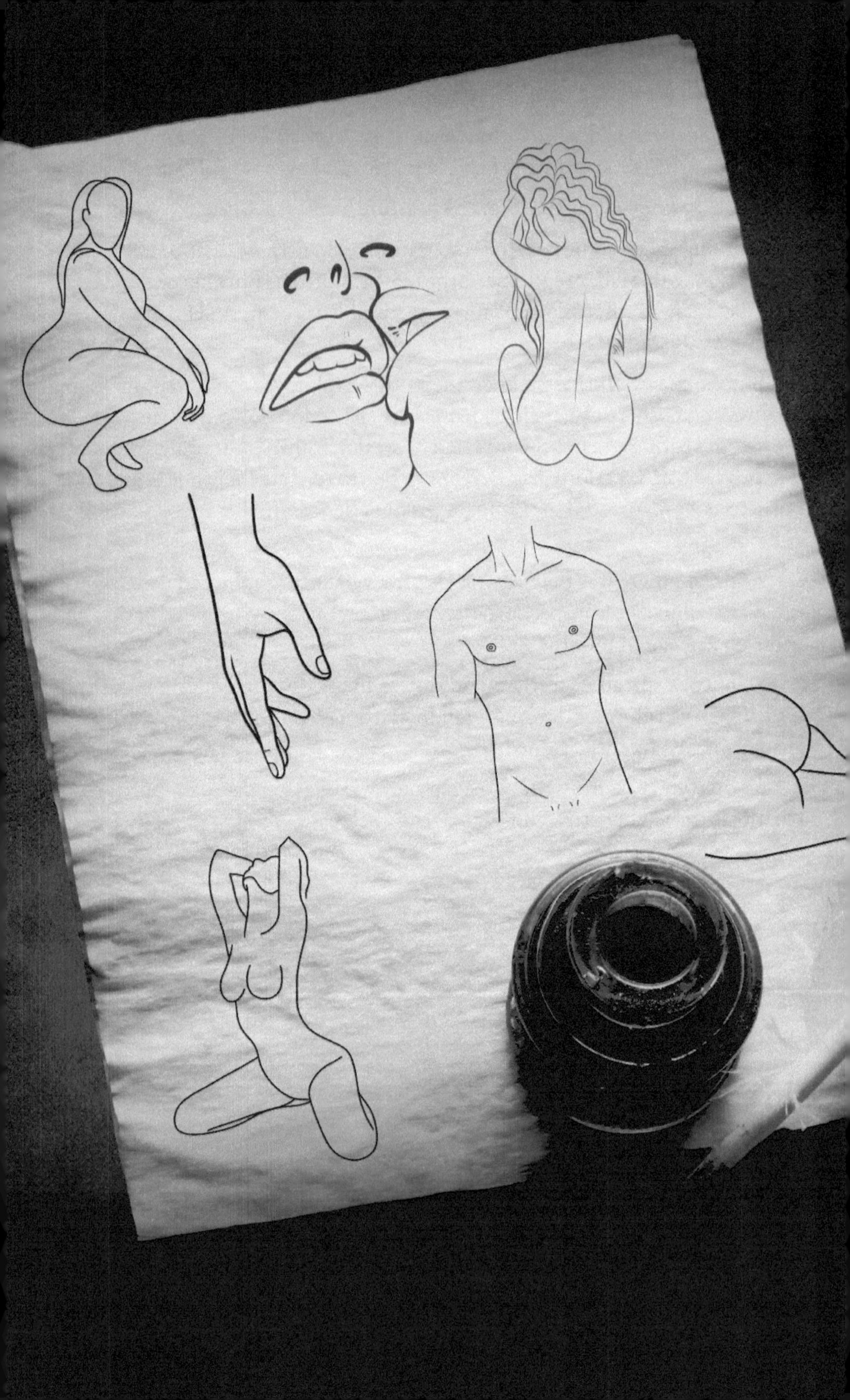

# Indelicate Illustrations

As the light of the sun faded, Ben added another log to the fire. Spring had enthusiastically bloomed before their very eyes, the dawn of a new beginning, yet the nights still held a chill about them—enough of one to require the occasional fire.

"My darling, how did the lady's brunch go today? Was it pleasing to you?" Ben said.

"Humanity is not perfect in any fashion; no more in the case of evil than in that of good. The criminal has his virtues, just as the honest man has his weaknesses."

With great effort Charlotte tore her attention from the enthralling words of Pierre Choderlos de Laclos. It was a gift from Ben's brother, Thomas, upon their engagement. An odd book to give as a gift, especially to one's future sister by marriage, but it was a gift she appreciated nonetheless. Les Liaisons Dangereuses, it was called.

"It was lovely. Your Papa insists upon having the pet bears along a chain in the front of the yard. He wants everyone to see them."

Ben rolled his eyes. "That macaroni man."

Macaroni. With a pang of sadness, she thought of Nelly. Ben noticed. He always had a way of noticing. He cupped her shoulders with his firm, strong hands.

"She lives on through you. In the lessons she taught you, the memories you made, and through the silly words she used which even I have picked up from you."

Her lips twitched. She couldn't help it. He invariably made her feel better.

Well, he did, and the Vetiver oil that Amir procured for her through his Papa's trades. That made her feel better too.

'Twas life changing.

Ben settled back into his favorite mahogany fireside chair and started scribbling in his notebook once more.

"What draws your attention so, my love?" She motioned to the notebook.

He smiled. "It's nothing. Merely the dull notes of a scientific nature. It's quite dense. You certainly wouldn't prefer it to your novels." His wink fluttered her heart.

"A cider sounds satisfying right now. Would you care for some?" He rose from the chair. She couldn't help but notice the tightness of his breeches, remembering in detail what lay beneath them.

"No thank you, darling." She winked. "Hurry back to me."

He knelt and rubbed his nose to hers then placed a kiss upon her head before walking out the door.

She could live like this forever.

And yet, over the pages of her book, Ben's notebook whispered to her.

Read Me! It called.

Not really, but it felt like it did.

Curiosity killed the cat, but then again, satisfaction brought it back, or so they say. One quick peek to settle her curiosities wouldn't hurt. She wanted to know him better—to find out his interests in earnest.

The door remained closed. The kitchens were downstairs, so there should be plenty of time.

But, perhaps this was an intrusion of privacy. He would show her if he wanted to share, or maybe it genuinely wasn't something she would be

interested in.

But his intellect enthralled her. He was the most gifted man she knew; a true visionary. He was a solver of most problems—it was highly impressive.

One glance couldn't hurt.

What crossed from one page to the next within the notebook startled her heart and confused her mind. Strewn about the pages were not the workings of science, nor anything of elevated intellect, but rather that of indecent, grotesque formations of women. They were unlike any drawings she had ever seen.

This was surely not Ben's.

Women of all shapes and sizes were fixated upon the page in drawings of the most lewd fashion. Pleasuring each other...fornicating in groups.

These depictions were of no encouragement to the sacred bond shared between a husband and his wife. Nay, these drawings were a celebration of sinful indulgences unbecoming to a child of God. Charlotte's stomach churned with unease as she turned each vulgar page, unable to reconcile these depraved images with the gentleman she knew Ben to be. She recoiled at a particularly shocking sketch, the obscene contortions eliciting a reflexive gasp, her mind unable to process how such things were possible. However, curiosity warred with shame within her, a heated flush creeping up Charlotte's neck despite being alone as she lingered on a drawing. Try as she might to suppress it, an unwelcome thrill coursed through her at the risqué drawings, leaving Charlotte conflicted about these scandalous new yearnings.

Footsteps sounded from down the hall. Charlotte hurriedly closed the notebook with trembling fingers, willing herself to take calming breaths as a storm of confusion swirled through her mind. She raced back to the chaise and quickly found a place within her book.

Still thy heart.

Don't react. He will know.

Ben entered, the sly grin of a fox fixed upon his chiseled jaw. "Did you miss me?" He smiled, lips pressed tightly together as he leaned in for a kiss.

"Mmhm." She was being too obvious. Though Ben's tender gaze usually brought her comfort, she found herself avoiding his eyes, suddenly self-conscious about what lurid thoughts he might be harboring.

He furrowed his brow. "Everything all right, darling?"

"Oh...um...yes. It's just—" Should she tell him the truth? She glanced at the notebook. He saw.

He narrowed his eyes and sighed deeply. "You looked...didn't you?"

"Possibly." She crossed her arms. "What need does a booklet like that fulfill for you? Is my body not enough?" She couldn't help but feel insulted.

He closed his eyes. "Charlotte, it's not mine." He pressed his lips with a slight frown. "It's John's."

John Priestly?

"But what use do you have with it?"

"I noticed it sitting here, he left it here on his last visit. Curiosity took hold, same as you."

But something was missing. "Did I not see you scrawl within it? Perhaps adding to the drawings?"

A slight smolder flashed in his grey eyes. "Charlotte. Let me share a word with you that I find appropriate for this situation. A wife shall never endeavor to deceive or impose on her husband's understanding; nor give him uneasiness--as some do very foolishly--to try his temper."

Charlotte froze. Ben continued. "Much the same as I do with you, one should treat another before marriage with sincerity, and afterwards with affection and respect." He surveyed her. "I was writing a joke to John. Nothing more. Put these pictures from your mind and think not of them again." Ben wrapped his arms around her. "You are mine. Your body is rapturous perfection. I haven't a need for any such drawings, my love. Trust in this."

She trusted him. With the truth revealed that Bethshua was behind the murders of her family, she had stowed away any accusatory thoughts concerning John. But these drawings were...unnerving. She wasn't sure she could view John Priestly with a similar perspective as before.

# Misbehavior at the Masquerade

The finest silk gowns to grace Philadelphia proper spun about the ballroom floor; their bejeweled owners taken with fine drink and merriment. This was Charlotte's first visit to Franklin Hall, their countryside manor, filled with exuberance and frivolity unlike anything her eyes had been blessed with to date. Velvet tapestries of the deepest crimson flowed among the ceiling and spilled down the walls, providing the perfect backdrop for masked couples as they twirled about the room. The eloquent sounds of Vivaldi, Telemann, and Handel filled the air, vibrations of brass married with woodwinds, harpsichords, and strings. It reverberated deep into her chest and plunged into her soul.

Ben led her to the floor, his black feathered mask only covering the top half of his face. His chiseled jaw and luscious lips were ripe for the taking, just as she liked it.

"Join me, my lady."

The ballroom buzzed alive with fire blowers, jugglers, and to her astonishment, performers walking on tightropes high above their heads, their bright outfits intimately close as if painted on their skin. How did they miss the chandeliers? God above, they were divine.

The masquerade was an incredible sight to behold. And she was here. With Ben.

How mundane she felt among such wonder. Beauty surrounded them and the wine flowed freely. She was surely in a dream...one that she wished to never wake from.

Ornamented tables piled high with rare delicacies enticed her palate, yet Ben continued to spin her across the room. He dipped her low, her bosom surely exposed to the rest of the guests.

Not that they would mind.

A sense of promiscuity lingered in the air—a palpable aura of mischief and madness emanating from the high society guests. Perhaps it was the wine, or the way Ben's stormcloud eyes peered from behind his mask, but something exciting stirred within her. 'Twas the inexhaustible, unquenchable thirst of desire. He was hers, and she his, and they would dance together for all of time.

The room swirled much faster than the dancers now. The fire blazed in her throat with the same ferocity of the flaming performers. They spun. They danced. She lost herself in the music and in his arms. She glided into an adjoining room with her love.

Through foggy vision she peered closer at the masks surrounding her. Something was wrong. With crushing despair, she realized they were distorted, grotesque depictions of men and women. Masks of goblins, witches, and nightmarish creatures she knew not the name of.

Chaise lounges and soft cloth coverings upon the floor of this room were filled with the naked, writhing bodies of a whole host of guests. Men kneeling, servicing all manner of pleasures. Moans filled the air. Women licked and kissed parts revealed of their companions. Her soul suffered great shock, yet she also tingled down below.

But this was sin.

Ben's eyes were wide, yet he, too, stumbled with drink.

An unmasked man but a few paces from her raised for breath from betwixt the taut thighs of his lover.

Dear God.

It was John Priestly.

He suckled her toes, licking from ankle to tuft, crawling closer in between her legs. Her mouth was filled with the member of a man who's back was

turned. Charlotte didn't want to know who, but feared she already did.

She turned to Ben. They needed to get away. But he stood unmoving.

His eyes were affixed on a sight so ghastly that when she settled upon what he was looking at, she, too, was a moth to the flame.

In the center of the room, bulging with the growing life inside her belly, surrounded by masked men and women who kissed and sucked and caressed every inch of her being was—Ben's sister.

Sarah's hand rested on the back of the man with warm chocolate hair, the man who stood with her at Christ church so many months ago.

A man thrusting and moaning between her legs, coupled together with her in ecstasy.

It was a man Sarah was raised with, and now coupled with.

Her brother—Samuel Franklin.

Sarah caught her eye and narrowed her gaze. Her lips split into a malicious grin.

"Hello, Charlotte."

Sarah threw her head back and cackled to the crows.

Charlotte stepped back. Sandpaper hands grabbed at her arms. They pinched her. Shoved her. This could not be.

They held her down with the strength of ten men.

Ben was out of sight.

As the masquerade swirled around her with malicious intent now clear, Charlotte scanned the faces in a panic, no longer certain who to trust or what might come next in this twisted game where even love had proved an illusion.

They bound her wrists, though she struggled to get away.

God, protect her now.

A length of silk gagged her, cutting her screams into a visceral silence.

"No! Please!"

Charlotte struggled to break free, but as the linen cloth came near, all she

could see beyond the writhing bodies on the floor was her beloved Ben, bound and carried as well.

Her last sight was of him as he vanished down stairs she hadn't noticed before.

# Stolen Away

Darkness...footsteps...pain.

Slimy and rough, the stone wall grazing her shoulder returned her to reality through a hazy fog.

They were moving with haste. Their heated, labored breaths warmed her skin. Sickness threatened to expel from within.

She had seen them—knew their secret. But it wasn't as if they were trying to hide it.

Her legs were below her head now. They were headed down a slope. Deeper into darkness. Charlotte's hands throbbed with the growing sting of numbness.

Mother....Papa...Priya....Nelly.

Now she.

They stopped. The clank of metal keys added to the sounds of heavy breathing and shuffled footsteps, but none had spoken. With a slow metal moan, a heavy door swung open, further adding to the question of where they had taken her.

She twisted, fought, kicked at them, but it was no use. Like a lamb to the slaughter, she'd been so easy to take. She'd been eager to stray from the Godly flock near the end. Was this the price of dipping into that well of pleasure? Had Eve the same thoughts after biting into her own forbidden

fruit and gaining the knowledge that she had; of good and evil?

"In here."

Without warning, she was launched into the air, forcefully flung into a stone cell. Her arms scraped against the coarse, moist floor, until she collided with something hard. Sticks or stones, perhaps. As she turned around to face them, the barred door clanged shut, her captors racing back from whence they came.

No. No!

She screamed. Begged. Cried. To no avail. There was no one to answer her.

The catacombs. That's where she was. She hadn't believed the rumors, but now, cold, damp, and stifled from the stench of death, she knew it to be true.

As with the first woman on earth, God had surely forsaken her.

***

Minutes passed. Maybe hours. Maybe days. She didn't know.

The silence of her cell was a deafening defeat, only broken by the rustle of tiny footsteps followed by shrill squeaks. Rats. She clung to the cold iron bars, unwilling to move, unwilling to breathe, careful not to move and displace any more of the hard sticks that littered the floor around her. Her blood rushed, the pounding of her ears drowning out all else.

But wait. She reached out into the dark, sliding her hands along the floor. Searching for what she landed on. The sticks were cold. Hard. Oddly shaped.

She picked up one of the large ones, finding it mostly smooth but with something grainy on its surface. Almost a powder. She fingered the rounded end, noting a rough edge protruding out from it. She lifted her fingers. Salt. Rust.

Blood.

Dear God no! She threw it away, furiously wiping her hands on her filthy dress. Bones. She was surrounded by bones. They had left her here to die.

A soft rasp, hardly above a whisper, emitted from a large shape in the corner, followed by a soft moan. In the darkness, she had pretended it was a

shadow, it wasn't there, but as her vision adjusted she knew.

Footsteps sounded from the tunnel again, men's voices talking and laughing as the faintest flicker of light danced across the wall again. The light was getting larger now, closer. She was not alone in this cell. Soon she would see what lay groaning in the corner.

"Time to fetch their bitch."

A ragged foot, tattered breeches, filthy skeletal hands came into view. The bony body of a corpse stared at her from the corner, greasy black hair falling into its eyes. A scruffy face did little to conceal the crooked teeth protruding from the corpse's mouth.

But it wasn't a corpse. Not yet.

She gasped. The torch light illuminated the whole of their cell now, bones and filth within clear view, along with the emaciated body of the coroner, Edward Robinson.

The door swung open. "Ahhh. You've seen a friend, then. He, too, discovered more than he should have." Rough hands grabbed her and roughly placed something over her head. "It's time."

# Taste of Terror

*"Beok Erhd Noksis Jayk*

*Atha Midira Immeck*

*Neddis Furock Re Amensa*

*Neftal Kab Lagoz Introibo Non"*

A whip cracked against her skin, a symphony of pain screaming down her legs. Too many hands caressed her body, rubbed her skin, reached under her shift. Their smooth hands settled between Charlotte's trembling thighs.

*"We call to you, Oh honored one!*

*Delight with us in Darkness."*

Those that held her yanked off the linen cloth that covered her head, painfully taking a few of her hairs with it. She surely now stood in hell. Walls made of stone. Torches lit with fire. Figures in black robes of all shapes and sizes lined the circular room. They wore masks with only holes for the eyes. One figure stood at the helm, the priest of their black mass, on a platform covered in bones. He was naked, erect, and wore the head of a bear on his own. She turned to the demon beside her, the one who had removed her own hood—the one with their fingers inside her.

Blue.

Only one man that she knew had such terrifying, intense, blue eyes as those.

Governor Hellsmith.

Lucifer! Your children await.

She wrenched at her bonds. The rope burned her wrists—she couldn't break free. The drenched silk gagged her, dampening her cries. Ben was by her side. He too, was bound to a cross of St. Andrew's. He remained clothed, save for his shirt. She took in the sight of deep scratches upon him, some long healed.

The call of death was upon them both. Its stench drew near.

*Beok erhd Noksis Jayk!*

*Atha midira Immeck!*

Not long ago she would have embraced it. She would have welcomed death with open arms. She would have greeted her family with a joyous rapture in the great beyond, whatever that held.

But after all of her pain and suffering, after the guilt of life when only she remained out of those she loved—still, she had chosen to live.

Why hath God forgotten her so?

She had not been grateful enough in life.

Was this her punishment for fornications with whom she was to wed?

No.

This was something of a sinister, demonic, possessive nature.

*Neddis Furock re Amensa*

In the center of the room a woman lay clothed in a sheer, black cloth, a macabre masquerade mask concealing her identity. She arched her back and moaned in ecstasy, her legs spread as a black, horned goat licked at her menstrual blood.

*Youth, Blood, Fire, and Bone*

*Bring us life, through the blood of our own*

Ben tried to get to her. Hellsmith's fingers defiled her. He removed them from her, licked her juices, and sauntered to the woman in the center.

He turned back to face her, removed his hood and wickedly grinned before untying his breeches. She couldn't look away from the outline of raven black hair beyond Hellsmith's thrusting hips.

She couldn't breathe. Couldn't move.

God have mercy.

*Youth, Blood, Fire, and Bone*

*Bring us life, through the blood of our own*

Ben jerked and twisted within his bonds, staring at the ritual with a ferocity she had never seen before. The flames of the torches upon the wall reflected in his eyes, the devil trying to crawl into his soul. With each movement, the ropes holding her wrists tightened, demons of hell holding her there. Dead eyes stared at them from iron maidens set within the walls. Ben tried shouting, but he, too, was gagged with silk. Hellsmith finished with a grunt, and the next hooded figure took his place. One by one, each member of the circle savagely defiled the woman. Men... and women.

*"Yes, Master! Fill me with the seed of your children!*

*Raise my desires, raze this world."*

The voice. She knew it.

"Quiet, you fools! Show respect for our Master. You will serve your purpose on this day."

"I like hearing them scream." A woman's voice.

An ornate iron door to the side creaked open. In walked Sarah, swollen with pregnancy and pulling the midwife Mary behind her by a chain and collar.

*"Neftal Kab lagoz Introibo Non"*

"So sorry for being late—" she snapped her head over to where they stood, "I was...preoccupied." Sarah giggled. Samuel stepped in behind her, wrapping one arm around her waist.

"We've come to offer a sacrifice, a servant, for the sake of our unborn child."

May the Lord of Fire delight in this gift.

Blood ran down Ben's bonds. His own family. He struggled to get free. Her own hands and feet pulsed with blood flow. Please God, please don't let them be next.

She wanted to live.

The erect man with the head of a bear, who had stroked himself as he watched from up on high, commanded them to bring him Mary. One who waited their turn with the woman brought a torch of fire to her skin. It seared. It burned. They chuckled.

Over the chanting, she heard moans coming from the woman in the center.

They knelt the midwife Mary before the bear, one pulling her hair, and her head, taunt over the immense bowl in front of them. The bear raised an axe high.

*Beok erhd Noksis!*

*Beok erhd Noksis!*

*Beok erhd Noksis!*

She closed her eyes. She couldn't watch. Her heart would surely stop beating before they sacrificed her too.

*We eat of this flesh*

*We drink of this blood*

She knew it was done when the masked demons cried to the Master. Her knees buckled, the restraints holding her to the cross. She opened her eyes. The bear man filled chalices from the blood that dripped from Mary. Others dipped into the large bowl.

God spare her and Ben.

Her sickness rose.

"Save some for me!" The woman in the center's laugh was as sinister as the deeds they were surrounded by. One of the hooded swung the head of Mary high above them. Droplets of blood landed on the hooded ones below. They opened their mouths, licked their lips—they wanted her blood.

God hath forsaken them.

They were lost.

They were next.

Their leader with the bear upon his head yelled down to her. "Care to join us, youthful Charlotte? Save yourself and embrace the light of Lucifer!"

They removed the cloth from her mouth. She could finally breathe.

Her bonds loosened. One of the hooded demons stood behind her and whispered in her ear.

"Shhhh. Do nothing. Do not move."

Charlotte shouted. "I will *never* join in this devilry! May God smite you all!"

Ben closed his eyes.

The one who released her leaned closer. Hot breath warmed her ear. "Go. Run away. Never look back to Philadelphia." Familiar eyes stared at her behind the mask. The demons still danced among their bloodlust, and hadn't noticed the exchange.

"Go!"

But Ben.

Ben looked to her with anguish in his eyes. He nodded yes. He wanted her to go.

Dear God. No. It wasn't supposed to happen like this.

"Go!"

She broke free from the cross, locked eyes with Ben for only a moment, then ran for the side door. Her tears obscured the way. Her breath would surely never calm again.

"After Her!"

Oh God. They came for her.

She grabbed a torch and ran blindly down the hall. Bones lined the walls. She thought they were under Society Hill, but they were in the countryside. Good God. That means—it reaches out here.

God. Tell me where to go. Tell me which way.

She passed rooms to either side. The hallway was lined with stone and bone. These were the bones of humans. She had to go. She had to get away.

A pair of footsteps were behind her. It was dark. Abysmally dark. She was tired. And Ben. Her Ben. And she left him.

Oh no.

The stone wall stretched in front of her. A dead end.

It would be her end.

The flickers of another flame.

"Charlotte!" A whisper. A man's voice.

"Charlotte it's me! He got me out!"

"Ben?"

It cannot be. Oh please. Praise God.

The man of her life. Her forever love. He rounded the corner and rushed straight into her arms.

"How did you escape? Surely now they come!" She couldn't believe it. He was here.

"Whoever that is, he didn't want to see us die."

His arms were covered in blood. She trembled.

"Charlotte, we need to go. Now."

"I– I don't know where to go."

"Neither do I, but we've got to try."

They stalked through the halls of Philadelphia's secret catacombs. Their experience kept playing through her mind.

Murder. Sacrifice. Blood. Sex.

She knew it was Hellsmith, but who were the others? And Sarah. And Samuel. And how could they stop it, when the most powerful men in the colonies were involved?

They would find her again. It was hopeless.

Ben took each turn with confidence. He said he was following the breeze.

They came to a door. Behind it were steps.

"Yes! This should lead us out, my love. Since a catacomb is underground, these steps should lead us back to above!"

Charlotte's body was nearly spent. She wanted to be far from here, but knew her legs were too weak to take her there. Ben, with an unknown strength summoned from his very depths, scooped her up into his bleeding arms.

They were tattered. They were worn. But with each step upward—they were headed to freedom. The two of them could run from this vile pit of corruption and evil. They could escape from the slithering, twisting, torturous snakes that surrounded them and flee far from Philadelphia. Perhaps they could go to England. The torches lining the stairway illuminated their path to a better life.

She clutched onto Ben's neck with what dwindling strength remained. In the final moments of her crescendo of anticipation, they reached the door at the top—their gateway to freedom.

Ben kicked the door with his foot three times.

Thump. Thump. Thump.

The menacing iron door of ornate and sharpened filigree designs swung inward, with the unmistakable sound of chanting reaching her ears once more.

# Alive, but Dead

This couldn't be. Charlotte collapsed further, the wavering flicker of safety now doused by despair.

Each step Ben took, he brought them deeper inside the ritual room. All feelings of hope drained from within her. The room swam in her vision, rocking, fading, floating away. Her body slumped, as she was numb.

Her love...her life. How could this be?

With each step forward, a deep gong sounded.

Charlotte knew she should leap from his arms and run, but the shattering weight of what this meant had frozen her limbs.

Not her Ben. Not her beloved.

Please, God. No.

Having risen from the floor, still dressed in the sheer black cloth, the woman from the ritual stood before them.

The man masquerading as a bear head raised his arms and giggled with sickening glee. He threw up his arms. "WELCOME...my son."

A pang jolted deep in her stomach, rattling her to the core of her being. No.

Great waves of emotion, as crushing as those found in the ocean during a colossal storm, battered her soul and crashed around her. She would surely drown.

She was leaning, falling, suddenly upon the ground. She clutched her hip, great bolts of lightning pain shooting through her side. Ben had dropped her unceremoniously on the cold, blood-soaked floor.

She drew her scraped and bleeding knees into her chest. This couldn't be happening.

Ben rose and stood tall, shoulders back with a smug look of pride plastered upon his malicious face. "I offer my final sacrifice. The final of five. My initiation into our order will finally be complete."

A terrifying hiss came from all those around. It sliced through her.

Final of five—oh God.

The scream that escaped from her throat shattered into a thousand shattered fragments of glass.

He...the killer....it cannot be.

She crumpled further, cold tears falling down her face. Please.

"Take her." So cold. So unlike the Ben she loved. This was not the man she knew. The man she loved.

Josiah Franklin removed the bear head with repulsive delight. He clasped his hands in joy. "Charlotte Scott! So happy you could join us this evening!"

One by one, the mouthless masks were removed by the figures in black cloaks around them. Some, not all, revealed their faces.

*Beok erhd Noksis Jayk*

*Atha midira Immeck N—*

The cloaked were those of high society. Most of them here, gathered together in the worst kind of sin.

Two members grabbed her by the arms. Charlotte kicked, clawed, spat—tried. None was enough. Searing pain. Dripping blood. She couldn't run even if she wanted to. They tied her limbs to an ornate stone altar. She could hardly fight them, but still she struggled against them.

Familiar faces met her eyes. Dear God. Mrs. Franklin—not her too.

Ben walked purposefully, seductively into the waiting arms of the woman from the center of the room. He caressed her raven black hair and pulled her face up towards his. He kissed her deeply, with a lust so palatable Charlotte nearly lurched. He removed the woman's mask.

Charlotte screamed again.

This could not be.

May God help her.

Moaning in satisfaction, an evil grin plastered on her youthful face, blood still running down her legs, the woman from the center of the room who kissed Ben now—was Bethshua Franklin.

But no! She was dead. Burned. The sight of burnt flesh and the smoky scent of death still lingered in her nose, ripped from her memory of not too long ago.

A slithering voice from the back of the room echoed loud. "Confused, little flower?"

Delphia Spencer. The brute bitch.

"You shouldn't be...you pegged her yourself." The deep tone of her malicious laugh reverberated into Charlotte's soul. "Discovered her little secret, didn't you?"

She couldn't look at Delphia, couldn't take her eyes from his. Ben smirked.

He ran his fingers through Bethshua's hair. "She truly is a witch, foolish girl."

Bethshua raised a hand and placed it on Ben's chest. She slid it down... down to stroke him.

"But...the fire—"Charlotte wasn't sure how she whispered the words.

Beth was rubbing harder upon Ben now. He closed his eyes and moaned, the sick sound of a twisted man she never knew. "Are you that addled to not realize who my Master is? Through Lucifer's love I am imbued with powers beyond your simple imagination."

Ben laughed. "I knew you were plain, but come now Charlotte. You mistake my intentions. I have no interest in a woman whose only asset is her ample flesh. I prefer my women with a bit of... refinement. "

Tears wet her face. For Charlotte, this was the end.

Bethshua turned her menacing gaze toward her prey and split her sinful lips into a grin. "I let you borrow my Ben for a moment, but only because we needed you. We needed your family. It seemed the perfect fit for his initiation—what with your harlot mother having served us before."

"Ahhh, Catherine." Hellsmith sighed.

The bastard.

Bethshua continued. "And it was easy enough to frame your weak Papa for it."

So that's why Papa's business slowed.

Ben broke from Bethshua and circled the room as a buzzard with its meal.

"Five sacrifices for the five points of the pentagram." He moved closer to her.

His face had darkened, rolling stormcloud eyes resting on his distorted features. This was not her Ben. He never was. Her cheeks seared as angry tears welled in her eyes.

"Plus, two as an appetizer." He pursed his lips. "Elizabeth came to learn too much—" he looked up to his father, "and needed to be dealt with." Ben slowed his walk, almost to a stop.

"She dared insert her thoughts about Sarah's child. The very child Thomas helped her care for with his herbs."

Charlotte couldn't believe it. How dare he. She remembered him comforting Thomas at the funeral. His own family.

Ben continued pacing. "The baker was merely for practice—to see if I could do it." He paused, the clack of his wooden shoes silenced, hardly an arm's length away from her now. "I hadn't experienced the pure, humanistic joy in sacrifice yet." He leaned closer, barely speaking above a whisper into her

ear. His heated breath was upon her.

"The first, the harlot, for promiscuity—Priya wished to be a whore." The skin where he caressed tingled at his touch. Charlotte burned with hatred for him.

"Such a shame. John had taken a true fancy to her, but when she found him with another—" Ben looked beside her, "she had to be dealt with. Isn't that right, John?"

The cloak that held her nodded his head. Dear God.

He began to walk again, arms clasped behind his back. "The second, the fool. That bastard Dirch had it coming to him. And when he dare imitate my crimes?" She thought of the window.

Ben shook his head. The chanting grew louder now, the circle of sinners closing in upon them. "The perfect, unwilling sacrifice."

Her world was burning, yet a rage stirred within her soul. How dare he.

Ben stopped at the front of their chamber from hell. Bethshua sank to her knees and took him in her mouth.

Bile rose in Charlotte's own.

"The third, the enemy, for resistance. Your Papa frequently forgot his place." Ben placed a hand on Bethshua's head. "He and his Rosicrusian lackeys threatened our order on more than one occasion." He raised his eyebrows. "If only he'd kept his place after the split and known it well."

Ben cracked a smile. It shook her to the bone. "No matter. His death was quite...electrifying."

Charlotte's pulse quickened now, veins popping in her neck. She stood still, no longer resisting her captors. She needed to gain strength.

Ben.

Her Ben.

Bethshua's Ben.

She would not die this day. By this man...this monster to whom she'd foolishly given her heart.

Ben spoke again through his moans of twisted pleasure. "The fourth, the servant, gave me pause. She had shown me kindness."

Poor, sweet Nelly. She wrenched within her captor's grasp, ready to rip the smirk off of the contorted face she once thought handsome. How dare he speak of her.

"I'll spare you the details—" he said, raising his eyebrows, "but please know that she brought me great joy before I left her there to burn."

Sick. Twisted. Bastard.

Charlotte struggled in their grasp once more. Her fury surged through her muscles... for all whom she loved, she would wrench free. "Ben Franklin...may you rot in HELL!" The power in her voice invigorated her.

He chuckled. "But alas, my portly little love, our joy is in ourselves."

The unmasked Luciferians took one step closer, chanting, staring at their prize.

"And my greatest joy will come with such sweet sorrow, for now—" Ben moaned, thrusting forward into Bethshua's mouth, raising a dagger in his right hand, "I require that you die."

Charlotte wrenched her arms, twisting her body to escape from the grasp of those that held her. He would not have his way. A guttural scream rose from deep within, the memories of her family and all those that had been wronged flooded forth to encourage her.

For Priya.

For Nelly.

For Mother and Papa.

Charlotte's eyes fixated on the ax lying on the floor, its sharp edge glinting in the dim, flickering light. It was within her reach, and she knew what she had to do. Summoning a strength fueled by the love of all those she had lost, and the rage she held in seeking revenge for them, she grabbed the ax. Memories of her mother and father, pain and fear, her feelings of worthlessness and lack of faith in herself, roiled together like a rolling storm gathering speed. The emotions were overwhelming, but she refused to let them consume her. They were the thunder; now she was the lightning. The axe was heavy in her hand, the rough handle threatening splinters, yet she couldn't care less. The scent of the old wood brought comfort among the dominating rust smell of blood. She could hear the sound of her own breathing, ragged and uneven, broken only by the metallic clang of the ax's blade as she lifted it off the ground. The chanting and sight of the others had faded, a mere foggy background as she narrowed her eyes at the source of so much suffering.

With unwavering commitment to her task, she bolted towards him, the axe held tightly in her grip, her mind focused on one action alone.

It was time for Benjamin Franklin to die.

Charlotte ran with wild abandon, slicing into the arm of one of the masked. He buckled to his knees, hood falling back.

Minister Horvath. She growled.

Mr. and Mrs. Franklin stood on their platform, the bear's head beside them. They crouched low in anticipation, grinning widely and licking their lips. Their hands were bared as claws.

Charlotte swung the axe again, aiming for Ben but instead hitting Sarah. Charlotte dragged the axe clean across her neck, landing with a thunk in the side of Bethshua's head. Her blood spurt across Ben's face; his dagger clanging to the floor.

Dear God. In a split second she watched as life left her victim's eyes. She had descended into the depths of sin with them. Unforgivable. Inexcusable.

But necessary to survive.

The Luciferians lunged, driving in to capture her. Kill her. She raised the axe to swing again, but someone grabbed her from behind. The axe clattered to the floor.

One of the hooded, in the chaos and confusion, threw a robe over her.

How? She couldn't imagine who it was, but thanks be to God for them.

Where is she!

Find the bitch!

Satan's flames will strike you down!

Yes! A rope hung on the wall, over by the door. It held the heavy iron chandelier above them. Her hooded accomplice picked up the axe that she'd dropped, shoving it into her hands.

"Go." They whispered.

Ben shrieked at his compatriots. "Stay here! We will search the catacombs! She's weak! She hasn't gone far!"

On their way out the door, she swung the axe one final time, cleaving the rope in two. Those frantically chanting and trying to restore the bodies of Sarah and Bethshua Franklin fell victim to the chandelier's crash.

This time, Charlotte didn't wait to see their fate.

She ran with her accomplice, the one who had helped her escape before. His hood had fallen, and as she looked back she realized who it was.

Thomas Franklin. He was among them. But why did he help her now?

It didn't matter. Now was the time to escape. She would flee from Philadelphia. Far from her previous need for the house and the husband and the "perfect" life according to societal expectations. She had sacrificed every better feeling to worldly advantage before, but no longer. She would live her life on her terms, and hers alone, empowered by her thoughts and memories instead of trampled by hysteria.

# *Two Years Later*

Boston, Massachusetts, 1742

"Welcome to Colonial Inn, Ma'am. Allow me to assist you." The doorman of the hotel smiled with a kindness that at one time would have warmed her. A strong scent of lemon and lavender, alluding to a general sense of cleanliness, comforted her.

Charlotte smiled at him in return. She was trying. They all were.

"Thank you, kind sir. We require a private room, removed from the hustle and bustle, you understand?" Aunt Abitha always had a way of getting straight to the point. Her consistent wearing of black and a long lace veil paved the way for privacy, which, these days, was much appreciated. Most assumed they were in mourning. Maybe they were.

"That's the last of it, I do believe." Thomas tipped his hat to the doorman of their rented carriage and offered his arms to them.

"My ladies." Thomas chuckled.

Charlotte smiled, wrapping herself around his arm. "Thank-you kindly, Sir Thomas."

He laughed, a deep rolling sound that resonated through her. "Maybe once we make the crossing to England, the queen will give me a true knighthood?" His grin was infectious. Her mood lightened, if only slightly. "Wouldn't that be grand?"

Charlotte hugged his arm to her and lowered her voice, "You surely deserve it, dear friend, though none know it.”

A roaring laughter greeted her ears as she noticed a friendly face heading towards them through the crowd. “Ha! A knight. You think quite highly of yourself, don’t you, Sir Thomas?” Amir flashed a cheeky grin, swirling to join them.

It delighted her to have him with them. His presence uplifted her spirits and kept the darkest of thoughts at bay. A reminder of Priya, which, as always, brought about a pang of sadness. He and Thomas would start again in Apothecary once they reached their new home. Amir’s Papa had many connections in England, which she hoped would serve them well.

Thomas tightened his lips. Charlotte would always be thankful to him for his help that fateful night—the night when High Society was revealed for who they truly were. She would not be alive without his assistance, of that she was sure. His resistance to their ways brought them out of the darkness and back into light. Now, they had started a new life and would soon be across the sea, never to return to the Americas, she hoped.

Aunt Abitha gathered her skirts and set forth with a gusto only recently acquired. She was done with the Americas. “Come now, you three. I’m exhausted from our travels.” She turned to them. “Let us retire and rise refreshed for our journey away from this ghastly place.”

Charlotte and Thomas grinned at each other. “Of course, Aunt Abitha.”

The delicious aroma of buttered croissants wafted in the air.

“Oh look!” Charlotte chimed, glancing at the posted menu. “They have roasted duck and cherry pie prepared for dinner this evening.” They wouldn’t want to dine among any others, of course. “Perhaps we shall have it sent to the room?”

Thomas eagerly nodded his agreement.

Charlotte turned to make her way to the innkeeper’s desk. The portly, cheerful man was deep in conversation with a finely dressed couple. Their backs were to her, and the maiden clung to the man’s arm, resting her head upon his shoulder.

Charlotte sighed, a twinge of sadness striking her heart. Young, naive love.

The man addressed the keeper of the desk. "Yes, we require the finest room available, if you please." He pulled his lovestruck lady closer. "No expense shall be spared on this, our honeymoon."

The woman with blonde curls and a delicate lace bonnet giggled.

But wait, Charlotte paused. That voice.

Time was a filter, a porous device that mercifully removed impurities and details from even the most traumatic of memories—but time had not removed this voice from her mind.

As recognition crashed through her, Charlotte gasped so sharply, the young woman glanced behind to look at them.

The keeper continued. "And what name shall I register the room under, Sir?"

The finely dressed man turned to face her. Piercing grey eyes met hers once more and a wicked grin cracked his lips. Charlotte found herself scanning the room for something, anything she could use to bring about justice. It may have to be her bare hands, and even that was acceptable.

"Benjamin. My name is Benjamin Franklin."

Thomas did well to hold her back. But soon she would overcome him, and then... she would strike.

# THE END

Coming Soon

# CHAPTER 1

## Florence, Italy, 1504

Tucked away in a quiet corner of the Palazzo Vecchio amidst a sea of crimson silk dresses and lavish lifestyles, Basil Hallward's brush faltered in its dance across his canvas. He had poured the essence of life into this piece, unlike any before. The opulent members of Florence's artistic elite surrounded him, their chatter and laughter battering the unseen walls he surrounded himself with when focused. He was intoxicatingly lost in his own world, consumed by creativity and the even stronger feeling of anticipation. The shadow of the final stroke of his most transcendent work of art to date loomed, with the thought of finishing this portrait shepherding in a mixture of rapturous accomplishment and gripping fear that coursed through his veins as a flood of sentiments.

Capturing the haunting beauty of Dorian Gray with each dip of the brush into paint he so carefully mixed, mirroring perfection in the balance between linseed oil and mineral pigments, held an unimaginable experience unique to each. These bittersweet moments were both devastating and divine, for as he crept closer to finality, knowing once the portrait was complete, the final note of his intermezzo of experience with Dorian Gray would echo into silence.

Basil sighed, his chest hollowing in preparation for the crater in his heart that was soon to appear.

The lavish chambers in which he worked were alive with a symphony of sensations, creativity flowing so thick through the air, Basil envisioned their collective melodies of mental mastery caressing his skin.

Da Vinci and Michelangelo were embroiled in lively debate, the former teasing the latter of his "melting masterpiece," to the delight of all gathered. Basil wiped the latest bead of sweat from his brow, undeniably in agreement with Michelangelo's jabs toward Leo (as only Basil and a few other long-time artisans called him.) He understood the concept behind what Leo attempted, but raised an eyebrow as the preposterous giant pots were brought into the lounge. The piles of wood within them had burned for three days, for God's sake! Not to mention the resulting heat they had nearly suffocated in made for ill-advised artistic accommodations.

Leo's depiction of the 1440 Battle of Anghiari, unfinished in the experimental "encrusto" technique, or whatever he had called it, seemed to melt down the walls, in stark contrast to the drying effect he attempted to create. The work was far too vast for all of the colors to dry, and thus they streamed down the walls as clearly as the sweat did from their brows.

"Look at him melt, fine illustrissimo!" Michelangelo laughed, clapping his competitor on the shoulder. "I believe your encaustic method was a bit too hot for us to handle!"

Basil sheepishly grinned at Leo, glancing at the preparatory drawings on Michelangelo's side of the hall. Piero Soderini and the prince of pranks, Machiavelli, had put them up to this dual of the arts. The Battle of Cascina, Michelangelo's charge, offered the perfect opportunity for him to enhance the scene in ways he was known for.

Basil chuckled.

Michel really did know how to make the male figures "stand out" in his work.

The Tuscan sun drenched the courtyard beyond the floor-to-jewel encrusted ceiling in golden light, silhouetting a lone magpie against the azure sky.

The paintbrush gripped the canvas, reluctant to let go of the masterpiece, of the journey it took to get there. With a deep breath, soothing to the soul, Basil summoned his strength and pulled the brush away, trailing the slightest of crimson droplets with it.

As if the portrait itself were bleeding.

Among the additive and spellbinding joy of the rest of the room, Basil mourned at his completion.

It was finished. His time with Dorian Gray was at an end.

An exuberant laugh shattered his reverie. "Now, Basil, you brood in this corner like a bereft widow!"

He would recognize the striking blend of red and gold hair that seemed to ignite as molten fire anywhere, to say nothing of the broad shoulders and marbled arms swinging towards him. Henry VIII, notably, soon-to-be King Henry VIII of England, clapped Basil on the back, nearly sending him sprawling. "Come, show me this enrapturing vision that has stolen you from our fun."

Basil swallowed, steeling as turned towards what could only be described as an intimate rendering on one he hardly knew, but was instantly enchanted by. Would Henry see what he did in Dorian? The haunting, androgynous beauty unlike any he had seen before; those fathomless gray speckled eyes that gazed with innocence and naivety. Her rosebud lips that Basil knew whispered poetry and obscenities so bemusingly in the same breath.

"Well?" Henry's eyes gleamed with avarice as he studied the portrait. "She is exquisite, I will grant you that." The young adult looked further, leaning close to the painting, blowing his hot, putrid breath that still reeked of his last whore's muffin tuft. "I must have her."

Basil's fingers curled into fists, the swift rise to anger a surprise even to him. "Dorian is not some trinket to be possessed."

"I want an introduction." Henry's tone brokered no refusal. Not surprising for one with a past and soon to be future such as his. "Arrange it, or I'll assume you wish to keep her all to yourself." A cruel smile twisted his youthful lips. "And we both know the price of denying me."

Basil swallowed bile and rage in equal measure. He couldn't refuse– but to surrender Dorian to this lecher's clutches?

Not in good conscience.

Basil's nails, desperately overdue for a trim, bit into his palms. If he'd had

319

a heartbeat, it would have hammered in his chest. In times like these, when trapped as a mouse before a viper, he could almost feel the long forgotten thump, thump, thump, which he only still recognized because of those he fed from. In the cavern where his shriveled heart rested, suspended for eternity by veins that were of no use to him any longer, there was only a leaden weight.

That, and the memory of panic– the same breathless apprehension that had seized him upon first seeing Dorian across the crowded hall at her arrival to that Hall of the Five Hundred in Palazzo Vecchio.

He had loved once before– a love that had cost him his life. Now love was ash, and he, a horror.

"As you wish." The words tasted of fiery cinders on the tongue as he spit them at Henry.

What a coward he was.  A selfish, underspoken, coward. A killer of many and yet a contestant to none. Conflict never suited him, for all these years.

Dorian's maintained innocence, unstained by the vanity and selfishness of this world, had slipped through his fingers like a falling leaf between the crooked branches of a withered and dying tree.

And yet, a friendship with Dorian could only ever be as ephemeral as the few trusting relationships he'd had over the last 90 years since the change.

An impossibility. A dream.

Basil sighed. Sweet Dorian was fated ensnarement in a web far more sinister than his own unrequited longing.

All for the sake of his worthless immortal life.

To Be Continued...

# Author

Dr. Marie Lestrange is a multi-passionate author, musician, and artist with a particular interest in historical Horror. She is the writer and illustrator of the Little Lestrange series, unique and chilling parodies of classic ABC "children's" books that are certainly not for children (S is for Serial Killers, T is for Torture). Additionally, Dr. Lestrange hosts and produces the Moths to the Flame podcast, drawing inspiration from her extensive research into the macabre, true crime, and occultish practices. Her most recent venture is chartering the Tennessee chapter for the Horror Writer's Association. She and her writer husband love traveling with their little Hobbit and his mischievous pup, Fire, outside of the East Tennessee mountains they call home.